Dominic pull[illegible]nd began to kis[illegible]he could ba[illegible]

She managed a strangled cry at last. "Dominic, no! We must not!"

He raised his head from hers and drew away a little. His eyes were black and unfocused.

"No?" It sounded more like a groan than a word.

"There are servants here. And I…" She indicated her masculine uniform. He laid his palms against her cheeks.

"There is only one servant in the house. My valet. He will not disturb us. We are quite alone. And as for your military garb…"

He put his hands to her waist and unbuckled her sword belt. Her fur-trimmed pelisse followed.

"Better," he said in a low voice that shuddered all the way down to the toes of her boots.

He wanted her, completely, desperately. As he had wanted her once before, at the masquerade. Then, he had denied himself, in order to safeguard her. Now he wanted to make her his.

"Alexandra?" He sounded a little uncertain.

She smiled and held out her arms to him.

* * *

His Cavalry Lady

Harlequin® Historical #936—March 2009

The Aikenhead Honors

Three gentlemen spies: bound by duty, undone by women!

Introducing three of England's most eligible bachelors:
Dominic, Leo and Jack,
code-named Ace, King and Knave.

Together they are

THE AIKENHEAD HONORS

A government-sponsored spy ring, they risk their lives—and hearts—to keep Regency England safe!

Follow these three brothers on a dazzling journey through Europe and beyond as they serve their country and meet their brides, in often very surprising circumstances!

Meet the "Ace," Dominic Aikenhead, Duke of Calder, in

HIS CAVALRY LADY

Meet the "King" and renowned rake, Lord Leo Aikenhead, in
HIS RELUCTANT MISTRESS
April 2009

Meet the "Knave" and incorrigible playboy,
Lord Jack Aikenhead, in
HIS FORBIDDEN LIAISON
May 2009

His Cavalry Lady

JOANNA MAITLAND

TORONTO • NEW YORK • LONDON
AMSTERDAM • PARIS • SYDNEY • HAMBURG
STOCKHOLM • ATHENS • TOKYO • MILAN • MADRID
PRAGUE • WARSAW • BUDAPEST • AUCKLAND

Recycling programs
for this product may
not exist in your area.

ISBN-13: 978-0-373-29536-4
ISBN-10: 0-373-29536-7

HIS CAVALRY LADY

First North American publication 2009

This edition published by arrangement with Harlequin Books S.A.

www.eHarlequin.com

Printed in U.S.A.

Available from Harlequin® Historical and JOANNA MAITLAND

Marrying the Major #689
Rake's Reward #697
A Poor Relation #709
My Lady Angel #737
A Regency Invitation #775
"An Uncommon Abigail"
**His Cavalry Lady* #936

*The Aikenhead Honors

This book is dedicated to my editor, Jo Carr.

Prologue

St Petersburg, 1812

The third door led into yet another magnificent room. Empty, just as the previous ones had been. There was nothing for it but to go on.

Adopting a brave posture—there could be no enemy here, could there?—the young cavalry trooper strode across to the door on the far side. There he hesitated, for just a second or two. Then, with a tiny shake of the head, as if telling himself to face his demons, he put his hand to the latch and opened it.

'Ah, Trooper Borisov. At last.' The speaker was a portly gentleman dressed in court uniform. He was smiling, but he did not bow or offer any other salute. 'I am Prince Volkonsky, Court Minister to his Imperial Majesty.'

The trooper came sharply to attention. 'Sir. I…' He faltered. His unease had been increasing with every one of those empty antechambers.

The Minister's smile broadened. 'His Majesty is waiting to meet you, young man. He has heard much of your exploits. And of your exemplary courage. Would that we had ten thousand more like you. We would have rid the world of the French scourge long ago.'

Borisov could feel his face reddening. He cursed silently. Why did he always have to react so? Only girls blushed. Not battle-hardened cavalrymen.

The Minister was waiting for an answer.

'Thank you, sir. You are most generous. But there are many brave men in the ranks of his Majesty's army and—'

'Indeed there are. But few as young as you, Borisov, or with such a record.'

Borisov said nothing more. Any response would sound like bragging.

'Now, if you will take a seat, my boy, I will tell his Majesty that you have arrived. He is occupied at present, but I am sure you will be admitted soon.' Without giving Borisov any time to respond, the Minister tapped gently on the further door and entered the room beyond, closing the door softly behind him.

Tsar Alexander himself is behind that door. The thought shivered through Borisov's mind. *The Tsar himself, the Little Father. And I am to meet him. This very day. The Tsar himself.*

Borisov began to pace. He needed to be moving. As just before a battle, he could not be still. For this meeting was as momentous as any battle he had fought.

It was only as the connecting door reopened that Borisov began to wonder what he should say to the Tsar. What if he asked—?

'Trooper Borisov, his Majesty will receive you now.'

Borisov swallowed hard, forced his body into his best military posture and strode through that terrifying door.

It was a huge room, hung with paintings and mirrors, but almost empty of furniture. In the far corner, under the tall windows, stood an ornate gilded desk with a single chair behind it. A distant part of Borisov's mind registered that visitors to this room were not permitted to sit.

The figure behind the desk rose and came round into the centre of the room. Borisov remained rooted to the spot by the door. He knew, without looking, that it had been closed behind him. He was alone. With the Emperor himself.

'Borisov. Come forward. Let me look at you in the light.'

Borisov bowed and obeyed.

The Tsar was the taller of the two. Unlike Borisov, he had a fine set of side-whiskers. He stood erect and imposing in his military uniform, looking his visitor over with bright, intelligent eyes. Assessing eyes.

He will spot where my jacket was mended for that sabre cut, Borisov thought suddenly, wishing he had been able to afford a new one.

'We have heard much about your courageous exploits during the wars. How many times did you take part in those cavalry charges? Five?'

Borisov's throat was too dry to speak. He nodded, blushing yet again.

'Your commanders report that you are totally fearless, throwing yourself into every skirmish. Even when it is not your squadron that is charged with the attack.' The Tsar smiled down at him, encouragingly.

Borisov swallowed. 'That was a…a mistake, your Majesty,' he croaked.

The Emperor raised an eyebrow but said nothing.

'I… It was my first battle, your Majesty. No one had told me that charges were by squadron. When I returned from the first one, I just… I assumed that I was to continue as before.'

'I see. But you stopped eventually?'

'Yes, your Majesty. The sergeant-major told me to remain with my own squadron and to charge only with them.'

The Emperor's eyes were dancing with good humour. 'But you continued to throw yourself into every battle? And you saved the life of an officer at Borodino.'

Borisov took a deep breath. 'He was wounded, your Majesty. I merely chased off the enemy. They ran as soon as they saw an unwounded trooper bearing down on them with a lance.'

'And you gave him your horse.'

'I...yes, I did.' Borisov did not add that, by the time the horse was eventually recovered, all the kit it carried had been stolen. And that, as a result, Borisov himself had almost frozen to death for want of a greatcoat.

'Saving an officer's life is a meritorious act, Borisov. That is why you have been summoned here to receive the Cross of St George. And...' the Tsar turned back to his desk and picked up a paper '...and for another reason.'

Borisov swayed a little on his feet. Please, no!

'I have here a plea from a distraught father, Count Ivan Kuralkin, who begs for help to locate his beloved child. This child ran away from home to join the cavalry and has been missing now for more than two years, serving under an assumed name. The father begs that the child, the comfort of his old age, will be found and returned to him. Do you think I should grant his request, Borisov?' He dropped the paper back on the desk.

The young man gulped, realising that his expression must betray his panic.

'You have no view on this, Borisov?' The Tsar's keen eyes were on him.

'I would not presume, your Majesty.'

The Tsar nodded to himself, as if acknowledging a good answer, then turned and walked to the long windows overlooking the vast garden of the palace. For several minutes, he stood, apparently contemplating the plants. Then, abruptly, he spun on his heel and said, in a voice so soft that it barely carried to where the trooper stood, 'I have been told that you are a woman, Borisov. Tell me the truth. Is it so?'

Borisov stood as if transfixed. His mouth worked but no sound came out.

The Tsar strode across the room until the two were barely a pace apart. He did not look angry or forbidding. He looked merely intrigued. And he was waiting for an answer.

It was not possible to lie to the Tsar. Besides, it was clear that he already knew. The young man managed just a thread of a voice. 'It is true, your Majesty.' He waited for the blow to fall.

The Tsar smiled broadly and clapped the trooper on the shoulder. 'I should never have believed that a woman could do all that you have done. Such courage and such dedication. You are a shining example to the army. Alexandra Ivanovna Kuralkina, I salute you.' He fastened the cross to her uniform, kissed her formally on both cheeks and took a step back, pausing to assess the effect. Then he turned back to his desk and picked up the paper again. 'And since you did not answer the question when I put it to you, I shall answer it for you now. You shall be returned to your family by the Tsar himself with all honour. Your exploits shall be fêted.'

No! Oh, no! The Emperor was going to send her back to her father and stepmother. She had fled one marriage to a man she had never seen. No doubt her stepmother would soon sell her to another. She would never be free again. Such a punishment was too much to bear. She threw herself at the Emperor's feet. 'Your Majesty, I beg you, from the bottom of my heart, please do not send me back to my father. I would rather have died for you on the battlefield than return there. Let me continue to serve you, to fight for you. The cavalry is all I desire in the world. I cannot serve you if you send me back to my father's house.'

The Tsar looked down at the man-woman at his feet. He frowned slightly and turned away, leaving her crumpled on her knees on the intricately patterned wooden floor. It was no position for a cavalryman to be in, but she did not dare to move. She held her breath, watching him pace. Was there a chance he might change his mind?

'How old are you?' he asked suddenly, waving her to her feet.

That was the last question she had expected. 'Twenty-two, your Majesty.'

'Indeed? You look no more than sixteen.' He paused, clearly digesting that information. 'Tell me, my child,' he said at last, 'what would you wish to do, if anything in the world were possible for you?'

'I would wish to continue to serve you in a cavalry regiment, your Majesty.'

'Any particular one?'

She hesitated. Did he mean…? 'A Hussar regiment, your Majesty, if I had a choice.' A vision flickered across her brain of herself in Hussar uniform, sabre drawn, taking part in a mighty charge. Oh, yes, a Hussar regiment.

'As an officer?' A small smile licked the corner of his mouth.

Her heart began to pound at the Tsar's extraordinary suggestion. Only men with written proofs of their nobility could become officers. Under her assumed name, Borisov, and with no hope of demonstrating her noble status, her only choice had been to enlist as an ordinary trooper. Her military life so far had been wonderful, exhilarating. But to be an officer! She could do it. Of course she could. Like her father, she had been born to do it. 'A commission in a Hussar regiment, your Majesty, would be like a…it would be the fulfilment of a dream I have always thought impossible.' She looked shyly up at him, wondering whether any of this could be true. Was he really about to grant her fiercest desire?

He nodded, twice. 'I shall commission you into the Mariupol Hussars.'

She gasped aloud. She could not help it. The Mariupol Hussars was a crack regiment. Noblemen fought tooth and nail for commissions in it.

'But not, I think, as Borisov. Nor under your own name, Kuralkina, obviously. You shall take my name. You shall be Alexandrov. Alexei Ivanovich Alexandrov of the Mariupol Hussars.'

'Oh, thank you, your Majesty,' she breathed. She wanted to burst with happiness. The Little Father himself had granted her dearest wish. It was a miracle.

'It is a fitting reward for saving the life of an officer on the battlefield. And since you will not be able to ask your father for the funds you will need, I myself shall supply you. Apply directly to me, through Prince Volkonsky. No one else is to know of this. You will continue to serve as a man.'

'Your Majesty, I do not know how to thank you. I—'

'There is one way to thank me, Alexandrov, and one way only. You have been given a new and honourable name. Let your conduct match it, on the battlefield and beyond. Let no stain of dishonour tarnish it so long as you bear it.' He stared down into her eyes, searching for commitment.

In that soul-searing moment, Alexei Ivanovich Alexandrov swore a silent oath of honour and service to Tsar Alexander. Until death.

Chapter One

Boulogne, June 1814

It was the smell that woke him.

For fully three seconds, Dominic lay quite still in the Lion d'Or's best bed, trying to make sense of the strange messages tumbling into his brain. Dark. Silence. Smoke? *Fire!*

He flung himself out of bed. Light! He needed light! And where the devil were his breeches?

A terrified neighing ripped through the pre-dawn silence. Then a whoosh, as if a giant were sucking in a monstrous breath. Followed by red, hellish light.

The smoke had turned to flames. The Lion d'Or's stables must be on fire!

Dominic threw wide the half-open window, stuck his head out and yelled at the top of his voice, *'Au feu! Au feu!'* It was surely loud enough to wake even drunken grooms.

He dragged on his breeches and crammed his feet into boots. A voice rang out below. At last! Then more voices. A woman's despairing wail. And the ominous crackle of the fire taking hold in dry straw and ancient timbers.

Dominic took the stairs three at a time. In the yard, the

silence was turning into utter chaos. Yelling, cursing men milling around in the eerie light. No one fetching water. No one saving the horses.

He grabbed the nearest groom by the shoulder. 'Get to the pump,' he ordered in crisp French. 'Start filling buckets. And you—' he seized another by his flapping shirt '—rouse all the men from the house. Get them into a line to pass the buckets. You two. Don't stand there gawping. Start getting the horses out.'

In the space of half a minute, Dominic had turned the commotion into the beginnings of order. The terrified horses were being led to safety. Water was being brought. But the flames had a head start. And they were winning.

The front part of the stables and one side of the doorway were ablaze. One panicked horse was refusing to be led through. It was fighting against the halter, rearing, eyes rolling, hooves flailing. With a cry of pain, the groom dropped to the ground. The horse fled back into the stables.

Dominic lunged forward, hefted the unconscious groom over his shoulder and raced across the yard to the inn. By the door, a maidservant stood motionless, wide-eyed with fear. 'You, girl.' He laid the boy ungently at her feet. 'Make yourself useful. Look to his hurts.' He did not wait to see whether she obeyed. He had to help save the horses. Only one other man left to do that. Not enough. Not nearly enough.

The smoke was now so thick that it was difficult to see. And to breathe. Dominic looked around for something to use as a mask over his face. If only he had thrown on a shirt. But he had nothing. He would have to continue as he was. Taking a deep breath of the cooler air in the yard, he plunged into the hell of the burning stables.

Still at least half a dozen terrified horses to save. Possibly more. He could barely make out the back of the stable. It was full of smoke, though not yet ablaze. But he could hear the sounds of hooves thundering against stall boards. At least some of the horses must still be tethered. He raced to the back of the building, keeping as low as he could, to avoid the choking smoke. Let the groom deal with the horses nearer the door.

Like a ghostly apparition, a slim shape in grubby white emerged from the swirling smoke, leading a horse. No more than a boy, from the little Dominic could see, and dressed only in a bedgown and boots. But a boy who knew horses, for he had covered the animal's eyes to quiet it. 'Well done, lad,' Dominic gasped as they passed. No reply. The boy had his mind on his task. Just as Dominic must.

It was taking too many precious minutes to rescue the horses. All the time, the fire was engulfing more of the building. Yet the boy in the bedgown was fearless, always going back into the most dangerous area of the stable. He had a way with the terrified beasts, too. More than once, Dominic fancied he heard the lad's voice, murmuring strong and low, urging the animal towards the flaming doorway. He had even started to cover the horses' nostrils against the acrid smoke. Part of Dominic's brain registered that he would find the lad after this was all over, and reward him for his bravery. He would have been proud to have such a boy in his own service.

Out in the yard again, Dominic caught a dripping cloth tossed to him by one of the inn servants. Gratefully, he covered his head, hoping that the boy had done the same. With this, there ought to be a chance of rescuing the remaining animals. Only a few more to bring out now. He ran back into the thickening smoke.

He found himself struggling with the tether of one of the last horses. The straining beast had pulled it tight in the iron ring. Its thrashing hooves were threatening to crack Dominic's head open. If only he had a knife. Damnation! The rope refused to come free. At this rate, they would both burn!

A strong, lean hand appeared out of the smoke, holding a knife. Bless the boy! A single slash cut the rope. Then the hand disappeared again. No time to say a word of thanks. The horse, suddenly freed, reared up to its full height with a loud and terrified whinny. Dominic ducked under the deadly hooves and grabbed the trailing rope, forcing the animal down. He had to get this horse out. The fire was really taking hold now. Soon the stable roof would be aflame. There would be no more rescues then.

At last, Dominic managed to coax the horse through the stable doorway. Someone had taken an axe to the blazing wood so that the gap was wider and the flames were less fierce. The broken, smouldering timbers lay on the ground. Dominic thrust the rope into a waiting hand and raced back inside, ignoring the prick of sparks on the bare skin of his back and chest. He had tiny burns all over his body now. No doubt he would look as though he had a dose of smallpox when this was over. But he had to be sure that there were no more horses hidden by the smoke.

It seemed the lad in the bedgown had had the same thought. His eerie figure was just visible through the swirling darkness, searching among the stalls. Dominic ran towards the boy. 'Is that all of them?' he yelled, trying to make himself heard above the noise of the fire.

Before the boy could say a word, there was an ominous crack above their heads. Dominic caught a glimpse of a huge, flaming beam dropping towards them. Towards the boy! Dominic bridged the space between them with a single stride, grabbed the boy and thrust him aside. The beam hit the stable floor just inches from where they stood, showering them both with sparks. In seconds, the boy's bedgown had caught alight.

Dominic made to tear it off him.

'Non!' It was a scream of anguish.

The boy must be an idiot. Surely he knew that it was better to be naked than to burn?

'Non!' the boy cried again, ripping the tail of his bedgown out of Dominic's hands.

There was no time to argue. And only one solution. Dominic pushed the boy to the ground and covered him with his own body, rolling them both in the dirt to stop the sparks from taking hold.

And then he understood.

This was no boy. The lithe body straining against his own belonged to a fearless, and extraordinary, girl!

His mind told him it was impossible. But his body knew better. It was threatening to go up in flames to match the blaze around them. Dear God, why this woman? Why now? Had he no self-control at all?

A loud groan brought him back to stark reality. His weight must be crushing her delicate form. And there was no time now to wonder what was happening between them. He had to get her out of this hellhole. The rest of the roof would fall at any second.

He leapt to his feet, dragging the girl up by the arm. *'Venez,'* he rasped from his parched throat. He started for the door. But the girl was trying to free herself from his grasp. What on earth was she about? This was no time for modesty. Yet still she fought him.

With a curse of exasperation, he grabbed her slight form around the waist and slung her over his shoulder. Her small fists started to pummel his bare back, but he ignored that. He simply held her even more tightly against his body. No time to try to reassure her. In any case, the scorching smoke was burning his throat so much that he was almost sure he could not speak. He must get her out! Ducking low, he staggered towards the stable door and out into the yard. It was full of smoke still, but no flames. The men seemed to be bringing the fire under control at last.

With a groan of relief, Dominic set the girl on her feet, supporting her shoulders until he was sure she was strong enough to stand. He needed to commend her for her amazing courage. And to apologize for manhandling her. *'Mademoiselle, vous—*

' It was barely a croak, but he was not allowed to finish. Her eyes had widened at his words. It could not be fear, surely? Not with this amazing girl. With a strangled cry, she wrenched herself away from him and fled in the direction of the inn door. He was left with a fleeting image, barely discernable through the hanging smoke, of huge eyes in a pale face, cropped hair, and a wet, filthy bedgown clinging to her slim form.

He started to follow. She must not be allowed to vanish, like a ghost. He must find out who she was. She—

'Monsieur! Attention!' One of the men grabbed his arm and pointed. With an enormous crash, the roof of the stables collapsed inwards. Sparks were flying everywhere. The fire was out of control again. If the men did not act immediately, the inn itself would catch fire.

Dominic grabbed a bucket and began to douse the inn wall, calling to the other men to help him. Provided they all stayed at their task, the inn should be safe. God willing.

By the time the fire was finally under control, all the men were exhausted. But they were triumphant. The yard was a sea of grinning teeth in blackened faces. Dominic knew he must look just as filthy as the rest of them.

For the first time in what seemed like hours, he relaxed his shoulders. His back was aching. And all those minute burns on his skin were beginning to hurt like hell.

The inn servants were working as an efficient team now. They no longer needed Dominic to direct them. So, with a sigh of relief, he made for the inn door and the staircase to his bedchamber. His room was deserted. His valet, Cooper, must still be down below, helping to fight the remnants of the fire, and unrecognisable under the dirt and sweat. No matter. Dominic had no need of him.

The reflection in the pier glass pulled him up short. It wasn't only his face that was filthy. His whole body was grimed with smoke. He grinned at himself. No wonder the girl had fled from him. He looked like a black demon. Even his own mother would not recognise him like this. He would have to bathe, but that would be impossible until the fire was out and the inn kitchen was working normally once more. Hot water would be the last thing on their minds at present. He would have to wait.

Sighing with exhaustion, Dominic sank on to the bed and pulled off one ruined boot. Even Cooper would be unable to save this pair. He grinned again, imagining the valet's consternation when he saw the state of them, and of his master. With luck, Cooper would have a pot of skin salve somewhere in his baggage. But, for the moment, Dominic did not care. What he wanted was to close his eyes, just for a few minutes.

He dropped the second ruined boot and lay back on the bed, allowing his head to sink into the feather pillows. Bliss. A few moments rest. Only a few.

He was just beginning to drift into sleep when her blurry image came back to him. That girl. What courage she had. Who was she? He must speak to her again and thank her. But only later, once he was clean again, and presentable. And once he was fully in control of his body's responses, too. He needed to show her that he was a gentleman, not a ravening demon. He found he could not quite remember her face, or the colour of her hair. It had all been too indistinct in the smoke. And later her head had been covered by a wet cloth, just as his own had been. But her hair had definitely been cropped, like a boy's. Very strange. Perhaps she had recently recovered from a fever or some such? Yes, that must be it. Still, it should be easy enough to discover her. There would not be many girls with cropped hair at the foremost inn of Boulogne. He would find her, and thank her. He'd give her a purse of guineas, too, if she would take them. She had certainly earned them.

So much courage. He *must* find her again. He must.

* * *

'Hold still, your Grace, if you please.'

Dominic cursed. Cooper was being particularly thorough with his confounded salve.

'Exactly so, your Grace. But if I don't catch all of these burns, they'll turn bad and then where will we be? Begging your Grace's pardon, o' course.' There was nothing in the least subservient about Cooper's tone, in spite of his words. He had been with Dominic for too many years and was particularly officious when he knew he was in the right. As now.

Dominic sighed and held himself still until his man had finished. Cooper eased a fine lawn shirt over Dominic's injured torso. It felt blessedly cool against his tormented skin.

'There. Works wonders, your Grace. You'll soon be right as ninepence. You'll see.'

'No doubt, Cooper,' Dominic croaked. His throat was still raw from the smoke. He reached for the tumbler of water and drained it. For a moment, it helped.

'I'll fetch up some honey in a moment,' Cooper said. He had been out in the yard, helping to pass the water buckets, but he had not inhaled nearly as much smoke as his master. He still sounded more or less normal. 'Once your Grace is fit to meet company again.'

Dominic groaned and reached for his cravat. He had wasted too much time already. He had not intended to fall asleep but, exhausted as he was, there had been no fighting it. He must find that girl. She would be injured too, her throat burned and her tender body scarred by flying sparks. He would offer her Cooper's salve. He would—

'Right, your Grace. You'll do now, I think.' Cooper nodded knowingly at his master's reflection in the glass.

Dominic assessed the image for a second. His mother would certainly recognise him now. It was as well that Cooper had cut out the scorch marks in his hair, though. The Dowager would certainly have had something caustic to say about those, if she had seen them.

He strode to the door and clattered down the stairs to find the landlord. He must find that girl.

'Monseigneur.' The landlord had instantly appeared, bowing so low that his nose seemed to be about to touch his knees. His thanks were effusive. And apparently interminable.

'Yes, yes,' Dominic said, with a dismissive wave. 'Anyone else would have done the same. Say no more about it.'

The landlord bowed again, even lower. It seemed he was about to start all over again, but this time Dominic cut him short. 'Landlord, there is a girl in the inn, with cropped hair. I wish to speak to her. Be so good as to bring her to me.'

'A girl, *monseigneur*?' He was looking thoroughly puzzled. He began to shake his head. Then, 'Oh, the girl with cropped hair. You mean that one.'

Dominic resisted the temptation to swear at the man. The landlord had just had a major fire at his inn, after all. No wonder his mind was at sixes and sevens. 'Yes, that one. I wish to see her. Where is she? And who is she?'

'You must mean the corn merchant's daughter, *monseigneur*. We have no other girl with cropped hair here. Poor thing, her father said they'd had fever in the family. Such a shame to cut off a girl's hair like that.'

'Yes, yes, but where is she? I require to see her.'

The landlord swallowed and stared at the floor. *'Désolé, monseigneur.* She has gone, I fear. Her family left several hours ago. While *monseigneur* was resting.'

Dominic swallowed a curse at his own weakness. He should have followed her at once. All his instincts had told him to do so. He frowned down at the landlord, but the man had not raised his eyes. 'But she has a name?' Dominic rasped.

The landlord hesitated for a moment. 'I…I do not have the girl's name, no. She was with the family Durand, of Paris. I assumed she was the daughter. Monsieur Durand gave me no precise address. It was not necessary, you understand. He—'

'So you have no way of contacting them?'

'I regret, *monseigneur*, that—'

'Oh, very well.' Dominic knew he was sounding bad-tempered. And he had no just cause. It was not the landlord's fault, but it was so frustrating that the girl had gone. Why did she have to have such a common surname? And no exact address? It was as if the whole of Boulogne was conspiring against him. With a shake of his head and a curt word of thanks, he left the landlord and strode out to assess the state of the yard.

Behind him, the landlord shook his head slowly. They were strange people, these English, even ones who spoke perfect French like the Duke of Calder. What on earth could he have wanted with a ten-year-old girl? Nothing good, that was certain. It was rumoured that the English had strange and perverted tastes. As an honest and patriotic Frenchman, the landlord could not take the risk of betraying the identity of the child, even to the English Duke who had been responsible for saving his livelihood. The English were the enemy of the Empire, after all. They had been responsible for exiling the Emperor.

The landlord sniffed in disgust. Then he smiled to himself. Giving the Duke a false name and address for the child had definitely been the right thing to do. And clever. By now, she was well on her way home. And not to Paris.

Dominic strode across to where the horses were tethered in the yard, as far as possible from the ruined stables. The grooms were milling around, trying to settle them. The pervasive smell of smoke was making the animals decidedly skittish.

Perhaps, with a fast horse, he could catch her? The family must be on the road to Paris, after all, and they could not be all that far ahead of him, unless they were travelling post. That was surely unlikely for a merchant's family?

He was on the point of calling out for a horse to be saddled. But then he remembered where he was. And the tasks that he was here to perform.

He could not leave Boulogne. Not even for an hour. He had to fulfil his orders from the Foreign Secretary, Lord Castlereagh. His lordship had treated Dominic with the utmost courtesy, but there had been not the least doubt that his soft-voiced instructions were to be carried out, and to the letter.

'On the face of it,' Lord Castlereagh had said, 'your task is simple. You will be attached to the staff of Emperor Alexander for the duration of his projected visit to London. The Russian court language is French but, of course, you speak it like a native, so you will have no difficulty there. You are to do everything in your power to smooth the Emperor's path during his stay. And you will ensure that none of his personal staff gets into any trouble while they are here.'

'On the face of it, sir? There is something more, I take it?'

Lord Castlereagh's smile was thin, and rather acid. 'You have just demonstrated why I was right to choose you, Calder. There is indeed something more. The government is somewhat concerned about the Russian Emperor. He is an able man, but he is not above doing deals with England's enemies. We know, for example, that he is unhappy about Princess Charlotte's proposed marriage to the Prince of Orange. It is possible he may seek to undermine it, for he knows how valuable a naval alliance with Holland would be to us. He would prefer the heir to the throne of England to marry a penniless princeling, I suspect. The Regent plans to offer him hospitality so that we may keep a close eye on who visits him. Your role will be to watch also, but on the inside.'

'If the Emperor is as astute as we are led to believe, sir, surely he will decline the services of a British liaison officer?'

'He might try. But I can assure you he will not succeed, Duke.'

And he had not. Or Dominic would not now be in Boulogne,

preparing to attend on the Emperor. Still, at least Dominic had had a little time to go home to Aikenhead Park. After spending so many months alone in France, spying for the British government, Dominic had needed a chance to relax.

It had proved to be a brief but enjoyable respite, especially as his youngest brother, Jack, had been there to welcome him home. And to roast him as usual. Although Jack was only twenty-four years old to Dominic's thirty-six, the bond between them was strong. They had become even closer over recent years, once Jack had become the third of Dominic's little team of spies, the Aikenhead Honours. Dominic, the eldest of the three Aikenhead brothers, was Ace, the leader. Leo, less than two years his junior, was King. Jack—Dominic always found himself smiling at the appropriateness of the name—was the Knave, and Jack's bosom friend Ben Dexter was Ten. The Aikenhead Honours lacked only the Queen, the Lady. Dominic had never found any woman who could be trusted with their secrets. Besides, it was often very dangerous work. No woman could be asked to do it. And none would have sufficient courage, either. Except, perhaps, that girl? Now she…

Dominic shook his head, shattering his wandering thoughts. He had no need of the Aikenhead Honours here in Boulogne, on such a straightforward assignment. And he must stop thinking about that girl. She was trying to haunt him and he would not allow it. He had work to do. He still had preparations to make before his first meeting with the Russian Emperor on the morrow. Everything must be exactly right.

He walked smartly back into the Lion d'Or, mounting the stairs two at a time. He must not let his frustrations rule him. She was only a merchant's daughter after all, no matter how courageous she was. Too high to be a mistress; too low to be a wife. He would soon forget her. Besides, he could barely remember what she looked like. And she had refused to speak to him. She had a low, melodious voice, he was sure, for he had heard her use it to reassure the terrified horses. But, for him, nothing beyond that scream of *'Non!'* even after he had rescued her from the burning stable.

Not even a word of thanks. Just wide-eyed fear. And flight. As from the devil himself.

Chapter Two

Alex stood on the dockside in Boulogne and gazed at the sea for the first time in her life. She had tried so hard to imagine what it would be like. She had thought about bigger versions of the many lakes she had seen. She had even tried picturing the steppes covered with water instead of earth. But she had not foreseen the movement. Yes, that seawater was definitely moving. The ships in the harbour were going up and down.

Her stomach lurched in sympathy and she felt a sudden foreboding. She had been overjoyed when she was bidden to join Tsar Alexander on his trip to England. But she sensed she was not going to enjoy this part of the journey one little bit.

In order to divert her mind from the horrors of the heaving sea, Alex at last allowed herself to remember that extraordinary encounter in the blazing stable. Until now she had not dared to think about the man. He had saved her life and she should be grateful to him. She was grateful to him. But when he had addressed her as *mademoiselle*, she had had no choice but to flee. Without even a word of thanks. He knew her secret and, all unwittingly, he would have betrayed it. She had had no choice.

She could still remember the feel of his half-naked body, lying on top of hers, and rolling them both around to stop the flames from taking hold. He had felt immensely strong. She was small, but she was no lightweight. Yet he had flung her across his shoulder as if she weighed nothing at all. If only she had dared to ask the landlord for his name. She could perhaps have sent him a note—an anonymous note—of thanks. Perhaps even now, she could—

No! She could not! To risk everything just to thank a smoke-blackened French servant? She did not even have the first idea what he really looked like. To seek him out, she would have to betray herself. It would be utter madness. She must force herself to forget the man, the stable and everything that had happened there.

She tried to focus on her mission instead, sternly reminding herself she must speak only French. She was under instructions from the Emperor himself not to disclose that her Scottish mother and her Scottish nurse had given her a perfect command of English. Her task was to listen, and report what she heard, no matter how unimportant it might seem. In other words, she was to spy for the Emperor. To serve Mother Russia.

A Royal Navy barge was coming in to dock. At first, it seemed tiny, and flimsy, against the vastness of the water, but eventually it moored alongside the jetty. Even tied up with ropes, it was still moving up and down. Alex felt ill just looking at it. In a desperate attempt to master her mutinous body and prevent the image of her rescuer from returning to haunt her again, she turned her back on the harbour and began talking to a group of French fishermen about their trade and their catch.

With luck, by the time she had to go on board, she would be back in control.

Dominic was leaning idly on the rail as the barge made its way into Boulogne harbour and prepared to tie up. He had satisfied himself that everything was in readiness for the Emperor on board the *Impregnable*. Once he set foot on

French soil again, his duty would begin in earnest. He would not have a moment to himself. There would be weeks of banquets, and balls, and speeches and all the endless ceremonial deemed essential for visiting royalty.

It would be exhausting, but he would have to remain vigilant throughout it all, just in case there was some little snippet of intelligence to be gleaned from a drunken officer or an overheard conversation. He would so much rather have been still at Aikenhead Park, even though his mother had been urging him to remarry, as she invariably did when he first arrived home. Though her eyes were always full of love for her firstborn son, she never managed to conceal a faint hint of exasperation with him. To be fair, she had cause. One failed marriage, one long-dead wife and no heir. Not a very good track record for a duke, especially a duke who had a habit of risking his neck on secret Government assignments. Yet in spite of his mother's hints, the Park always provided Dominic with a peaceful refuge, where he could refresh both mind and body.

That was what he needed in a wife. He could see that now. He had made such a wretched business of it, the first time, allowing himself to be seduced by the façade of Eugenia's beauty, wit and vivacity. As a companion, she had been aloof and chilly. As a bedmate, she had had the ability to freeze a man's ardour at ten paces. He would not make that mistake again. His new wife must be a woman of calm and serenity, who would make his home both welcoming and relaxing. A woman whose soft, mellifluous voice would stroke away the cares of the outside world. A woman—

A sudden shiver ran down his spine. From somewhere on the harbour side, he could hear a woman's voice, speaking educated French in just the low, musical tone that he had been imagining. Just like the voice of that girl in the stable. Was she really there? Or was his mind playing tricks?

He scanned the quayside impatiently. He needed to see

where she was, to see her face properly at last. The moment the ropes had been secured, he strode down the gangplank. He had to find the owner of that rich and wonderful voice. It was her. It must be.

'Je vous félicite,' said the voice. *'Et je vous remercie, aussi.'*

The voice seemed to be coming from among a large group of French fishermen, standing just a few yards from the barge. A Russian officer in uniform was with them, his back towards Dominic. Was the elusive girl there, too, hidden by the Frenchmen's burly backs?

The officer turned away from the group of fishermen. *'Au revoir,'* he said, raising his hand in farewell and starting across the quay towards the barge.

Dominic's stomach clenched in horror. Before he could stop himself, he uttered a savage curse. He was losing his wits! He had been weaving his missish dreams around a voice that belonged to a man!

A tall, dark man in civilian clothes had stepped off the military barge. He looked rather pale, as if he, too, did not enjoy the sea. But he also looked important. He certainly had an air.

Alex saluted him. 'Captain Alexei Ivanovich Alexandrov, at your service, sir,' she said smartly, in French.

For a second, the older man looked shocked, but then he returned Alex's salute with a tiny bow. 'Calder, appointed as liaison between his Majesty's Government and your Emperor,' he replied, in impeccable French. 'My task is to ensure that his Imperial Majesty's stay in England is as pleasant and enjoyable as possible. And if anyone in the Emperor's suite should need assistance, please ensure he asks me. It is precisely why I am here.'

Goodness. He seemed a rather exalted personage to be performing such a relatively menial role. For the moment, however, Alex merely thanked him, as courtesy demanded.

'Will you please to come out to the *Impregnable*, Captain?' Calder indicated a warship at anchor in the bay. 'You will wish to see where your Emperor is to be housed during the voyage.' With that, he made his way back on to the barge.

Alex hesitated. Her companion looked remarkably at ease on that flimsy plank of wood, even though it had dipped a little with every step he took. Courage! she told herself. Forward! She stepped on to the plank and marched along it, resolutely ignoring the swaying under her feet. She was an officer of proven courage. What was a little water to her?

Safely on the deck of *Impregnable* at last, Alex allowed Calder to lead the way down a steep ladder and into a large, light cabin at the stern of the ship. It had been laid out with sumptuous furnishings: gilded furniture, paintings, plate, delicate glassware, and every other comfort that a high-ranking traveller might desire.

The ship moved suddenly, just as Alex turned to close the cabin door behind her. She reached for the latch, missed, and stumbled into a small table alongside.

'You'll get your sea legs soon enough, Captain,' Calder said. 'But, until you do, it will be wise to hang on, if you are moving around the ship. Especially going up and down the companionways.'

'Companionways?'

'The stairs between decks,' he explained. 'The Navy has its own language.'

'You will forgive me if I say so, sir, but I am extremely surprised to meet an Englishman who not only speaks perfect French, but understands naval slang as well.'

'My mother is French,' he replied quickly.

'That would explain it. Though I would be astonished to learn that she had served in the Navy.'

Calder almost smiled. '*Touché*, Captain. No, of course she

did not. But I, myself, have often ventured to sea. We are a maritime nation, we British. It's in our blood. Whereas for you, I imagine, the vast tracts of steppe play the same role.'

He was right. He was a man of insight, this Mr Calder. Unless…? 'Have you visited Russia, Mr Calder?'

He looked slightly startled for a moment, but he replied easily enough, 'No, Captain, I have not. You will understand, being a military man, that travel has been…ah…a little difficult for civilians, these last fifteen years or so. However, now that Bonaparte is safely settled as Emperor of Elba—' he made a sound in his throat that could have been a snort of derision '—now that he is Emperor of Elba,' he repeated, 'the English are again indulging their love of travelling. Especially to Paris, of course. Perhaps even as far as Russia? It repays the effort, I am sure.'

'Oh, indeed, sir. For Russia is such a vast country that we have everything.'

'Except…' said Calder softly, pausing on the word, 'except the sea.'

At that moment, the ship lurched again. Alex felt as though her stomach had remained fixed in the air while the rest of her body sank by a foot.

'May I suggest you sit, Captain? Then you will not have to put so much effort into trying to keep your balance.'

He sounds almost paternal, Alex thought, wonderingly. Why should a rather stern-faced Englishman take the least trouble over a Russian soldier who looked barely half his own age? But she sat, nonetheless.

'I can imagine how you feel. I do not suffer from seasickness myself, but I have a much younger brother who goes green at the very sight of a ship.'

'I see,' Alex said automatically, feeling increasingly queasy.

'But it does mean that I am well acquainted with all the best remedies. If you should start to feel ill on the voyage, I will have the galley prepare you a special tisane which will relieve the symptoms, I promise.'

'You are more than kind, sir.' With the swell now worsening, she felt real gratitude to this strange Englishman. He might yet turn out to be her saviour.

'However, to business.' In clipped tones, Calder described the practical arrangements that had been made for the Emperor's comfort. There was nothing that Alex could cavil at. Calder, and his naval colleagues, seemed to have thought of just about everything. 'Emperor Alexander's host on this voyage to England will be his Royal Highness the Duke of Clarence, the Prince Regent's brother. He is a naval man himself. I should perhaps warn you that he has…um…a tendency to be a little bluff. I hope that the Emperor will not take offence. Naval language can be a little ripe, on occasion.'

Alex smiled. In her years as a common trooper, she had probably encountered a great deal more ripe language than any prince of the blood royal would use in front of the Tsar. 'His Imperial Majesty,' she replied carefully, 'is a man of impeccable taste and manners. He will certainly not do anything to put his host out of countenance.'

'Excellent, thank you.'

'At what hour is the Emperor's party expected to come on board?'

'About an hour or two before the tide, I expect,' Calder said. 'The captain of the *Impregnable* will give us exact information shortly. Tell me, Captain Alexandrov, does his Imperial Majesty travel with a large suite?'

'No, not on this occasion,' Alex said. 'He did not wish to impose on his host.' She went on to list all the people who were travelling in the Emperor's immediate entourage.

Calder remained inscrutable throughout her recital. He could clearly be a difficult man to read, when he chose.

'The Prince Regent has had a splendid set of rooms prepared

for the Emperor at St James's Palace. I am sure his Imperial Majesty will be most comfortable there. His suite also.'

'Oh dear.' The words were out before Alex had time to think.

Calder's eyebrows rose. 'There is a difficulty?'

'His Imperial Majesty—' She stopped, trying to collect her thoughts. 'You will be aware, I'm sure, Mr Calder, that his Imperial Majesty's sister, the Grand Duchess, Catherine of Oldenburg, is already in London, on a private visit.'

Calder nodded.

'His Imperial Majesty has no desire to inconvenience his royal host, but he is extremely fond of his sister, and he has decided that he will reside with her, at the Pulteney Hotel. I assume that will be in order?' She tried to say it in the airy voice of real assurance, knowing that the Tsar's mind was absolutely made up on the issue. By failing to forewarn the Prince Regent of his plans, he had also ensured that nothing could be done to thwart them.

'The Regent, like his Imperial Majesty, is a man of impeccable manners. I can assure you, Captain Alexandrov, that everything shall be done exactly as the Emperor wishes. Provided, of course, that the Pulteney Hotel is able to offer the necessary accommodation for such a guest.' He quirked an eyebrow.

Alex had a feeling she was blushing. She knew perfectly well that the arrangements had already been made, by the Grand Duchess. 'I am sure that his Majesty will be more than happy to accept the Prince Regent's hospitality if the Pulteney fails to come up to scratch. But since it is his Majesty's own choice, I do sincerely hope that the Pulteney can provide adequate facilities.'

'No doubt it will,' Calder said laconically. 'No doubt it will.'

'I have explained the arrangements to the Emperor's junior aide-de-camp,' Dominic said to the captain of the *Impregnable* a little later. 'You may have a spot of bother with him on the voyage. He turns green at the slightest lift of the deck.'

'Poor lad. He has my sympathy.' Captain Wood smiled. 'He doesn't seem old enough to be an aide-de-camp.'

'He doesn't seem old enough to be in uniform at all. But he must be. Firstly, he's a captain, though I suppose that could be a temporary promotion. But also—did you notice?—he wears the Cross of St George. That's one of Russia's highest honours for gallantry. He must have seen action, in spite of his youth.'

Dominic was still finding it difficult to account for his own initial reaction to the young Russian. Alexandrov looked nothing at all like Dominic's admittedly hazy memory of the amazing young woman at the stable fire, though that was the image that the sound of Alexandrov's voice had conjured up in Dominic's mind. Apart from the short hair, there could be no similarity. Dominic's smoke-fuddled brain must be playing tricks on him. Alexandrov was a small, thin young man with closely cropped hair and unremarkable features, but he seemed a nice enough lad, and one whose quick wits would make him good company. Dominic would just have to learn to ignore the melodious richness of his voice and to banish the memories of that girl for good. That should not be too difficult, surely? After all, he had no chance of ever finding her again. The only practical course was to forget about her.

'Tell me, Duke, is it true that the Emperor has brought dozens of Russian hangers-on?'

'Yes. But console yourself. Your fellow captain on the *Jason* will have not only the Prussian King, but also two of his sons, at least one of his brothers, and various uncles and nephews to boot.'

'Well, the Royal Navy is big enough to deal with whatever they send. They have armies, but we have the Navy, and that's what matters. And it will be even stronger once we have the Dutch alliance, from Princess Charlotte's marriage.'

Dominic nodded. 'How soon do you expect to sail, Captain?'

'In about two hours. With the wind in its present quarter, we should make Dover in very good time.'

'Dare I hope that the voyage will be quick enough to save that young lad from too much distress?'

'You are generous, Duke, to concern yourself with him.'

'Perhaps.' Dominic tried again to banish the embarrassing memory of that quayside encounter. 'But, as the British liaison officer, I'd rather not have an invalid on my hands. Not when I have to house them all. And, incidentally, to explain to the Regent that the Emperor has spurned his very expensive hospitality.'

'Truly?'

'So it appears. Young Alexandrov tells me—that is to say, it rather slipped out—that the Emperor is determined to stay at the Pulteney Hotel along with his sister, the Grand Duchess. So the Regent's plans to house him in the utmost state in St James's Palace have come to naught. The first round goes to the Emperor.'

Alex groaned yet again. How could she possibly be so sick when everything inside her was one vast, aching emptiness? At least, the Emperor had excused her from attendance on him. If only she could just—

'Ah, Alexandrov.' The cabin door had opened to admit Calder, followed by a swarthy seaman carrying a steaming mug. 'Give that to me now, man,' Calder said in English, gesturing towards the mug. 'I'll take charge of our guest.'

'Aye aye, your Grace.' The sailor passed the mug to Calder. 'Prefers rum meself,' he said, casting a look of profound distrust at the strange brew. 'Sovereign, rum is, for most any ailment.'

'You may return to your duties,' Calder said sharply, slipping a coin into the seaman's hand. The man knuckled his forehead and left, with the slap of bare feet on wood.

Alex had tried to ignore the English. But one thing she had understood quite clearly. The seaman had addressed Calder as 'your Grace'. Surely that title was given only to dukes? Was Calder a duke? If so, his role as a liaison officer was even stranger than she had thought. The ship lurched and she groaned again.

Calder—the Duke?—put an arm under Alex's shoulders and raised her enough to bring the mug to her lips. 'Drink a little,' he said in French. 'This will help to settle your stomach.'

The smell was slightly perfumed, and spicy. It was— The nausea overcame her again, and she tried to push the mug away.

'Believe me, it will be worth the effort. Come now.' He brought the mug back to her mouth.

Trying to ignore the smell, she sipped. It did taste of spice. Ginger, was it? She swallowed. The nausea did not immediately return.

'Good. Now a little more.'

She sipped again. Soon she had drunk about a quarter of the tisane. It warmed her aching stomach.

'I will leave it here by your bunk. It is best drunk hot, but, even cold, it will help. Now, you should sleep, if you can, or, better still, come up on deck.'

The thought of walking up the steps, and standing on that swaying deck, made Alex's head reel. Would she ever stand upright again?

He must have seen the reaction in her face, for he said, 'I know it sounds like the least attractive prospect in the world but, believe me, the fresh air in your face will make you feel much better. So, which shall it be? Sleep? Or fresh air?'

'I shall follow your advice, sir.'

Calder smiled suddenly. It transformed his rather harsh features. 'You *are* feeling better. I am glad of it. We shall soon be able to see the white cliffs of Dover. And that, my fine young friend, will be where your ordeal will end.'

Alex groaned. Just at the moment, she was sure it never would.

'I do understand,' he said. 'You feel as if you are about to die and nothing can save you. But, after five minutes on dry land and with some food inside you—'

She clapped a hand over her mouth at the very thought.

'With some food inside you,' he repeated, ignoring her distress, 'you will feel quite yourself again. And we shall be able to join the Emperor's suite on its way to London. You would not wish to be left behind, would you?'

'Oh, no! I am here to serve his Majesty. Where he goes, I must follow, no matter what the circumstances.'

'You're a brave lad,' Calder said, patting her shoulder. 'Come now, let's have you up on deck.'

She sat up slowly, trying to control the dizziness. Then she swung her legs to the floor. Surprisingly, she felt rather better. That tisane was working miracles. He offered an arm, but she ignored it. 'I can manage,' she said, putting her weight on her legs.

He caught her just as she started to fall. 'You are stubborn, Alexei Ivanovich.'

She was surprised to hear him use the Russian form of address. Something else to ponder over when her brain was fit to think once more.

'Curb your Russian pride for a moment, my fiery young steed, and allow me to help you up on deck. I promise I will not do more than is absolutely necessary. Your standing as a brave soldier will not be undermined in any way.'

'You are more than kind, sir,' she said, allowing him to take her weight.

Within five minutes, they had negotiated the steep stairs and Alex was managing to support herself at last, leaning against the rail. The fresh air was indeed making her feel much better. And, in the distance, she could see land. 'That is England, I suppose?'

'Yes. The white cliffs of Dover, a beacon for returning British sailors, for centuries. It means they are home, and safe.'

'I imagine it was very difficult when the rest of Europe was closed to you?'

'Well…' He smiled again. She fancied it was a rather enigmatic smile this time. 'Mainland Europe was never really closed to the Royal Navy. We had bases all round the Mediterranean. We were not short of places to land or to resupply.'

'And no doubt you could penetrate inland, too, if you wished?'

'I imagine so. Not being a Navy man, I cannot be expected to have knowledge of such things.' On a sudden, he sounded rather wary.

'But you have sailed, sir. You told me that you had.'

'It is true. I have. A little. Enough to know that I prefer my feet on dry land. As I fancy you do, too.'

At that moment they were joined by the ship's captain. 'I am delighted to see that you are on your feet, Captain Alexandrov,' he said, in rather hesitant French. 'The Duke has certainly looked after you very well.'

Oh, dear. It was true. 'The Duke?' she said, in her best imitation of total surprise. 'But *monsieur* introduced himself as plain "Calder".'

'It is his way, Captain Alexandrov. He is Dominic Aikenhead, fourth Duke of Calder. I fear he has played a trick on you.'

The Duke straightened, as if very much on his dignity, but there was a decided twinkle in his eye when he said, 'I beg your pardon, Alexei Ivanovich. I supposed that we were going to have to work together during your Emperor's visit. I thought too many "your Graces" might get in the way.'

'Indeed, your Grace,' Alex said, trying to prevent herself from smiling. 'I will try not to allow too many "your Graces" to get in the way of our working relationship, your Grace. Will that suit your Grace?'

The Duke burst out laughing. 'Confound the boy. He gives me back my own again.'

'You deserve it, too,' said Captain Wood.

'Aye. Probably.' He turned back to Alex. 'We can agree, I hope, that I shall be plain "Calder" to you? And that you shall be "Alexandrov" or "Alexei Ivanovich" to me. Agreed?'

Alex felt the beginnings of warmth around her heart. 'Agreed,' she said.

Chapter Three

'How are you now, Alexei Ivanovich?'

Alex was not at present on duty, and so she was standing near the front of the immense crowd, watching the proceedings. Had the Duke sought her out merely to ask after her health? Strange, if true. And yet another example of his kindness. 'Better, thank you, Calder. Much better,' she answered politely. 'I find I like the steadiness of Dover very much.'

'Have you eaten?'

'No.'

'Why not?' he demanded sharply.

She bristled. She was grateful to him, but he had no right to order her life. 'On board ship, I could not, even if I would have. And now that we are on land, there has been no opportunity. I must attend on his Majesty. I cannot take time out to fill my belly, however hungry I might be.'

Several voices hushed them angrily. The assembled dignitaries were now about to present their address, on behalf of the inhabitants of Dover.

Alex stood motionless throughout, trying to look blank. She understood it all, of course, though it was remarkably dull and pretentious.

The speech of welcome ended, and the Emperor stepped forward to reply. 'Although I understand your language,' he began, to murmurs of surprise all around, 'I do not feel myself sufficiently acquainted with it to reply to you in English; and I must therefore request those gentlemen of the deputation who speak French to be my interpreters to those who do not.' He then continued in French. His speech was received most warmly.

'That was a considerable surprise, Alexei Ivanovich. Were you not aware of your Emperor's talents?'

'I…I have not been an aide-de-camp to his Majesty for very long, Duke. I…I have had no occasion to discover that he speaks English. How would I?'

'How indeed? Do you tell me that no one in the Emperor's suite speaks English?'

'I think it was assumed that most of our hosts would speak French,' Alex said, avoiding the question as best she could. Somehow she did not want to lie to this man. If she did, he would know it. She was sure of that.

'Not everyone in England speaks French, you know, though most of the nobility does, I suppose. The royal family speaks German, so the King of Prussia and Marshal Blücher will be well served on that front. But if you, and others of the Emperor's party, go out into London, you will not be able to make yourselves understood. That could be dangerous. Even for allies.'

'Then we shall have to trust to our good-hearted liaison officer to rescue us, shall we not?' she asked impudently.

He gave a snort of laughter. His eyes were dancing. 'That, Alexei Ivanovich, is the sort of reply I should have expected from one of the sharp-tongued Cyprians of London, not from a battle-hardened cavalryman such as yourself.'

'Don't worry, Calder. I may not have your language, but I do have my sabre. I fancy it will be able to rescue me. Even if you do not.'

* * *

Major Zass, the Tsar's principal aide-de-camp, smiled round at the group of young officers who were now assembled in the Pulteney Hotel. 'That all went off very well,' he said, 'in spite of the problems on board ship.'

Alex felt the beginnings of a blush on her neck. He meant her seasickness. If it had not been for the Duke of Calder, it would have been even worse. He had been so very kind, so very thoughtful. Almost like a brother.

What a strange fancy to have. Was that how an elder brother would behave? She had no way of knowing. Her only brother was still a child. Yet Calder—

Zass was allocating various duties to his officers. 'You, Alexandrov—' at the sound of her name, Alex's daydream evaporated and she came smartly to attention '—you will attend on his Imperial Majesty when he rides out on horseback and when he makes visits to the sights of London. We will not involve you in the balls and receptions, though. We all know, don't we, gentlemen—?' he cast a laughing glance round at the others, who were all smiling knowingly '—that Captain Alexandrov is no dancer. Indeed, I'd wager that he is actually frightened of ladies.'

Alex's protest was drowned in the wave of laughter from her companions. There was no point in arguing. For it was true. She did avoid the company of ladies whenever she could. There was too much risk that they might see through her disguise.

'More seriously,' Zass continued, 'you will all have met the Duke of Calder, who has been assigned to us as a liaison officer by the British Government. He appears to speak no Russian, only French and English. But it may be that he has some Russian, too. So no one—' he looked sternly round at the assembled officers '—no one is to take any chances in his company. Do *not* assume he will not understand what you are saying. I trust I make myself clear?'

'Sir!' the officers said, in chorus.

'Good. Alexandrov, you seemed to be particularly friendly with the Duke.'

'Sir, it…it was simply that he was kind to me when I was ill on board ship.'

'That may well be true, but—' He stopped in mid-sentence, frowning. 'I think I need a private word with you, Alexandrov,' he said, beckoning her into an empty side-room. The other members of the Emperor's suite were left to continue gossiping and joking together.

'It would be particularly useful, Alexei Ivanovich, if you were to become friendly with the Duke of Calder. We believe he is not quite what he seems. Why, for example, is a duke, no less, acting as liaison officer? There must be many officers of the British army who speak French well enough for the task. It is beneath him. So, why does he do it?'

'You suspect he is a spy?' Alex breathed wonderingly. He had been so kind to her. She had accepted it, had even begun to return his warmth. Was it all just playacting, a means of gaining her trust? But why? She was the most junior member of the Emperor's entourage. She knew nothing. Nothing at all.

'It is possible. The English have stood alone against Bonaparte for many years, trusting no one. We may be allies now, but there have been moments…'

Alex caught her breath. Was Zass about to criticise the Tsar? Surely not?

Zass laughed harshly. 'I am sure the allies did only what was necessary for the sake of their countries. As did our beloved Tsar. But from England's point of view, it would not have seemed so. For them, all the allies were fickle, and unpredictable. The English have never trusted Russia. Which may go some way to explaining your Duke's presence here.'

'*My* Duke?' Alex exclaimed. 'I have only just met the man.'

'He is yours, Alexandrov. His Majesty gives him to you.

To find out everything you can about him. For your country. Is that understood?'

'Perfectly, sir.'

'Excellent.' He made to leave, but turned suddenly. 'The Duke does not know about your background, does he? I mean your command of English?'

'No, sir. I have been taking pains to look particularly stupid and uncomprehending every time English is spoken.'

'Good. Make sure it stays that way. I will expect your report, on a daily basis. Everything, you understand, no matter how trivial.'

'Of course, sir.'

Satisfied, Zass left the room without another word.

Alex allowed her shoulders to relax. She let out the breath she had been holding. Zass made her nervous. His Majesty had promised that the secret of her real identity would be shared only with Court Minister Volkonsky. And yet, Zass was very close to the Emperor. He might even know—

No! There was absolutely no point in speculating. She had to behave as if she were indeed Alexei Ivanovich Alexandrov, commissioned officer in the Mariupol Hussars, and temporary aide-de-camp to his Majesty. A temporary ADC whose task was to spy on the Duke of Calder, and to discover as much as possible about the intentions of the British Government.

It was such a messy business. Her instincts had been telling her to trust the man, to offer him true friendship. But that was impossible now. The coldness of duty was fixing itself around her heart, freezing the warmth that had begun to settle there. Duty! Only duty! Emotion was for females!

So the Duke of Calder lowered himself to become a spy. Possibly. It sat uncomfortably with his exalted station. Spying was a very dirty business.

That last thought made her laugh aloud. If spying was a dirty business, Alex herself was now immersed in it. Up to her neck.

* * *

'His Grace the Duke of Calder, sir.' The waiter bowed low and then withdrew, his eyes goggling.

Zass stepped forward and bowed. 'Your Grace,' he said smoothly, in French, 'we had not expected the pleasure of your company again this evening.'

Dominic smiled at the aide-de-camp and looked slowly round the room, marking each man. About half Zass's officers were present, but there was no sign of young Alexandrov. A pity. He was an entertaining young cub.

'I have come to serve as escort to his Imperial Majesty.' No response. Dominic tried again. 'For his Royal Highness the Prince Regent's banquet. At Carlton House.' There was something wrong here. Most of the officers were gazing at their boots. And Zass was avoiding Dominic's eye. 'Is there some problem I am unaware of, Major?' Dominic asked coolly.

Zass licked his lips. 'Perhaps you were not told, Duke. His Imperial Majesty plans to dine here. With his sister, the Grand Duchess of Oldenburg. I had understood that apologies had already been conveyed to the Prince Regent. The fatigues of the journey, you understand—'

'Of course, sir. You need say nothing more.' Dominic cursed silently. Fatigues of the journey, indeed! The Emperor's energy was boundless. He was simply refusing to go. Prinny was already furious that the Emperor had declined the apartments in St James's Palace. When he discovered that Alexander was refusing one of his sumptuous feasts as well, the Regent would probably sink into another childish sulk.

'Thank you, Duke. I shall ensure that his Majesty is fully informed of what has happened. He will be very grateful to you.'

Dominic bowed his acknowledgement. But he was not so easily bested. 'I have to tell you, Major, that no apologies have been conveyed to the Regent. Perhaps one of your officers… er…overlooked his task?'

Zass was looking thoroughly embarrassed now.

'If the officer in question cares to present his apologies to me, I will convey them to the Regent. Along with those from his Imperial Majesty, naturally.'

Zass looked to be about to have an apoplexy. At that moment, young Alexandrov appeared, as if from nowhere. His slight form must have been hidden behind one of the bigger men. 'Duke, it is my fault,' he said simply, stepping forward to stand alongside Zass. 'Major Zass tasked me with passing the Emperor's apologies to you earlier today and I…I am afraid that I forgot. It must have been the seasickness. It…er…it put everything else out of my mind.'

The lad was not a very convincing liar, but Dominic knew he would have to pretend to believe him. Dominic was sure where the responsibility truly lay. 'Perhaps, Major Zass, you would like to accompany me to see the Regent, to present the Emperor's apologies in person?' The man paled. Good. Dominic did not relish being made a fool of, especially with the connivance of a lad he had gone out of his way to help.

'Captain Alexandrov will go, Duke,' Zass said quickly, adding cruelly, 'It was his mistake, after all.'

Dominic was appalled. That was no way for a senior officer to behave to his subordinates. But he said only, 'Very well. When you are ready, Alexandrov, my carriage is at the door. We can ride to Carlton House together.'

Alex clattered down the staircase to the entrance hall, her spurs ringing. She settled her plumed shako on her head as she reached the last step. The Duke was standing by the main door, waiting for her. He was staring out into the street but, even from this angle, he looked magnificent in his full evening dress. Forbidding, too, she had to admit. He must have been very annoyed to discover the Emperor's change of plans. As, no doubt, the Prince Regent would be also.

She had yet to have even the briefest glimpse of the Prince Regent, but all of Europe knew his reputation. Meg, Alex's Scottish nurse, had said he was as handsome as a prince in a fairy tale, but that had been decades ago. He was no longer young, or handsome.

At that moment, Calder turned and saw her. She felt herself go bright red with embarrassment. She swore under her breath. Of all the difficulties of playing her role as a man, this was the worst. She had never been able to control it. And of course, this time, she had reason to blush. Calder was going to make her appear before the Prince Regent and take responsibility for the Emperor's whims. Why had she put herself forward? There had been no real need, for Major Zass would undoubtedly have found a way out of the difficulty. But that might have involved some implied criticism of the Emperor. Such a thing was unacceptable.

'There you are, Alexei Ivanovich. It is time we left.'

'My apologies, Calder. My orderly had taken my shako away to brush it.'

Calder looked her up and down. 'I must admit that the Hussar dress uniform is a most splendid one. Though perhaps,' he added with a smile, 'not the most practical.'

Alex relaxed a little. They were getting back to their earlier friendly banter. It felt very comfortable.

'Come,' he said briskly, 'we had better go. The carriage had great difficulty getting here and may have even more in leaving.' He shouldered his way through the press of people and flung open the door of his waiting carriage.

Alex had to admit he had remarkable presence in that powerful body. She followed in his wake, removing her shako. Its white plume was too tall to be worn inside the carriage.

'Carlton House,' Calder ordered sharply. 'Quick as you can.'

The carriage moved off, but only slowly, for the crowds were in no mood to make way for anyone less than a visiting monarch. Alex glanced back at the hotel. The Tsar, his sister, and various of his officers were standing on the balcony. The crowd was cheering itself hoarse.

'I fancy this may be quite a tedious journey,' Calder said with a sigh.

Alex nodded and leaned back in her corner.

'You will forgive my curiosity, I hope, Alexei Ivanovich, but I cannot help remarking that you are very young to have seen even one battle. Yet I know from the cross you wear that you must have done. It was won at Borodino, I was told.'

Alex launched into the answers she had long ago learned by rote. 'I am not nearly as young as I look, Duke. I have been serving in his Majesty's army for more than five years now.'

'Borodino was not your first battle then?'

She shook her head. 'I suffer from my lack of beard, but my comrades soon become accustomed.'

'I'm sure they bait you unmercifully.'

She shook her head again. 'The amusement soon palls. My youthful appearance has long been accepted. It is only when I meet new people, such as yourself, that it is remarked upon. What matters to my comrades is that I should be an efficient officer and that my soldiers should obey me without question. As they do.'

'I'm sure they do. You seem to me to be a remarkably resolute young man.'

'Not so very young, Duke. I am twenty-four years old.'

His eyebrows rose. 'Indeed? Now that I would not have believed.'

She laughed. Usually, at this point in her recital, she would be feeling uncomfortable. But, with this man, it had not happened. Perhaps it was that brotherly kindness? She told herself that it could be nothing else.

The carriage stopped so suddenly that they were both thrown forward. The Duke swore. Then, letting down the glass, he stuck his head out to speak to the coachman. Returning, he said, with a grimace, 'We are stuck here, I fear. Marshal Blücher has arrived at Carlton House. Even a man on horseback cannot get through.'

Alex picked up her shako. 'Shall we walk, Duke?' she asked, with a slight smile.

'If you wish.' He reached for the door handle. 'But wearing that fine Russian uniform, you, too, may find yourself being mobbed.'

Alex put a hand to the hilt of her sabre. 'Have no fear, sir. If you should be attacked, I will spring to your defence.'

The Duke looked down at her from his superior height. For a fraction of a second, he appeared totally thunderstruck. Then he burst into laughter. 'With you at my side, Alexandrov, I do believe that anything is possible.'

At the gates of Carlton House, the crowd was enormous, the noise deafening. Dominic had had to use his height and weight to force a path through. For all young Alexandrov's bluster, he would never have been able to do it by himself. He was fiercely proud, and as brave as a lion, but physically he was as slight as a girl. Such a strange combination in a young man. Yet an immensely likable character, nonetheless.

Dominic decided it was impossible to go any further by the direct route. The crowd was shouting for Blücher, with even more enthusiasm than their earlier huzzas for the Emperor, outside the Pulteney. 'Come, Alexandrov. Let us go round by the stables.'

The young Russian nodded and followed, holding his sabre tight against his side so that it would not impede their progress.

'At least I won't lose you, even among all these people,' Dominic shouted over his shoulder. 'With that incredible plume, I could find you in a throng of thousands.'

Alexandrov grinned his response.

The lad responded very well to being roasted. No doubt he was used to it. Yet he had begun to look a little nervous now, probably at the prospect of apologising to the Regent in person. Dominic suddenly felt ashamed of himself for tricking the lad into believing he must do so. That had never been his intention. Was he seeking revenge for the fact that Alexandrov's voice disturbed him still? Unworthy, if so. It was not Alexandrov's fault that Dominic's mind was playing tricks on him.

The stable gates were closed and manned by soldiers. 'Let us in,' Dominic ordered. 'I am the Duke of Calder and this officer is on the staff of his Majesty the Russian Emperor.'

'Daren't do it, sir. Er...your Grace.'

'Nonsense. Open up at once.'

The soldier stood stiffly to attention. He made no move to obey Dominic. 'We've only just managed to get these gates closed, sir. We opened them for Marshal Blücher's carriage and were almost crushed by the people flooding in around him. There are still hundreds of them inside the house. You'll have to go in by the main gate. Sorry, sir.'

'Fetch your officer.'

It did not take Dominic long to convince the young lieutenant that he ought to be able to open the stable gates just enough to admit two gentlemen. And that, if he was any kind of officer at all, he should be able to ensure that none of the milling crowd could force a way through.

Within minutes, Dominic was leading the way into Carlton House. They arrived in the grand hall just in time to see the Prince Regent and Marshal Blücher emerge from the Regent's private apartments. The crowd cheered ecstatically. For Blücher, of course. But the Prince had not lost his sense of theatre. In the midst of the huge throng, he invited Blücher to kneel so that he could fasten a medallion on the old man's shoulder. Dominic fancied that the portrait on the medallion was of the Regent himself. That was very much his way. The

Marshal, however, seemed to be overcome by the honour. As he rose, he kissed the Regent's hand.

'Wait here,' Dominic shouted into Alexandrov's ear. 'I'll go and make sure the Regent's aides know about the Emperor's change of plans.'

'But if I am to apologize—'

'You are not,' Dominic said firmly, glad to be able to clear his conscience at last. 'I'll say all that is necessary on your behalf.'

'But you cannot—'

Dominic did not wait to listen to the young man's protests. All he wanted now was to pass his message and then to escape from this infernal circus. Prinny might delight in it all. But for ordinary mortals, the next few weeks were going to be a continuing trial.

Chapter Four

Dominic ushered Alexandrov through the front door into the sudden quiet of the spacious hallway. Withering, the Aikenhead family butler, bowed as he took their hats. 'Lord Leo has just this minute arrived, your Grace. I believe he is in the library.'

'Excellent. Thank you, Withering.' Then, reverting to French, 'Come and meet my brother, Alexei Ivanovich. Must say I wasn't expecting him.'

'Perhaps he could not resist all the London festivities, Duke?'

'I take leave to doubt that. But you shall judge for yourself. Come.' Almost as an afterthought, Dominic said, 'Send in some of the best Madeira, would you, Withering?'

'It is already done, your Grace. Lord Leo—'

Dominic laughed. 'I should have known. My brother makes free with my cellar whenever he favours me with his company.'

As Withering flung open the double doors to Dominic's library, the solitary figure in the room rose from the leather armchair and strode towards them, grinning widely. 'Dominic! Hadn't thought to see you tonight, old man. Assumed the Regent would have you running round in circles until dawn.'

'In other words, you thought you'd have hours yet to make

free with my Madeira,' Dominic retorted, trying not to show just how pleased he was to see his brother.

'But of course,' Leo said smoothly, throwing a questioning glance towards Dominic's companion.

'Forgive me, Alexandrov,' Dominic said quickly, reverting to French. 'That was bad manners on my part. You will allow me to present my brother, Lord Leo Aikenhead? Leo, this is Captain Alexei Ivanovich Alexandrov, one of the aides-de-camp to his Majesty the Emperor Alexander.'

The two men bowed to each other and exchanged courtesies.

'Surprising that you are both off duty so early,' Leo said in his accentless French. 'Or are you?'

'Yes. Until tomorrow morning. Is that not so, Alexei Ivanovich?'

'His Imperial Majesty has no further need of me this evening. He dines with the Grand Duchess. However, if he rides out before breakfast, as he usually does, I shall be on duty then.'

'No hard drinking for you tonight, then, Captain? What a pity. Thought to introduce you to some of Dominic's better bottles.'

'I—'

'I must ask you to forgive my brother, Alexei Ivanovich,' Dominic said quickly. 'He is incorrigible. And in spite of his efforts to paint himself as a drunken sot, I can assure you that he is only trying to humbug you. And me.'

The young Russian smiled first at Dominic and then at Leo. 'Believe me, I have had much worse from my compatriots. But I should perhaps warn you that I very rarely drink.'

Leo's eyes widened, but he was too polite to make any comment. Dominic, by contrast, was not at all surprised. It was such a pity that they were, so to speak, on opposite sides, for Alexei Ivanovich was a remarkable and admirable young soldier, the kind whom Dominic would have been happy to call his friend. Alexandrov had an inner core of steel. In the space of only a day or so, Dominic had learned that he was not the sort of man who would conform where it did not suit him. And that he was definitely a man who should not be underestimated.

Alex put down her half-empty glass. Her invariable rule was to permit herself no more than one glass of wine, and always with food. On this occasion, she had been very tempted to break her rule for the Duke's splendid wine. But she did not dare. Not with gentlemen as astute as the Duke and his brother.

The Duke tried again. 'Will you have a little more wine, Alexei Ivanovich?'

Alex shook her head, smiling across at him. 'No, Calder, I thank you. Your wine is truly excellent, but I never have more than one glass.'

'Haven't even had that,' Lord Leo interposed, gazing pointedly at her glass. 'If I were a betting man, I'd be tempted to wager that you don't really like wine at all. Am I right, sir?'

'I—'

'Don't bother to reply, Alexandrov,' the Duke said quickly. 'My brother has a disreputable habit of trying to provoke others, even when they are our guests. I have spent years trying to cure him of it.' He sighed theatrically. 'I'm afraid I have failed.'

'Not true, brother mine. Never provoke *my* guests. Only yours.'

Alex, astonished, looked from one to the other. The Duke was trying, unsuccessfully, not to laugh at his brother's wicked comment. Lord Leo had an expression that was…almost angelic. Angel laced with grinning devil. Was this what it was to be brothers, and to be truly close? It seemed more than wonderful. With no sisters, and only one, much younger, half-brother, Alex had never experienced anything like this. What's more, as a mere female, she had been expected to spend all her time acquiring domestic skills. Even if she had had sisters, she doubted that her stepmother would have permitted anything bordering on frivolity. A girl's role was to learn what she needed in order to be a good daughter first, and then a good wife to a man chosen by her parents. Duty was everything. Enjoyment, and laughter, had no place at all.

As she stared, wide-eyed, at the Aikenhead brothers, she was visited by a subversive thought. If her own Scottish mother had brought her back here, would her life have been totally different? Would she have been happy to have remained in the role of a girl? Her restlessness had been largely her father's fault, of course, for he had brought her up in a military environment while he himself was serving in the Hussars. She had absorbed the life through every single pore of her body until she had been living it every minute of every day. She had ridden like a Hussar, eaten like a Hussar, thought like a Hussar. It had become the life she loved and the life she wanted. So, when her father had left the army in favour of a civil post, it had been as if Alex were cast into prison. Particularly so when her father had married again, to a shrewish woman who believed that the role of an unmarried girl was silence and sewing. And to be addressed, formally, as 'Alexandra', rather than the familiar Scottish 'Alex' that had always seemed so loving.

The butler returned to clear the plates. 'Lord Jack has just this minute arrived, your Grace,' he said quietly.

Calder raised an eyebrow. 'Strange. The wine is in here and Lord Jack is not. You must have seen an apparition, Withering.'

Alex looked down at the table and pursed her lips hard, trying to conceal her amusement. Calder must not suspect that she had misled him about her knowledge of English. Oh, this was becoming so very difficult.

'Lord Jack,' Withering said in a lofty tone, 'was informed

that your Grace had a foreign guest at the supper table. He therefore repaired to the library.'

'And my Madeira,' laughed Calder, slapping the table with his hand. 'Not an apparition then. Tell my brother, if you please, that we shall join him shortly.'

The butler bowed and withdrew.

Calder then explained, in French, that his youngest brother had just arrived. 'I should warn you, Alexei Ivanovich, that Jack is something of a scapegrace. In fact, he's even worse than brother Leo.'

'Thank you, Dominic,' Lord Leo said calmly.

Calder's mouth quirked at the corner, by just a tiny fraction. He continued, as if his brother had not spoken, 'Jack will lead you astray, if you give him half a chance. He is about your age, and he thinks that Leo and I are now old and staid, quite beyond redemption. He will try to lure you off to gaming hells, and heaven knows what else.'

Alex hoped fervently that she was not blushing again. 'I am grateful to you for the warning, Duke. But I do not gamble.' The brothers' surprise was evident. Alex decided to give them her usual lie. 'I'm afraid I cannot afford it. My family may be noble—as you probably know, that is a requirement for officer status in the Russian army—but that does not mean we are rich. I cannot, and will not, wager my next meal against the turn of a card. I apologize now if that is a disappointment to you.'

'Not to me, Alexei Ivanovich,' Calder said. 'The Prince Regent tasked me to take particular care that the Emperor's officers did not get into trouble through playing for high stakes here in London.'

'And how, pray, were you supposed to ensure that?' Lord Leo asked innocently.

'No idea.' Calder grinned. 'Perhaps Prinny thinks I have a magic wand?'

Lord Leo grinned back, shaking his head.

Alex swallowed, feeling a little embarrassed. Was it permissible to criticise the Regent in this way? No Russian officer would ever say any such thing about the Emperor. Never.

'Forgive me, Alexandrov. I did not mean to embarrass you. Like all monarchs, the Prince Regent sees it as his role to issue commands. It is for others to find ways of carrying them out. Practicalities are for underlings. Among whom I number myself.'

Alex's eyes widened. A duke? An underling?

She felt a slight draught as the door opened at her back.

'I've finished the Madeira, brother,' said a new, younger voice. 'Would you have me start on the brandy now?'

Dominic was glad that both his brothers had arrived to help entertain the young Russian. It gave him an opportunity to watch the lad, to judge his motives. And to rid himself of that strange fancy, from Boulogne. Alexandrov's remarkable voice still seemed to be able to stir strange feelings, deep in Dominic's innermost core. He must banish them. He must. Alexandrov was a man, confound it! All that smoke must somehow have addled his brain.

Dominic forced himself to concentrate on his mission. He would have to find some way of testing the lad, even though he was definitely on his guard. He thought carefully before he spoke. On the other hand, his face did sometimes betray his emotions. That was one of Dominic's mother's failings, too. It was excusable in a woman, but not in a soldier. Alexandrov had clearly shown his astonishment, for example, at the Aikenhead family banter. He must be a lad with no older brothers.

'What have you seen of London so far, Captain?' Leo asked. Leo knew that Dominic's ability to judge a man was better than his own, and so he willingly drew all the attention on to himself, leaving Dominic to observe. And deduce.

The young Russian seemed to have relaxed a little. He

smiled at Leo and sat forward in his chair, picking up his half-full wine glass and turning it round and round in his strong, lean hand. It was a ploy, Dominic was sure. Had there been, somewhere in his past, a drunken episode of which he was ashamed? He struck Dominic as the kind of lad who would take such indiscretions extremely seriously.

'His Majesty arrived only today, Lord Leo. So far, I have seen the inside of the Pulteney Hotel, the inside of your brother's carriage, though not for long, since it proceeded at a pace resembling a one-legged snail, and—'

'Do snails have legs in your country, Captain?' Jack had adopted that high-handed tone which meant he was bent on mischief. 'In this country, they seem to have lost their legs, somewhere along the way.'

'I meant…I meant…'

Good grief, the young man was blushing. Well, well, well. He really was just like the Dowager. Not so manly after all, perhaps? No wonder he was avoiding alcohol, if it was so easy to put him out of countenance. It could be useful to know that.

'It is…it is a…a family joke, which does not translate well. I meant only that Calder's carriage was unable to proceed. And so we had to walk to Carlton House,' Alexandrov continued, more fluently than before. 'It is very grand inside.'

'Far too much gilding for my taste,' Jack muttered.

'You must excuse my brother,' Dominic said quickly. 'His taste tends towards the furnishings of gambling dens and the like. We don't often let him into polite company. In fact, we've been telling the world that he's not our brother at all, but a changeling.'

Jack gasped and started to rise from his chair.

'Unfortunately,' Dominic continued calmly, 'he looks so much like me that no one will believe us.'

Alexandrov nodded, rather pensively. 'Perhaps you are both changelings, Duke,' he said with an air of studied innocence. 'Perhaps the true heir is Lord Leo, who looks nothing like either of you?'

Jack burst out laughing.

Beside him, Leo was grinning, too. 'Seems to me that our Russian guest can give as good as he gets. I'd watch your tongue if I were you, Dominic.'

'I shall clearly have to. I fancy that Captain Alexandrov must spend a lot of time being roasted by his fellow officers and sharpening his wit on them. Is that the way of it, Alexei Ivanovich?'

'I find it does not do, Duke, to accept jibes meekly. The occasional riposte reminds my comrades that my role is not solely to provide sport for them.'

'How true,' Dominic said thoughtfully. He waited a moment more before striking. 'And what, would you say, is your role, exactly?'

There was a decided pause before the Russian spoke again. 'I…why, I am a captain in the Mariupol Hussars and have been honoured with the appointment as an aide-de-camp to his Imperial Majesty. You are already aware of that, I think.'

Dominic nodded slowly. 'Just idle thoughts that came to me.' He picked up his glass and took a long swallow. 'It seemed to me that his Imperial Majesty already has a great many young officers in his suite. I simply wondered why you had been added to their number.'

'Oh, that is easily explained, Duke,' Alexandrov replied smoothly. He was fully in control now. 'His Majesty had not seen me for some years, since he did me the honour—' He reddened slightly and touched the Cross of St George on his breast. 'His Majesty was gracious enough to wonder about my progress. Court Minister Volkonsky suggested that I might be attached to the staff for the duration of this visit.'

Now that, Dominic thought, was a well-rehearsed line, but he doubted that it was the whole truth. What kind of monarch remembered to check up on the progress of one young officer among so many? Especially one not seen for years? The fact that Alexandrov had a ready tale suggested that he had something to hide.

Dominic leant forward. 'When did you—?'

The door opened again to admit the butler. Dominic raised his head, frowning. This was just the wrong moment for an interruption.

'Excuse me, your Grace, but a messenger has this moment arrived. I understand it is a matter of some urgency. Will you see him?'

Dominic rose. Withering had given no indication of who the messenger was. Which meant that the man was possibly from Horse Guards. Or from the Foreign Secretary himself.

'Thank you, Withering. I will come at once. No doubt it is yet another concern of the Regent's. Possibly about the colour of his coat.'

The moment the door closed behind the Duke, Lord Jack launched into a stream of questions about Alex's home and her family. She answered as best she could, trying to betray as little information as possible, but still she found herself saying more about her parents and her home than she had intended.

The two brothers had just begun a lively discussion on the dangerous topic of boxing when the Duke returned. He was looking grave, but his face softened at the sight of his brothers. 'Arguing again? And in front of our guest, too.' He shook his head. 'I thought you had better manners, Jack.'

'I'll have you know, Dominic—'

'Excuse him, if you would, Captain Alexandrov. He has always been an unruly brat and, unfortunately, Leo has never yet learned to keep him under control. He spoils him, you see.'

'If you weren't my brother, Dominic, I'd call you out for that!' Lord Jack had jumped to his feet, fists clenched.

'After that comment, I'm first in the queue,' Lord Leo growled.

The Duke grinned. 'I wouldn't dare take you on, Leo. Even if I had choice of weapons, you'd best me every time. Jack, on the other hand… Well, Jack is improving with his fists, at least.' He strolled forward to the table, lifted his wine glass and sipped. 'And now, if you will allow me, Alexandrov, I will escort you back to the Pulteney.'

'There is no need, Calder. I can certainly make my own way back.'

The Duke snorted. 'This, from a pint-sized sabre-carrier who speaks not a word of English? No, my friend, the Regent has charged me to offer all assistance to the Emperor's suite. I should be failing in my duty if I allowed you to be trampled underfoot.'

It would be most impolite to argue further. Besides, the Duke probably had business to discharge. Business resulting from that urgent message. She must do what she could to find out about that. Major Zass would be expecting her report on the Duke. 'You are very good, Duke. And I willingly accept your company, if it is not an inconvenience. If you are required at Horse Guards, I could easily take a hackney back to the Pulteney.'

The Duke's mouth twitched. 'You might take one, but I doubt it would get you there. There are still crowds of people in the streets.' He turned for the door. 'Now, if you are ready, Alexei Ivanovich…?'

Alex felt a sudden glow. It must be his continued use of the Russian form of address, she decided. Familiar. Friendly. It could not be the Duke himself, for he was a daunting figure, one to beware of.

But then, as he ushered Alex out into the hall, he dropped an arm across her shoulders, in a brotherly fashion. Her heart stopped dead. Her insides plummeted down to her boots.

Suddenly, she felt quite light-headed, as if she had drunk far too many glasses of champagne.

How could she think that, she who had never drunk more than one glass in her life? What on earth was happening to her?

Chapter Five

Late though it was, the streets were still packed with people. They seemed to be generally good humoured, but there was no mistaking the pervasive smell of gin. Looking over his shoulder as they pushed their way through towards the Pulteney, Dominic realised that young Alexandrov looked incredibly small and vulnerable. That sabre of his—which had no doubt tasted blood in battle—would be no help here in London.

'Oi! Who d'ye think ye're pushin'?' A couple of feet behind Dominic, a man with arms like prize hams had turned a furious face on Alexandrov. The ruffian was at least three parts drunk and seemed to be spoiling for a fight. He raised a huge fist to strike the Russian.

Alexandrov's hand went to his sabre-hilt and began to draw, just as Dominic moved to put himself between them. 'Sheath it,' Dominic cried, keeping his eyes fixed on the drunk. If he had to, Dominic could easily knock the man down, but that would be almost as risky as Alexandrov's damned sabre. A fist fight could quickly turn into a street brawl and then a full-scale riot.

'This is one of the Russian Emperor's officers.' Dominic was almost shouting to make himself heard. 'We're here to cheer the Russians, aren't we?'

The drunk was beginning to look confused. His clenched fist had slackened a little. Around him, the crowd was muttering. One or two were trying to pull the drunk away.

'Three cheers for the Emperor Alexander,' Dominic cried. To his relief, at least a dozen voices responded. By the third cheer, it was probably fifty. And the drunk was cheering, too. His furious face now wore a beatific smile.

Dominic breathed a sigh of relief and pushed on through the crowd until they were out of danger in a fairly quiet side street. He had to warn Alexandrov about the risks he was taking. The young fire-eater would not always have Dominic at his side to calm the mob. 'May I suggest, Alexei Ivanovich, that you would be unwise to brave the London streets alone?'

The young man bristled visibly and started to protest.

'I intend no slur on your honour,' Dominic said quickly, putting a hand on Alexandrov's shoulder and gripping it lightly. He might need protection, but he was much too proud to admit it. 'Your bravery is beyond question. I meant only that, with the London mob, it is remarkably easy to provoke a riot.'

Alexandrov had not attempted to shrug off Dominic's hand, but he had become rather flushed. It seemed he was just as quick to anger as he was to put his hand to his sword.

'I do not for a moment suggest that you would do so intentionally, Alexei Ivanovich. But if you had actually drawn that sabre of yours, their mood could have changed in the blink of an eye. They're not overfond of foreigners, you see, even foreigners who have helped to defeat Bonaparte.'

'Helped?' exclaimed the young man, with savage emphasis. 'You mistake, Duke. If one compares the losses of the Russian army with your own—'

Very quick to anger, Dominic decided. 'I do not seek to belittle you, Alexandrov, or the Russian army.' He patted the lad's shoulder in what he hoped was a reassuring way. It did not seem to be helping, for Alexandrov flushed even more. 'I seek only to assist you. You do accept that, I hope?'

As soon as Dominic removed his hand, Alexandrov's angry flush began to subside. He even made a half-hearted attempt to smile. Did he feel he was being patronised? Was that the cause of his evident ill temper?

Another burst of cheering drowned Dominic's attempted explanation. In the distance, he could see that Emperor Alexander had appeared once more on the balcony of the Pulteney Hotel. The crowd's reception was rapturous.

'That does not look to me like a lack of fondness for foreigners, Duke.'

'Agreed. But please remember, Alexei Ivanovich, that the London mob has one characteristic above all. It is fickle.'

The young man appeared to consider Dominic's words with rather more care than before. 'I do understand your warning, Duke. I admit I was rash. And I ask you to forgive my display of…of ill temper. It was unwarranted.'

'Doing it too brown, my friend. You have nothing to apologize for.' Dominic smiled with relief. He had found himself unaccountably warming to this strange young warrior with the hair-trigger temper. The last thing he wanted was to offend him, even inadvertently. 'Look! Your Emperor is leaving the balcony. Poor man, it seems the cheering crowd will give him no peace. Is he received in this way in Russia?'

'Yes. No. Not exactly. The Tsar is "the Little Father" to his people. The…the relationship is not the same.'

Dominic frowned, wondering. A father to his people? For a second he imagined the Prince Regent in the role. It was so absurd that he had difficulty in keeping his face straight. A sideways glance showed him that Alexandrov was set to take offence again. He was quick to see slights to his beloved Emperor, was he not? 'Forgive me, Alexei Ivanovich. In my mind, I could not help but compare your

Emperor with our Prince Regent. He has been called many things, but "a father to his people" would be the most unlikely of all.'

'You are not very respectful, Duke.' Alexandrov looked puzzled.

'It is our way, Alexandrov. The English are fiercely loyal to throne and country, but unwilling to be blind to their faults. And the monarch does not have absolute power here. The scandal sheets and the cartoons lampoon the Regent, his mistresses, his extravagances… It is our way.'

Alexandrov shook his head wonderingly. It was clear that he was finding it difficult to grasp the English attitude, so different from Russian ways. Yet he was at least trying to understand which, in Dominic's experience, was unusual. Definitely an intriguing young man.

Dominic clapped his companion on the back. 'Worry not, my friend. Such things will not happen to your Emperor while he is here. Besides, all London is determined to celebrate. What better figurehead than your young and virile Emperor?'

Alexandrov had flushed again. He swallowed. 'Our beloved Tsar is a great man,' he said simply.

They had reached the entrance to the Pulteney. Dominic fancied that the crowd was now beginning to thin a little, possibly because it was so late. It would be thoroughly unreasonable to expect the Russian Emperor to appear again. As the pair passed into the foyer of the hotel, he said as much to Alexandrov, adding, 'But that will probably not prevent them from trying. I doubt that your "Little Father" and his suite will get much sleep tonight. Or any other night.'

'The Emperor does not seem to need much sleep, Calder,' Alexandrov said with a touch of pride. 'I dare say you will see for yourself in the next few days. He is a man of enormous energy.'

'If you can keep up with him, Alexei Ivanovich, I am sure

that I can also. I'm not *that* old, you know.' Dominic raised an eyebrow, expecting a witty retort.

Instead, Alexandrov reddened like a schoolboy. 'I beg your pardon, Duke.'

Dominic shook his head and grinned widely. The boy had much to learn.

Alexandrov relaxed a little. 'What I meant was that the aides-de-camp do not go everywhere with his Imperial Majesty. We each have specific duties. I, for example, attend his Majesty when he goes riding. But I am not required to attend him to balls, and such social events.'

'Your are fortunate. Balls can be remarkably tedious affairs, I find.'

The lad was blushing again. 'I…I have not attended many balls, Calder. But I would not say that those I have attended were…er…tedious.'

'Oh? How would you describe them?'

From the look on the lad's face, Dominic fancied the appropriate word would be 'terrifying'. Now, why would he be afraid of such an event? Surely most young men would be delighted to be in the company of pretty young ladies?

'I am afraid that I do not dance, Duke. When Mother Russia was fighting for her very survival, it would have been dishonourable for a soldier to spend time on learning such frivolous skills. Sabre-drill was much to be preferred.' He spat out that last statement with considerable pride.

Dominic knew better than to pursue the matter. 'Will Major Zass go riding with you, do you think?' Riding in the park would provide a good opportunity to make contact with the Major in an informal, friendly way. Zass might even let slip something useful.

'He may do. He does ride when he can be spared. His Majesty insists that we all ride, for the benefit of our health. Exercise is most important, he maintains.'

'And his Majesty is right, of course. Tell me, Alexandrov, how shall I know whether his Majesty plans to ride in the mornings? Does he decide these things the previous evening?'

'I fear not.'

'Ah. Then I must send a servant here each morning, to find out what his Majesty's plans are. May I instruct the servant to ask for you?'

Alexandrov smiled. 'Of course. I always rise early, usually at first light.'

Dominic allowed himself a theatrical groan. 'You would not do that if you had been dancing till four in the morning.'

'No, perhaps not. Though his Majesty does. Often.'

'I must be getting old,' Dominic said ruefully. 'Now, I must not keep you from your duties, Alexei Ivanovich. My servant will wait on you tomorrow. Will six o'clock be early enough?'

Alexandrov put his head on one side. 'Well…' he said slowly, 'his Majesty often sets off before seven. Would six o'clock give you enough time to prepare yourself, Calder?' He allowed his gaze to roam over Dominic's immaculate evening clothes. 'I have heard that London gentlemen take many hours to dress for the day. The tying of a cravat, I am told…' He shook his head slightly.

Dominic felt his mouth twitch. 'That may be true of Brummell, Alexei Ivanovich, but it is not true of me,' he said, vehemently. 'I have not slept with my horse on the eve of battle, as you have done, but I can assure you that if my servant brings me word before half past six, I can be riding in the park by seven.'

Alexandrov grinned mischievously. 'Always assuming, of course, that you have not been dancing till five? I take it, Duke, that you are not going to a ball after you leave here?'

'No, I am going to— I have a number of calls to make, Alexandrov. You have still to discover exactly what your monarch plans to do tomorrow. I must do the same for mine, even though my main duty is to attend on your Emperor. No doubt we will meet in the park tomorrow. I look forward to it. Meanwhile, I will bid you good night.' He bowed to his companion and turned for the door.

'Calder.'

Dominic turned back. Alexandrov was smiling at him, looking very small and trim in the huge foyer of the hotel. The picture of a boy soldier. Except that he was not a boy.

'You did not give me a chance to thank you for your hospitality this evening. And for your help with the crowd. Thank you.' He bowed formally.

'My pleasure, Captain. And my brothers'. By the way, don't believe everything they tell you. I am not nearly as bad as they paint me.'

Alexandrov merely bowed again and turned towards the stairs.

Smiling to himself, Dominic left the hotel and walked into Piccadilly. He was an interesting young man, Captain Alexandrov. And an entertaining companion, especially when he gave his wit free rein. It would be a pleasure to cultivate him further, Dominic thought warmly. Then icy duty intruded, spoiling his sunny mood. Alexandrov would have to be used, to provide an entrée to Major Zass and possibly to others of the Emperor's court. And Dominic must say as much to Castlereagh, who would now be waiting impatiently for his report.

Tomorrow, in the park, Dominic would hope to further his acquaintance with Major Zass. And to judge just how well young Alexandrov sat a horse.

Alex managed to run nonchalantly up the stairs and round the first landing. Once she was out of sight of the foyer, she stopped, gripping the baluster rail tightly for support. Her free hand was shaking.

On the landing above, a burst of laughter forced her back to the present. Her brother officers had obviously been enjoying an evening off duty. One of them might spot her at any moment. She forced herself to straighten her back and march up the stairs, with her normal jaunty gait. No one must see any difference in Captain Alexandrov's demeanour.

Almost all of the Tsar's suite was in the reception room on the first floor. Some of them had clearly been indulging very freely in their Emperor's hospitality. A couple were stretched out on the sofas, snoring loudly.

'Alexei Ivanovich, where have you been?' cried one, lurching towards Alex as if to fling an arm round her shoulder.

She sidestepped neatly. 'Where is Major Zass? He is expecting my report.'

'Wha' report?'

Her thoughtless words had penetrated the drunken fog in the man's brain. What report, indeed! She had been tasked by the Major in private and now, stupidly, she was talking about her mission in the midst of her drunken comrades.

Concentrate, Alex! What has happened to you? You are not usually so unaware. You have plenty of experience of dealing with men such as these.

But not with men such as the Duke of Calder, said a little voice from somewhere in the recesses of her mind. Calder had upset all her equilibrium. The moment he touched her, she had—

'Alexandrov. At last.' Major Zass emerged from the side-room where he and Alex had spoken earlier. Unlike his comrades, Zass was still sober. He ushered Alex into the room and closed the door.

'You are very late, Alexei Ivanovich. I hope that is a good sign. Tell me, what have you discovered?'

Alex forced herself to focus on the Major, and how best to answer his questions. Briefly, she recited what had happened at Carlton House and, later, at the Duke's London home.

'And what have you discovered about the Duke himself? It sounds as if you had plenty of opportunity to probe.'

'The Duke of Calder is a very careful man, Major. I learned more about his brothers in ten minutes than I learned about the Duke in all the time I was with him.'

Major Zass frowned.

'But that, in itself, is interesting,' Alex continued, realising as she spoke that she knew more about the Duke than she had imagined. 'The Duke of Calder takes great pains to avoid direct questions. I am almost sure that he has something to hide.' She was right. She was sure of it. The way he had avoided her questions. And her eyes. Even on such a mundane thing as his plans for the rest of the evening. 'He tried to convey the impression that he was returning to Carlton House for further instructions. I do not believe that was the case.'

'You should perhaps have followed him?'

She had not thought of that. She had been in too much of a hurry to get away from him, to find space to put her ravelled thoughts in order, to mask the traitorous reactions of her body. Avoiding the Major's eye, she said simply, 'It would have been difficult for a Hussar in uniform to follow the Duke. He told me himself that he would always be able to pick me out by the white plume on my shako. However, I am sure that I could—'

'No, no. You are quite right. We must find another way of discovering what the Duke intends. For the moment, Alexei Ivanovich, I want you to stay close to our illustrious liaison officer.'

Alex gulped. She could not help it. Closeness to the Duke, touching the Duke, was so very disconcerting. It seemed to banish the rational thought on which she had prided herself for so long.

'And now you had best rejoin the others. They must not suspect what you are doing, Alexei Ivanovich. Their tongues are too easily loosed by alcohol.'

'Of course, sir.' Alex tried to forget that she had made one mistake there already. 'Has his Majesty decided whether he wishes to ride in the morning, Major?' She was pleased to note that her voice sounded appropriately businesslike.

'I expect that he will. You will be ready to accompany him?'

'Of course, sir.'

'Excellent. Let us hope that the Duke of Calder is equally prepared.'

For a second, Alex found herself hoping that the Duke would not appear after all, that she would be spared another difficult encounter, so soon after the last. But then, duty reasserted its grip. Her role was to discover the Duke's plans and whatever she could about his actions. Her own feelings were of no account, compared with her duty to her Emperor.

'One word of warning, Alexei Ivanovich. Do not become too friendly with the Duke of Calder. He is a powerful man and, by all accounts, quite ruthless. Get close to him, by all means, but never let your guard down.'

Excellent advice, Alex thought, but given much, much too late.

Alex hardly dared to relax, even when her bedchamber door was safely locked and she could be sure she would remain undisturbed. She placed her shako and gloves carefully on the chest of drawers by the door and unhooked her sabre belt. With her usual meticulous care, she laid it down and began to strip off her tight-fitting Hussar jacket.

Only then did she begin to breathe normally.

What a day it had been. What a night! And the Tsar's visit to England had barely begun. Alex would have to accompany his Majesty for some weeks yet and always, always, the Duke of Calder would be there, like a malign shadow at her side. No. That was unfair. She was sure—almost sure—that his intentions were not malign. Not to her. Indeed, he seemed to be rather paternal, in some ways. It was just… It was just that she didn't want him paternal. He was a man, a man who made her blood pound and her heart race, a man for whom she wished to appear as a woman, for once, instead of as a strangely youthful-looking captain of Hussars. She shook her head, wonderingly. How was it that she was thinking such strange thoughts? She knew nothing of the feelings between a man and a woman. Was this the passion, the lust, that so often seemed to drive her comrades?

Alex flopped heavily onto the large bed and closed her eyes for a moment. What a coil! How was it that this man had got under her defences? A foreigner, and a man so much above her own station, besides? She had never before felt the slightest attraction to any man. She had seen them as comrades and, sometimes, as friends. That was all. Yet she sensed this man could be so much more. What was it about him?

She could not tell. She barely knew him, after all, having been in his company for only two days. And yet it felt as if she had always known him, as if he were part of her, and she of him. It felt as if they were meant for each other.

Nonsense! And impossible! It must be lust! Or else she was going out of her mind. He was an English duke. Only their royal family ranked above him. Whereas she was merely the daughter of a minor Russian noble, a female who counted for nothing in Russia, who did not even have a say in her own marriage. The fact that she had fled from her family home, and had turned herself into a man and a soldier, made her all the more unsuitable for the Duke of Calder. He would see that, even if she did not.

No. He would never see that. He must never discover that she was anything other than the Hussar officer she appeared to be.

She opened her eyes and tried to focus. As she moved, her spurs caught on the bed cover. A loud ripping sound brought her back to earth.

Shocked, she sat up. 'Alexei Ivanovich Alexandrov,' she whispered aloud, addressing the mahogany bedpost, 'you may be a soldier of proven courage, but you are a hopeless fool when it comes to men. When it comes to this man. He is a foreigner. Possibly even a dangerous foreigner. You will be forced to be in his company for a few weeks. So? That is all that's required of you. Is that so much to endure without a word? Can you not keep your counsel for just a few weeks? You have done so for years, after all, and it has never given you a moment's pause.

'Yet now you want to confess. To him. Madness! And for what? In hopes that he might smile upon you for a second? He would not. If you betray who you really are, he is bound to recoil from you. While you will be ruined completely, exposed as an outrageous female masquerading in a man's uniform. You will certainly be returned to your father's house in disgrace. Remember, Alexei Ivanovich, remember what will happen to you then.'

Shaking her head vehemently, Alex ripped her spur clear of the torn bed cover and stood up, gazing at herself in the looking glass by the clothes press. What she saw was still a young cavalryman, even though he was only half-dressed, in boots, breeches and shirt, with short-cropped hair and a beardless chin. She ignored her heightened colour.

Hesitantly, she put her hands to her chest and allowed them to slide slowly down to cover her small breasts. They felt strangely tender. And larger than normal, as if they were swollen. Through the fine material of her shirt, she could feel her nipples becoming erect under her hands. It was almost painful when she moved her fingers across them.

She looked again in the mirror. And groaned aloud. Her eyes were drawn to her shirt, to the sudden swell of her breasts through the thin white fabric, to the pouting nipples. This time, she could not overlook the rosy colour on her cheeks and on her throat. Nor the tell-tale brightness of her eyes.

What she saw now was not a man. Not any longer. The

figure in the reflection was definitely a woman. In spite of her soldier's clothing.

A woman inspired by passion. And—Heaven help her!—a woman longing for one man's touch.

It was good to be back home, and enjoying a quiet brandy in his own library. Dominic let out a long sigh of contentment, stretching his feet towards the small fire that had been lit against the lateness of the hour. It had been a long and tiring day. And that final confrontation with Castlereagh had not helped. Precisely how was Dominic supposed to discover all about the Tsar's intentions in the space of little more than twenty-four hours?

'There's something strange about Alexandrov, don't you think?'

Jack's question jolted Dominic out of his reverie. He had thought much the same himself but, for some unfathomable reason, he did not want Jack to pursue it.

'Strange?' Leo put in. 'In what way strange?'

'Not sure. I just felt…oh, I don't know, I just felt he was slightly odd.'

'Well, a decorated soldier with no beard is bound to seem a little out of the way.' Leo leaned forward to refill his glass. 'Besides, he's a Russian. Very different from us. Not surprising if he seems a little strange to you.'

Jack sat up a little straighter in his chair, preparing to take issue with Leo.

Dominic, recognising the signs, decided that he must stop this. Now. It wasn't just distasteful. It felt somehow intrusive. He would not allow his brothers to dissect Alexandrov's character as if he were a beetle pinned to a board. Assuming his bored older-brother voice, he said, 'Don't start, Jack. I've come home for a few hours of peace, not to listen to a ding-dong battle between the two of you.'

'But—'

'Look, Leo meant no insult. You bristle too quickly, you know. And he's right that they *are* different,' he added, forcing himself to sound more conciliating. 'I've rarely seen officers so thin-skinned where their honour is concerned. They would probably drop a challenge as easily as you or I would drop a visiting card. We have a lot to learn about the Russians. All of us,' he finished, with emphasis.

Jack sat back in his chair and took a long swallow of his brandy. 'You're probably right,' he said at last. 'And yet I still think there's something about Alexandrov—'

'Confound it, brat, do you never stop?' Leo had picked up a book and now threw it at his brother.

Jack ducked quickly. Then he grinned. 'Losing your touch, Leo.'

Leo groaned theatrically. 'If I'd wanted to bowl you, brat, it would have been straight through, middle stump. Think yourself lucky I only lobbed it.'

Jack said nothing, contenting himself with trying to look superior.

Dominic allowed himself a sigh of relief, running his fingers through his hair and then over his chin. His stubble was pronounced. Alexandrov must have thought him remarkably unkempt, and if— No. That was wrong. When they parted at the Pulteney, Alexandrov had been twitting Dominic about how long he took to make an appearance in the morning, as if his dress were on a par with Brummell's. The lad had wit, but he was an impudent young pup, too.

Dominic smiled to himself. He would show Alexandrov. Tomorrow.

Chapter Six

Dominic woke with a start.

'Five and twenty minutes after six, your Grace,' Cooper said quietly, placing Dominic's usual cup of black coffee on the nightstand. 'The Emperor rides at seven.'

Dominic managed to grunt an acknowledgement. Why on earth did his head feel so thick? He hadn't drunk that much last night. So what—?

There wasn't time to wonder about such things. He had barely twenty minutes to dress, if he was not to become the butt of Alexandrov's wit.

It was only when Dominic was trotting through the gate into Hyde Park and feeling rather pleased with himself, that the picture flashed into his mind. Of course. Cooper had woken him up in the middle of that strange dream. No wonder he had felt so groggy. He had been deep asleep, and somewhere else entirely. Where? He could not say. In fact, he could remember precious little of it now. He fancied he had been sitting at table, opposite an unknown, shadowy figure. All he could make out was a single, lean hand, toying with a glass of wine. And then a second, identical hand had materialised in the gloom, holding what appeared to be a dagger. Most peculiar. Dominic hadn't been able to see the owner of that hand, either. But most peculiar of all was that the dagger had then lanced down, shattering the wine glass and spilling red wine all over the hand that held it.

Dominic shook his head, trying to clear that disturbing image. Dreaming of disembodied hands? Ridiculous! There must have been something wrong with that last bottle of brandy.

It was wonderful to be on horseback again. Liberating. Alex allowed her mount to dance across the dewy grass. It was not the same as being on the back of dear old Pegasus, who had carried her many a mile, and through many a battle, but this gelding from the Royal stables was no slug.

She took a moment to gaze around the vast expanse of Hyde Park. She had wanted, perversely, to draw an unfavourable comparison with the parks and open spaces of her homeland, but, to be fair, she could not. This was absolutely splendid.

As the little group trotted across the brilliant green grass, she searched again. The Duke of Calder had said that he would certainly ride with the Tsar this morning. Alex had dutifully despatched the servant at about a quarter past six to tell the Duke that the Tsar would be in the park by seven, at the latest. It was now after seven and neither the Duke, nor any other Englishman, was to be seen. Alex allowed herself a small, satisfied smile. So much for his arrogant proclamation that he could go from bed to saddle in less than half an hour!

His absence made her feel much more in control. She must resolve—she had resolved—to avoid the least physical contact with him. His slightest touch seemed to set her skin on fire and her pulses racing. It nagged at her mind that she should react so to any man, for she had never before been plagued in this way. Was it lust? Or something deeper? She could not tell. But the more often it happened, the less control she would have; and the more difficult it would be for her to conceal the effect he was having on her. Eventually, he would realise, and that would certainly provoke a crisis. He might even think that she had a schoolboy crush on him. He would be bound to avoid her if he thought that! And others would soon begin to speculate. She could end up having to admit to her female gender in order to avoid being accused of something even worse!

She shook her head sharply. She must not succumb to her insane longings for the Duke of Calder! The reins jangled with her sudden movement and her unfamiliar horse stumbled a fraction, unsure of what his rider intended. She leant forward and ran a gloved hand firmly down his glossy neck, murmuring softly to him in English. It was safe enough to do that here among the Tsar's suite. They were unlikely to make out her words, but if they did, they would probably ignore them as some kind of unknown gibberish.

'Come, gentlemen,' said the Tsar, raising his riding crop. 'There is no one about and we certainly need some exercise after all those days cooped up in carriages and ships. A race, I think. Let us attempt a cavalry charge to yonder oak tree. What say you?'

His question produced whoops of delight from the younger officers, including Alex. It would give her a chance to test the mettle of this borrowed horse. She rode much lighter than all of her companions. She had an excellent chance of winning, and she intended to make the most of it.

By seven o'clock, Dominic had ruthlessly banished what he knew were only idiotish fancies and forced himself to focus on his duty for the day. He had naturally assumed that the Emperor's party would enter Hyde Park by the gate near the turnpike, closest to Piccadilly. Yet there was no sign of them.

He allowed Caesar, his black stallion, to walk slowly in a tight circle while he considered what to do now. The Emperor could have been delayed. Or else he was here already and had, for some unfathomable reason, entered the park by a round-about route.

Dominic stood in his stirrups, straining to see across the park. Nothing. He cursed under his breath and sat back into his saddle. Caesar, recognising the anger in his master's softly spoken words, laid back his ears. 'Well, old fellow,' Dominic said, clapping the stallion's neck, 'we can cool our heels here, or we can assume we have missed the rendezvous and stretch our legs. Not a choice, really. You are tired of waiting. And I need to shake these confounded cobwebs out of my head.' Caesar pricked his ears. As soon as Dominic touched a heel to his side, he was off down the ride.

Dominic held him to a steady canter, while he looked around for any sign of the royal party. The park seemed strangely deserted. Where were they all? Had the arrival of the two monarchs changed everyone's habits already? Too many banquets and late-night balls, probably.

Ah, yes! There! In the far distance, Dominic spied a small group of riders in colourful uniforms. He could see the tall, spare figure of the Emperor himself, mounted on a huge bay horse, in the middle of the group. He thought he could even see Alexandrov, in his blue uniform and plumed shako. And one of the other figures might just be Major Zass. Excellent.

Suddenly, they set off as one, at the gallop. Dominic watched with interest, assessing them. As they thundered across the grass, the riders soon became slightly strung out. It was obviously a race of some kind, and no quarter was being given, even to the Emperor. He was near the front, but he was not in the lead. It seemed that he did not expect his officers to let him win. What a very unusual trait in a monarch! Dominic felt a tiny twinge of envy as he watched the Russians outstrip their Emperor.

Young Alexandrov was soon a good ten yards ahead of his comrades, bent low over his horse's neck. Unless the horse stumbled, the lad would certainly win. That would be a fine result against seasoned cavalrymen. And an Emperor. If the boy could do it. Dominic held his breath, waiting.

Alexandrov reached his goal and gave a shout of triumph. Then he put his horse into an elegant pirouette, just to demonstrate the extent of his control. Dominic grinned to himself, sharing the lad's delight. An impressive performance, especially on an unfamiliar horse. No doubt Alexandrov had been born to the saddle. And his years of military service would have improved his skill still further. Dominic felt himself warming to the lad again, in spite of his attempts to remain distant. Why on earth was he becoming so soft, on a sudden? Strange things were happening, of late. That was certain. He shook his head, wonderingly. It must be that Alexandrov was so very like Jack: young, gifted, enthusiastic and full of life. Full of mischief, too, probably. Alexandrov might not drink or gamble, but he gave the impression of a man of rare qualities, a man who could become a staunch and valued friend. If only they were on the same side.

Instead of riding out across the grass, Dominic decided to make his way round behind the shelter belt. He found he did not want Alexandrov to know that he had been watching his race. He did not stop to wonder why. He told himself that he would just turn up ahead of them and let the lad enjoy ringing a peal over him for arriving late on parade.

Five minutes later, having made his bow to the Emperor, Dominic pushed Caesar between Alexandrov and Major Zass.

'You are late, Calder!' Alexandrov exclaimed, not even attempting to hide the note of triumph in his voice.

'True,' Dominic replied. 'But it is a beautiful morning. What think you of our park, Major?'

Major Zass replied, as form required, with compliments. Alexandrov, who was still looking flushed from his gallop, said, 'It is indeed fine, Calder, though if you cared to visit Russia, you would find many such.'

Dominic raised his eyebrows. 'No doubt. But you do have just a little more land than we do, here in England.'

Zass guffawed. And so, to his credit, did Alexandrov. '*Touché*, Duke,' he said. 'I shall not try to catch you out in future.'

'Quite right, too,' Major Zass said, with a smile in his voice. 'A junior captain should have a care when addressing an older man. Especially a duke.'

'No, no,' Dominic said quickly. He would not permit Alexandrov to be cowed in any way. 'We are all gentlemen here, and all equals. Alexandrov may roast me as much as he likes. I may tell you, Major, that he has already had some practice, for I was foolish enough to introduce him to my brothers. Both of them can give lessons in how to insult their elders.'

Alexandrov threw Dominic a glowing look and said, in a low, confidential voice, seemingly for Dominic alone, 'Thank you. You are more than generous.'

A frisson of response ran down Dominic's spine. For a split second, he was back in the burning stables. What on earth was the matter with him? That little *bourgeoise* was haunting him still.

Almost without pause, Alexandrov spoke again, in a louder, airy tone. 'You are fortunate in your family, I think, Duke. It is a good thing, is it not, when brothers are also friends?'

Dominic seized on the opportunity to recover his control. 'If you knew my brothers better, Alexei Ivanovich,' he said, with a somewhat hollow laugh, 'you would not call them friends.' Then, with an exaggerated grimace, 'Tormentors, possibly. Or spawn of the devil.'

The others laughed. The tension—if anyone but Dominic had felt it—was broken. His mind had been playing tricks again, because of the boy's sometimes remarkable voice. That was all it was. He must learn to ignore it.

With comradeship established, they rode on together for a quarter of an hour. Dominic had recovered enough control to concentrate on using all his guile to turn the conversation towards the information he was to seek. He asked the Major about his Emperor's likes and dislikes, about his plans for the visit, and, more obliquely, about his relationship with the Prussian King. But Major Zass did not give away any useful information. In the end, Dominic had to give up, before his curiosity became too obvious. He had no choice but to turn his attention back to Alexandrov. 'You seem to have remarkable sympathy with that horse of yours, Alexei Ivanovich. Have you ridden him before?'

'No. He has been generously loaned to me from the royal stables.'

'As have all our mounts, Duke,' Major Zass put in. He gestured suddenly with his whip towards the Emperor, who had ridden apart with two of his young officers and was now trotting towards the gate. 'Come, Alexandrov. His Majesty is leaving. You may be off duty for the rest of the day, but some of us,' he added with a grin, 'have work to do.' With that, he put his spurs to his horse's flanks and galloped off in pursuit of his Emperor.

Pausing only to raise a hand in farewell, Alexandrov did the same, shouting over his shoulder, 'Farewell, Duke. Enjoy your ride. I shall send the messenger earlier next time. I would not have you delayed again, on that account.'

'Impudent young rascal!' Dominic said aloud. But he could not help laughing. Young Alexandrov was such an engaging companion that there was no room for unease. Moreover, his prowess on a horse, and his clever tongue, had set Dominic's mood for rest of the day.

And now it was buoyant.

Several days had passed with no change in the routine, and no real progress. Dominic would accompany the Emperor when he rode in the park in the morning, or when he walked with his sister instead. Alexandrov was always in attendance, Major Zass only rarely. Dominic was perversely glad of it, for he was coming to value the young man's company more and more. Unfortunately, it did not help his mission one jot.

'The Emperor certainly has boundless energy,' he complained to Leo, very late one evening, after yet another interminable royal banquet. 'He seems to want to visit all the places of interest in London. But Major Zass is often absent, and so is Alexandrov. It makes me wonder… Do you think they might be plotting with the Prussians?'

'If they are,' Leo said thoughtfully, 'it will be to undermine the marriage. Have any of the young Prussian Princes called on Princess Charlotte, d'you know? They're personable young men. That's where the danger lies, I'd say, for she doesn't like the Prince of Orange above half.'

'You're right. I should have thought of that myself.'

'You're tired, Dominic. You can't think of everything, you know.'

Dominic grimaced, but nodded his agreement. On the spur of the moment, he decided to ask his brother's advice about a notion that had been worrying at him for days now. 'You know, Leo, I've been thinking about Alexandrov. He's a truly remarkable young man. I thought perhaps…' He paused, reviewing his train of thought yet again. Was it wise to do this? It was certainly an unusual step to take. But, then again, why not? 'I thought I might ask the Emperor's permission for Alexandrov to stay behind in England for a month or two. After all, Bonaparte is safely ensconced on Elba and Europe is at peace, at last. There wouldn't be any harm in granting him some leave. I doubt he's had any for years, in spite of his long service and distinguished conduct. What do you think?'

'Yes, why not? We would enjoy his company. Jack certainly would, since they're much of an age.'

Dominic nodded. 'Of course, if Jack is to be involved, I

shall have to make sure he behaves. Can't have him taking Alexandrov to one of his gaming hells.'

'Not much risk of that, is there? Alexandrov doesn't gamble, remember? Knowing Jack, he'll take the lad to a whorehouse instead.'

'He'll have me to reckon with if he does.' Dominic could not keep the distaste out of his voice.

'Would it be so very bad, Dominic? After all, as long as the girls are clean…'

Dominic shook his head forcefully. He was absolutely sure he did not want Jack to introduce Alexandrov to London brothels. It did not matter that they were both young, single men, with wild oats to sow. Alexandrov had an impetuous spirit, certainly—only a bold fighting-cock would have tried to draw a sabre in a London street—but beneath his serious manners and his blind devotion to his Emperor there was a kind of innocence. It should not be corrupted. 'No, Leo. I won't allow that, and I shall tell Jack so, in terms. If he takes Alexandrov to a whorehouse, I'll have his hide.'

Leo looked surprised. 'Do you mean that?' The look on Dominic's face must have confirmed it, for he added quickly, 'I can see that you do. And since Jack knows that you are much better with your fists than he is, I imagine he will take the hint.' He yawned and rose. 'I'm for bed, I think. You?'

'Yes, as soon as I've finished my brandy. Have to be up even earlier than normal tomorrow. We're off to Oxford for a couple of days. The Emperor and the King are to receive honorary degrees.'

'Ah! And Prinny will be dressing up again, no doubt. Lots of gold braid and flowing robes.' Leo shook his head and made for the door. 'Rather you than me, Dominic. Night.'

Dominic leaned back in his chair and sipped thoughtfully at his brandy. What was so intriguing about Alexandrov? He was certainly a strange combination, a battle-hardened cavalryman, with the pride and courage of a man of honour, yet with the build and the beardless chin of a girl. And—just sometimes—the voice of a siren.

Was that the reason for Dominic's recurring unease? That voice, and the searing embarrassment he had felt at Boulogne, on realising he had been weaving fancies around a man? It was not the Russian's fault that Dominic had made such a stupid mistake, and it would be wrong to make him suffer for Dominic's weird imaginings. But, try though he might, Dominic had been unable to put that voice totally out of his mind. It was the little *bourgeoise*, of course. He could not forget her. It was probably because he had been so long without a woman that his mind was playing tricks on him. Once this mission was over, he would have to remedy that. Perhaps it was time he took a lover.

If Alexandrov decided to accept Dominic's invitation to remain in England, they would get to know each other better. Without the need to serve opposing sides, they would be able to meet as friends, real friends. And that would be very good for both of them. Dominic would soon get rid of his bizarre notions about Alexandrov. No doubt of that. And Alexandrov… What of him?

He swallowed the last of his brandy, reached for the decanter, and then thought better of it. Young Alexandrov would not sit here like this, filling and refilling his glass. He was a man of rather stern morals, it seemed. He barely drank and he never gambled. Probably didn't have much to do with women either, judging by his aversion to parties and balls. Or was it that he preferred women of a lower class? Somehow, Dominic doubted that. The very idea that Jack might take the Russian to a brothel had been repellent. Dominic had known that Alexandrov would never countenance it.

It was beginning to trouble Dominic that he and Alexandrov could have reached such a degree of understanding in so short a time. It was not at all what Dominic had intended. And yet it had happened.

'Well, Alexei Ivanovich, what do you think of Oxford?'

Alex cursed inwardly. She had been congratulating herself on having avoided the Duke all day. But now she was trapped. She determined that, this time, she would be calm and matter-of-fact. She would keep her wayward responses under control. So, from her vantage point under the gallery of the Radcliffe, she surveyed the scene. Slowly. Making him wait for his answer. There were hundreds of dinner guests, all dressed in their finest: the myriad colours of court dress, and regimentals and scarlet academic robes, all lit by thousands of candles.

'It is a fine sight, Calder, I'll grant you that,' she said at last. 'Though it is becoming oppressively hot in here. And with all the press of common people in the gallery…' She wrinkled her nose.

Calder laughed shortly. 'Not long now, I promise you. The Regent intends to go out to admire the illuminations.' At that very moment, the guests of honour rose and started to make their way to the entrance. Blücher was so drunk he could barely set one foot in front of the other, but eventually even he swayed out of the grand hall. The Duke gave a long sigh. He might have been trying to conceal a yawn. 'Are you still on duty now the banquet is over, Alexei Ivanovich?'

Alex shook her head.

'Then perhaps we may go for a stroll, to enjoy the sight of Oxford by night?'

What could she do but agree? Holding her sabre tight against her thigh, she turned and marched briskly out into the night, leaving him to follow in her wake. Outside there was less of a crush of people, she was glad to see. The last thing she wanted was to be pressed up against the Duke's intimidating body, even by accident.

'Come, let us walk.'

He had taken his stance a couple of paces from her, as if he had noticed that she wanted to keep a distance between them. She was glad of it. And yet she was not. Her rebellious body still ached for him.

'Is there anything in particular you would like to see, Alexandrov?'

'No, Calder.' They began to walk. 'I have seen so many colleges, and libraries and chapels today that I cannot remember which is which.'

Calder nodded, but said nothing. He just kept walking along, at an easy pace, swinging his silver-topped ebony cane.

Alex matched him stride for stride, in spite of her lack of height. She discovered it was very pleasant to be together this way, not speaking, not touching, just enjoying the illuminations and the beauties of the city. Many of the buildings were glowing rich gold in the soft light. It was a memory she would always treasure.

After a while, Alex felt relaxed enough to speak. 'Are you an Oxford man, Calder?'

'Yes. Oxford is a splendid life for young men, though I'm afraid I did not study as much as I should have.' He was smiling ruefully.

'You mean you were sent down?'

'No, it wasn't as bad as that. I did receive my degree. In the end. But I was unfortunate enough to lose my father while I was here, you see. I was not yet twenty-one, but suddenly I was the master of a vast estate. And a duke. I'm afraid I became rather wild.'

Alex was overwhelmed with sympathy. To have lost one's father so young! She herself had left home at only nineteen so, in some ways, their cases were similar. But Alex's father was still alive, still at home in Russia, still ready to love his daughter in spite of everything. The Duke's loss must have been devastating.

'Your silence is eloquent, Alexei Ivanovich. You disapprove?'

'Er...no, of course not. It would have been strange if you had not become a little wild. In the circumstances.' She sounded stiff and unconvincing. She knew it. And she imagined that he knew it, too.

'Well, I did reform a little. Eventually.'

There was a thread of humour in his voice. Here was a man who was happy to laugh at himself, Alex decided. That took a degree of self-knowledge. It was yet another remarkable trait in this intriguing man. It was becoming ever more difficult not to admire him. And to desire him. But she must not!

'And you, Alexei Ivanovich, were you, too, a wild youth?'

'I...er...I barely had time to be wild,' she managed at last. 'I joined the army when I was just nineteen and we have been fighting almost ever since.'

'Now that, I am sure, is a bouncer. All the officers of my acquaintance—and there are many—tell me that the mess is a place of wild goings-on, except when they are actually fighting. I cannot believe that the Russian army is any different from the English. Why—'

A tremendous clap of thunder drowned the Duke's words. A second later the rain began pouring down on their unprotected heads.

The Duke cursed roundly. 'We are going to be soaked,' he cried. 'Come, Alexandrov, let's try to find some cover.'

He put an arm round Alex's back in order to shepherd her into the lee of the nearest building. Faithful to her earlier resolve, however, she shook him off, without pausing to wonder how he might react to such rudeness. She felt his instant withdrawal, as if a chill wind had started blowing between them. It cut to her heart. She looked up at his face, trying to gauge his mood from his expression. It was hard to see him at all, for the torrential downpour had made it much, much darker than before.

And then the last of the illuminations was doused by the rain.

Alex gasped in shock. She was unable to see anything at all. Instinctively, she put out her hands, searching for something to cling to. Her questing fingers met the Duke's sodden coat. Underneath, she could sense the strength of his warm, vibrant body. For a second, she let her hands rest on his chest, feeling his life force coursing through him and into her. Just for a single second. And then, recognising her own madness, she snatched her hands away. 'Forgive me, Duke, I—'

'It's nothing,' he said. 'No need to apologize. Now, if we stand here for a moment or two, our eyes will become accustomed to the dark, and then we may make our way back to Merton. I hope you have brought a spare uniform with you to Oxford, Alexei Ivanovich. That jacket is tight enough already. If it shrinks after this, your collar will strangle you.'

Dominic glanced out of his carriage window. He could not see the stars, or even the sky, for the sheeting rain. At this pace, it would take hours to get back to London. If he had had a choice, he would have stopped at an inn, to find shelter for himself and his servants. By now, his coachman must be wet through and half-frozen. But they could not stop. The Emperor was ahead of them and would certainly be in London before morning. So, Dominic must be there, too.

Poor Alexandrov! Unlike Dominic, he was on horseback, riding escort to the Emperor. By the time the royal party reached London, Alexandrov would be even wetter than on the previous night. It was extraordinary that there had been two such storms on successive nights. But tonight's had been predicted. Whereas last night's had been so very sudden, extinguishing all Oxford's illuminations as easily as snuffing a candle. It had brought the celebrations to an end, instantly.

Dominic stroked his chin thoughtfully. The young Russian must have lost his bearings in the dark, to reach out like that. He had clearly been startled, as Dominic himself had been. There was no other possible explanation for what Alexandrov had done. Not from a cavalryman who had spent years on campaign and must be well used to moving around in the dark. It had been just momentary confusion, understandable in the circumstances. But highly embarrassing for the boy.

It would be most inconsiderate of Dominic ever to mention it again.

With a sigh, he leaned back in his seat and closed his eyes. He had been very short on sleep, these last few days, so he might as well have a little rest now. If the Emperor continued at his current pace, there would be precious little sleep for Dominic in the days to come.

Not just one soaking, but two! Alex stripped off her spare uniform jacket and assessed its sorry state. Why on earth did it have to rain so much in England? The Emperor was now back in his Pulteney suite, changing his dress for Lady Jersey's rout. Thank goodness someone else would be accompanying him. It was nearly three o'clock in the morning, and Alex had been on duty for over twenty hours. If she had to stay on her feet much longer, she would be asleep where she stood.

She summoned her orderly and gave him both her jackets, as well as her shako. He had managed to remove bloodstains in the past. He would surely be able to deal with a little water. She was yawning widely as she closed the door on him. She really must sleep. Tomorrow…no, later today, she would be on duty again.

She was asleep almost before her head touched the pillow. But it was not the quiet, restful sleep her exhausted body needed. It was sleep filled with weird, disturbing dreams. In one, she was drowning, pushed under water by a mass of soggy woollen cloth. She clawed at it, trying to push it away, trying to reach the surface, but she could not. It had a mind of its own. It seemed to be living and breathing, and determined to finish her off. She woke with a cry of fear, to find she had been wrestling with her own bedclothes. Nothing more.

But there was more. Of course there was. Her whole body was bathed in sweat. That nightmare had been all too much like reality. And terrifying.

She lay in the dark, staring up into nothing, wondering. She could remember the feeling of drowning from her dream. The fear gnawing at her gut. It had seemed as if it were actually happening. A shudder went through her body at the mere thought of it. She had never had nightmares in all her years of service, even after bloody battles. So why now?

It was all too obvious. It was the Duke of Calder. And her feelings for him. Feelings which were growing with every day she spent in his company, in spite of all her efforts to put him out of her thoughts. In spite of the fact that she hardly knew him at all.

No, that was not true. Knowing him was not a matter of time. Not for her. She had understood him from the first. She recognised that now. This must be more than lust, surely?

As she gazed into the dark, trying to make out the shadows of the bed canopy above her, she remembered how she had touched him, against her will, when they had both been plunged into darkness in Oxford. She had reached for him, as a protector, automatically. Why? She had never sought a protector in all her years in the guise of a man. Why now? Why this man? It must be more than lust.

She remembered the feel of his wet coat under her questing fingers. And his warm body beneath. That was what she had been fighting in her dream. Not the bundle of wet cloth trying to smother her, but the living, breathing man beneath, the man whose image was now haunting her, waking and sleeping.

Muttering a string of the foulest Russian curses, she flung herself out of bed and began to pace the floor in the dark. The oaths got rid of her anger and frustration, but only for a second or two. Then his image was back, piercing her unwilling mind, twining itself around the heart that had, until now, been totally immune to the charms of men. It was more than lust. And more than desire.

She abandoned all thoughts of sleep. She did not dare to face those dreams again. Awake, she might manage to think of other things. Asleep, she was at the mercy of her innermost thoughts and desires. She felt for the tinder box on the night-stand and lit her candle. Then she took it across to the looking glass and peered at her reflection.

Huge, haunted eyes stared back at her from a pale face. It was no longer the face of a confident young soldier. It was the face of a woman who had been forced to recognise her own fate. Love. An impossible, unattainable love. A parting, very soon. Followed by a life alone. And bleak despair.

Chapter Seven

'Are you on duty this evening, Alexei Ivanovich?' Captain Petrov said politely.

'Yes. But later. His Majesty has gone to dine with Lord Castlereagh. Afterwards he is going to the opera. I am to attend him there.'

'At least you will have time to relax tomorrow, when I am on duty.'

'I shall still rise early. If one wishes to go riding in London, it must be before the fashionable people are about. It seems that they do not believe in exercise, simply in displaying themselves.'

'Which you do not, of course?' Petrov let his gaze run over Alex's fine blue uniform jacket with its gold braid and white Cross of St George.

'If you wished to have a handsomer uniform, you should have joined a more illustrious regiment, Petrov. Like mine!' She grinned wickedly at him.

He grinned back at her. As the two most junior members of the Emperor's entourage, they were well used to this kind of sparring. 'Shall you go to the masquerade ball, Alexei Ivanovich?'

Alex began to shake her head. 'You know I do not dance.'

'Ah, but his Majesty has given us all leave to go. He says it is to be our reward for the hours of service we have all given on this visit.'

Alex shook her head again. There would be ladies there. No one had a better eye for a fraud than Society ladies.

'Tell you what, Alexei Ivanovich. Why not go dressed as a woman? After all, you've done it before. Everyone knows you went into that French camp, dressed as a Russian peasant woman.'

It was true that she had done it, though she had been a bit younger and rasher then. By offering to sell them provisions, she had been able to go round their camp, listening to conversations between soldiers and officers, and gleaning a huge amount of information. But the masked ball would be a different matter altogether.

'What's that?' cried another young officer who had just entered the room. 'Is Alexandrov to disguise himself again? What a rattling good jest! But you will never get away with it, Alexei Ivanovich, even wearing a mask. I wager a hundred roubles that you will be discovered before the night is out!'

'And I wager two hundred that he will not!' Petrov replied immediately. 'Do you dare to take me on?' Within moments the room seemed to be filled with young officers making bets on whether Alex could sustain the masquerade.

'But I have not agreed to do it!' she cried, trying to make herself heard above the din. 'You have no right—'

'I suggest you give in gracefully, Alexei Ivanovich,' said Major Zass's serious voice behind her. 'And it might be useful.'

She tried one last protest. 'Where am I supposed to get a lady's clothes? I would need a wig, and shoes, and— It's impossible.'

'Not at all,' Petrov said. He now appeared to be the ringleader in this mad escapade. 'You go off to the opera. Don't worry about such trivial issues. We will procure everything you need. No one will ever suspect that it is for a man.'

Dominic could not believe how full the theatre was. And there seemed to be thousands of people outside, pushing to get in. He shrugged his shoulders and continued to wait. The opera certainly would not begin until the royal visitors arrived.

Alexandrov appeared in the doorway, looking around anxiously, as if he thought he might be late. Dominic raised an arm and called out his name.

A strange expression crossed the young Russian's face. Dominic fancied he saw both pleasure and disappointment, perhaps even a flash of concern. What on earth had he done to provoke such a reaction? This young man was truly an enigma.

'Good evening, Calder. I had not expected to see you here. I had assumed that you would be attending the dinner with his Majesty and the Regent.'

Dominic shook his head. 'I am merely a liaison officer. My role is to smooth your Emperor's path, to remove obstacles, to open doors. A sort of…er…a sort of aristocratic doorstop, if you like.'

Alexandrov took one look at the expression on Dominic's face and burst out laughing. 'A doorstop! I shall remember that. And remind you of it, too.'

The hubbub outside grew so much louder that Dominic had to shout to make himself heard. 'Come, Alexandrov.' He put a hand on the lad's shoulder to pull him towards the entrance. 'The royal party must be arriving.'

Alexandrov reddened and tried to shake off Dominic's hand. Still a very touchy young cub, Dominic decided. It was all part of his fiery character. Perhaps it was the Russian way.

The cheering crowd outside parted for the royal party to move into the foyer. The Prince Regent was in the lead, bowing and smiling on both sides, as if the cheering was all for him. The Emperor followed, with his sister on his arm, and then the King of Prussia. Dominic and Alexandrov slotted themselves smoothly into the procession behind Major Zass and mounted the stairs to the royal box.

The national anthem struck up almost at once, and the huge audience began to sing lustily. The Emperor, Dominic noticed with surprise, joined in with the singing. Alexandrov did not, of course. Unlike his Emperor, he had no English. He simply stood to attention, staring at nothing.

When the members of the royal party were at last able to take their seats, Dominic allowed himself to relax a fraction and to lean one shoulder surreptitiously against the back wall. It was nearly midnight. It was going to be a long night. Out of the corner of his eye, he could see that Alexandrov was still standing trim and erect. No doubt he could do so for hours without moving a muscle. Admirable dedication to duty, however unpredictable he might be in other ways.

Suddenly, the audience was on its feet, clapping, stamping and shouting. And they had turned their backs on the royal box. They were gazing at the figure who had just entered the box opposite. There, clad in silk and diamonds, and with a black wig on her head, was the Princess of Wales.

Dominic straightened. And cursed silently.

Alexandrov, moving to his side, whispered, 'Who is that?'

'The Princess of Wales. And there's going to be trouble.'

Princess Caroline stood at the front of her box, smiling round at the people and acknowledging their love with a gracious wave of her hand. She was very good at this. Even the Regent would have to admit that.

The Regent had seen her. The back of his neck was almost crimson. No doubt he was furious at being upstaged by the wife he detested. And he had not yet risen from his place.

The Emperor, however, was equal to the occasion. No sooner had he recognised the lady opposite than he rose, took a step towards the very front of the box and bowed low to her. Behind him, the King of Prussia did the same.

Poor old Prinny, Dominic thought. Even you don't deserve this.

The Prince Regent also rose. He had no choice, of course. But when he bowed, he directed it to the people in the auditorium, as if he were responding to their protestations of loyalty.

Opposite, the Princess of Wales, smiling a little, sank into a graceful curtsy.

The crowd went wild with joy. Someone was even heard to cry, 'Three hearty cheers for an injured woman!'

The Princess of Wales had had her moment of triumph.

It was very uncomfortable for Alex to find, when they eventually left the opera in the wake of their royal masters, that she and Calder were the only two occupants of a carriage back to the Pulteney. She buried herself in one corner, well out of touching range. The Duke took his seat in the other corner. He seemed thoughtful. Or perhaps he was just tired? It was very late, and he had been on duty for at least as long as Alex.

'That was a very odd encounter between his Royal Highness and his wife, Duke. Do they really hate each other so much? Is there truly no prospect of a reconciliation?'

'I think reconciliation is impossible,' he replied grimly. 'They took against each other on sight, I understand. Thank God, they did at least produce an heir.'

'And she will need a husband, will she not?'

'Yes. In due course.'

'Oh? I understood that she was about to marry the Prince of Orange.' Alex hoped her voice held just the right tone of airy unconcern. For this was important. A marriage between Princess Charlotte and the Prince of Orange would cement an alliance between Britain and Holland that Russia most definitely did not wish to see. The Tsar's sister had been in

London for several months now, and one of her principal aims was to scotch that potential match.

The Duke sat in his corner, staring fixedly ahead, as if he were watching a distant scene, invisible to anyone else. 'I understand that the marriage is no longer to Princess Charlotte's taste. After that unfortunate display at Ascot, the Princess has acquired a disgust of him.'

'What happened at Ascot? I was not there.'

'Had you not heard? The Prince of Orange made a fool of himself at the races, by getting roaring drunk. Princess Charlotte decided she could not marry such a man. She sent the list of potential wedding guests back to her father with the groom's name crossed through. A neat gesture, don't you think?'

'By Jove! No, I did not know. So now, the Regent will be seeking a different match for his daughter.'

'Not yet. He still has hopes for this one. She must marry a royal prince, and, as with all arranged marriages, there is a possibility that the couple will hate each other.' He shook his head, rather sadly. There was still a far-away look on his face, as if he were talking of something more important than the royal marriage.

'You do not approve of arranged marriages, Duke?'

'I think marriage is a state which is necessary, but which a man must enter into with caution. A man may fall in love with a woman's pretty face, or her ready wit, but does he really know what she is, what she may become? Look at what happened to the Regent and his wife. Her manners and habits disgusted him. But, by the time he had discovered it, it was too late. They were married. And the same could happen to any man who was rash enough to take a wife from a different milieu. Or a wife he did not really know.'

Alex felt her gut tighten and her face redden. She hoped it was dim enough in the carriage that he would not see. For he might have been talking about her. She swallowed and then said, in a voice that was almost normal, 'You do not believe in the power of love, then, Calder?'

He snorted. 'I think not. At least, I have never seen the so-called *coup de foudre*. I'm not sure I believe that such a thing exists.'

Alex groaned inwardly. It did exist. She knew that now. Only too well.

'I think my parents grew into love over many years. Perhaps that is the better way.'

'You mean they did not know each other when they married? And yet you said such marriages are to be avoided.'

'I think a man must make very careful enquiries about the woman he is minded to take to wife. Not only must he talk to her, walk with her, dance with her and sup with her, but he must consider the opinions of other people, too. His parents, for example, if they are still living. His friends.'

'It seems an immensely serious and daunting business, Calder.' She tried to sound light-hearted. 'I am not surprised that you are still single.'

'Strictly speaking, I am not single,' he said carefully. 'I am a widower.'

'Oh. My condolences on your loss.'

'Thank you, but my wife has been dead these many years.'

He had withdrawn behind some kind of protective shield. Clearly he would not talk about his late wife, but Alex sensed—no, she knew—that his marriage had been just as much of a disaster as the Regent's. No wonder he now spoke with such cold calculation about the business of selecting a wife. He would have to marry again, since he had no son, but he was certainly determined to make a more successful match than before.

No doubt his late wife had been beautiful, and an accomplished hostess. She had probably been a great lady, too. And yet their marriage had been a failure. Alex herself would not even begin to compete in Calder's eyes. Not beautiful, not accomplished and not a lady at all, far less a great one.

An outrageous woman from a foreign culture was the very last wife he would choose. No matter how deeply she might love him.

Alexandrov had fallen silent. Dominic was very glad of it. Why on earth had he been so indiscreet? There was something about Alexandrov—that natural rapport between them—that prompted Dominic to talk more than he normally would. And more than he should. He had made it a rule never to discuss his late wife. He should have stuck to it.

Yet the sight of the Regent and his wife at the opera had brought back so many bad memories. Men married in order to sire an heir and in hopes of life-long companionship, perhaps even love. So often, what they found was none of those. In Dominic's case, there had not even been an heir.

Unfortunately he was going to have to go through it all again. Soon. Once this royal visit was safely over, he would have to start looking about him for candidates to be the next Duchess of Calder. It was his duty. He could not avoid it. Thus far, he had seen no woman to whom he was in the least attracted. Not a woman of his own class, at least. There had been that astonishing girl in the stable fire. He would certainly have met her again if he could, for she had an amazing quality…

But she was a *bourgeoise*. Totally unsuitable as a duchess. Fate had clearly been looking out for Dominic when she was spirited away so quickly. And yet…

And yet, sometimes he saw her in his dreams, even now. In his dreams, he could see her face clearly, but whenever he awoke, the memory was veiled once more. It was useless. If she was haunting him, she was making a pretty poor fist of it, for he would never be able to recognise her, not even if she were sitting beside him.

He glanced across to Alexandrov's corner, half-expecting his seductive ghost to be sitting there, still wreathed in smoke and flames. But Alexandrov—who, to be fair, also had remarkable qualities—was all too real, all too male, and staring vacantly into the distance.

It was a pity that Dominic had felt that instant attraction to the courageous *bourgeoise*. Not that attraction had any place in Dominic's plans. Not this time. This time he would ensure that his head dictated his choice. He would find a sensible woman who would make him comfortable. What was wrong with that?

Nothing. Except that it was well-nigh impossible, on the London marriage mart, to discover whether any woman was sensible. And as to whether she would make him comfortable…? Impossible to judge.

Thinking about a future wife was frustrating in the extreme. He was beginning to feel irritated, and confused. He was losing control. He found himself saying, 'Alexandrov, I had been wondering. What say you to remaining here in England for a few months, once the royal visit is over? I should be delighted to offer you hospitality. If you would like it, I would happily apply to his Imperial Majesty for permission.'

From the opposite corner came a noise which sounded like a strangled gasp. 'I…I…I…' Alexandrov stammered and then stopped. Eventually, he said, in a rather strained voice, 'You do me too much honour, Duke. I am touched by your thoughtfulness, but I fear it would be impossible.' His voice had begun to sound stronger. 'I have duties back in Russia after the visit. I could not shirk them for an expedition of pleasure, much as I should enjoy it. I do thank you for your invitation, however. Very much. And I am truly sorry that I am unable to accept it.'

It sounded like a pretty lame excuse, but in many ways Dominic was grateful for it. He had known that it could be dangerous to issue the invitation. Common sense had been urging him to steer clear, even though his instincts had been telling him it was the right thing to do. In the end, he had issued the invitation anyway. Without conscious thought. He should probably be thankful that the decision had been made for him. Close friendship between the two of them was not to be.

'What on earth is that strange noise?' Alexandrov asked sharply, breaking into Dominic's melancholy train of thought.

Dominic let down the glass and stuck his head out. There was no mistaking it. Turning back to Alexandrov, he said, 'If you let down the glass on your side of the carriage, you will be able to hear better. It is the final proof of the folly of marrying the wrong woman.' He could not keep the note of bitterness out of his voice. 'The people of London desire to show their love for Princess Caroline. So they are hissing the Prince Regent.'

Alex locked the door of her bedchamber and turned to survey the full horror of the items spread across her bed. There was no going back now. Like the Prince Regent, faced with his diamond-bedecked wife, Alex was well and truly caught.

She picked up the nearest item, a pair of fine silk stockings. Her fingers were not quite steady. Without thinking, she ran her hands over the delicate material, but the calluses on her palms snagged on the silk. She turned her hand palm up, to look. It was a small, strong hand, and the palm bore evidence of years of hard riding and fighting. It was not a lady's hand. A lady's hand was soft and white. Hers could never pass for a lady's hand.

She threw the stockings back on to the bed. The pit of her stomach was churning. She would be forced to go through with this. She would be discovered. And she would be disgraced, in front of the Duke of Calder. Would they discover that she was a man disguised as a woman? Or a woman disguised as a man disguised as a woman? It did not matter. Whatever the outcome, she would be ruined.

Alex sat down heavily on the bed and dropped her head into her hands. How had it ever come to this? For the first time since she had left home to join the army, she began to weep bitter tears.

At that same moment, there was a rather hesitant knock on the door. She rose, scrubbing at her eyes with the back of her hand, and checking automatically in the looking glass. Those few rebellious tears had not reddened her eyes. And her dress was proper enough for a cavalryman. She straightened her back. 'Who is it?'

'It's only me, your Honour.' It was her orderly. 'Captain Petrov told me to check with your Honour, to be sure that you have everything you need. Captain Petrov said—'

'Hold your tongue, man.' Alex hastily unlocked the door before he could reveal her intentions to the whole of the Pulteney Hotel. 'Come inside,' she snapped. 'Now, what instructions did Captain Petrov give you?'

The orderly was a fraction taller than Alex, but he quailed before her anger.

'Well?'

'I laid out all the lady's clothes for your Honour. Like Captain Petrov said. But he wasn't sure that you had... He thought there might be some things missing. He said I was to tell him, so's he could get them. That was it, your Honour.'

There was no point in taking out her anger on a common soldier. If anyone was to be blamed for this mess, it was Petrov. Biting back a curse, Alex turned to examine the selection of clothing on the bed. Petrov had been clever. Knowing that Alex would have to wear a wig to cover her cropped hair, he had acquired a masquerade costume from decades before. Including a grey wig. There was a beautiful gown, in a style that Alex recognised as a *polonaise*. Her mother had had something very similar. This one was in a pale shade of apple-green, with blonde lace at the throat and sleeves. There were matching satin shoes, too, with high heels, pointed toes and silver buckles. They even looked to be about the right size.

She picked up the gown and examined it carefully. The bodice was fitted, but the open skirt was to be caught up on either side at the back, to show the quilted petticoat beneath. Apart from the tapes, the fastenings were all at the front. That was something, at least.

And then she saw the corset. It laced up the back. So someone else would have to be present while she dressed. The fine silk chemise that Petrov had provided to be worn next to her skin would not serve to disguise her female sex. She picked up the corset by one of its shoulder straps. 'I can't be expected to wear *that*,' she said, with obvious distaste. 'Good God, man! I wouldn't be able to breathe in a thing like that!'

'But, your Honour, ladies always wear stays. And without them, how will the gown be made to fit?'

'That is Captain Petrov's problem. Tell him that he must find me some easier stays, ones that fasten at the front, so that I may loosen them myself if they become intolerable. Tell him that I am not about to collapse in a heap for lack of air, not even for his two hundred roubles.' She thrust the corset into the orderly's hand and pushed him towards the door.

She was pensive as she relocked the door behind her orderly and turned back to look again at the costume. On a sudden whim, she stripped off her uniform and donned the silken chemise. It slithered over her skin like a lover's caress. It was a long time since she had touched anything so fine. It brought back memories of her mother, but she did not dare to allow them free rein. They would bring too much pain. Instead, she picked up the grey wig and settled it snugly over her hair, arranging the long curls so that they fell over one bare shoulder. Then she turned to look in the glass.

A woman stared back at her. The long hair made so much difference. And the chemise was so thin that the outline of her woman's body was easily visible through it. What would Calder think if he could see her like this? Would he find her attractive enough to overcome his decided dislike of foreign women? And what would it be like to be in his arms? To be his Duchess, in his bed? That image turned her insides to a hot, churning whirlpool of desire. She tried smiling at herself, aiming for the kind of flirtatious effect that might help her to captivate him. But he was a man who definitely did not intend to be captivated. Especially by a woman such as Alex. Even if he found her half-naked, like this. It was hopeless.

In any case, he would never see her dressed so shamelessly. No one would.

She fought down the sudden panic that assailed her. It was known that Alexandrov was a very private man. No one would be surprised if he insisted on donning his disguise alone. More important, however, was ensuring that she could carry it off in public. She scrutinised herself carefully in the glass. There were too many betraying signs. Her complexion, for example, was much too brown, from having spent years in the open. But that could be remedied. Ladies of that period had worn face paint, as well as hair powder. She could easily create the white skin she needed.

Her hands? They were strong and brown and roughened, as she had discovered when she had stroked the silk stockings. But, for that, there was also a remedy: gloves. She glanced around. Petrov had forgotten to buy any gloves. They would be easy enough to acquire, she supposed. And then she thought, mischievously, that she would not make it easy for him. I shall demand a pair of elbow-length gloves, she decided, in apple-green kid, to match my gown. Let Petrov search London for those. And I hope it takes him hours!

She grinned at herself. She was back in control now. And since she had been forced into this idiotic deception, she might as well enjoy it. She stepped into the petticoat and tied the tapes around her waist. Then she put on the deeper green underskirt and the overgown, using the cords to sweep it up into soft folds to expose the embroidered quilting on the underskirt. The bodice was rather more difficult, but after two unsuccessful attempts, she finally managed to lace it up. The gown was quite flattering, and very feminine, but it did not look quite right without a corset beneath. The bodice should have been straight and flat, pushing her breasts up into the low lace-edged neckline.

But she was supposed to be a man! She was not supposed to have breasts at all! She examined her reflection yet again. Did she look like a man disguised as a woman? Or like a woman? For her comrades, she needed to be the former; but for the Society ladies at the masquerade, she needed to be a woman. It would all depend on the corset. She needed a corset that made her look like a flat-chested girl.

With luck, it could be done. It might even be an enjoyable challenge, to fool them all. *Even Calder*, said a little voice in her head, threatening her hard-won control yet again. She forced herself to ignore it and slipped her feet into the green satin shoes. They seemed to fit well enough. But then she took a few steps and groaned aloud. It would be torture to spend an evening in these. They were much too tight for walking, and certainly for dancing. Petrov would just have to bespeak another, larger, pair.

She chuckled to herself. She was already making a very satisfying dent in Petrov's hoped-for two hundred rouble winnings.

Chapter Eight

'And they must be pale green kid. Nothing else will do.' Alex was enjoying this. Petrov, riding alongside her, was looking increasingly beleaguered. 'In addition, I require white *maquillage*. A lady would never appear looking as brown as a nut, even under a mask. Also rice powder, rouge, and hair powder, of course. Oh, and a fan to match my gown. Are you making any progress with the new shoes, Petrov?'

He shook his head. So far, all he had managed to procure was a new corset, which laced at the front as well as the back. Alex needed a great deal more in order to dress herself convincingly as a lady.

'Let it be on your head, my friend.' Alex grinned wickedly at him. 'If you cannot provide me with everything I require, I will not be able to go through with this masquerade. You must acknowledge that.'

Petrov nodded glumly.

'And, sad though it would be, you would just have to sacrifice your two hundred roubles. After all, since you laid the wager without even consulting me, it is hardly my fault if it goes awry. Don't you agree?'

The roar of a royal salute from twenty-one cannon drowned

Petrov's reply, just as the royal procession reached Hyde Park Gate for the military review. Alex was glowing with pride, just to be here. This was her milieu. This was the cavalry, where she belonged. And where she would stay. As a man.

The royal party was making its way back to Hyde Park Gate when Calder appeared at her flank, riding the same black stallion he always favoured. Maddeningly, Alex felt herself colouring at the Duke's approach. She cursed inwardly. She was a sorry excuse for a man now. Before, she had blushed only when he touched her. Today, it seemed that his mere presence was enough. Not only that, but her insides had started to churn. Did that mean she was afraid of him? No! Impossible! She knew him to be a man of principle, and integrity. He had been kind to her. He was almost a friend. There was nothing for her to fear.

Provided he never saw her as she had been two nights ago, practically naked in a silken shift, and most definitely a woman.

'Good afternoon, Alexei Ivanovich. What think you of the review?'

'A splendid turnout, Calder. And commendable discipline.'

Calder bowed in acknowledgement of the compliment to his country. 'Your Cossacks are fierce-looking warriors. I imagine there will be a fashion for long mustachios after this, perhaps even beards. After all, the ladies have been adopting Cossack fashions. Why not the gentlemen also?'

Alex smiled. He had succeeded in putting her at her ease once more. She certainly could not fault his manners. 'That is not for me to say, Duke. It will depend on whether the English favour the Cossack look, or the Imperial one. You will have noticed that our illustrious Emperor has neither mustachios nor beard.'

'True. But then, he has to compete with Marshal Blücher, and *he* does.'

'Yes, he is most definitely their favourite,' Alex added.

This light-hearted banter was exactly what was needed. It gave her a chance to be herself, the Russian cavalry officer, and to suppress the strange female longings this man evoked. 'Just listen to them cheering him now!'

They walked on in silence for some way, and then Calder asked, 'Are you on duty this evening, Alexandrov?'

'No, I am not.' Damn! Why had she admitted that? What was he about to ask her to do? She should have lied. She must try to keep her distance from him.

'My mother, the Dowager Duchess, has come up to town. I am hosting a small dinner for her tonight, and I wondered if you would care to attend. My brothers will be there, and several others whom you may have met during your visit.'

Alex did not know how to reply. She could plead a prior engagement, she supposed. On the other hand, tomorrow was the Emperor's last day in London, and tomorrow night was the masquerade ball. It could be that she had only another thirty-six hours to be in Calder's company. Possibly less, if he had decided not to attend the masquerade.

Her tumbling emotions overcame her reason. 'Thank you. I...I should be delighted to attend.'

He grinned suddenly. 'I should warn you, perhaps, that my cousin Harriet—Miss Harriet Penworthy—will also be there. She is a sort of unofficial companion to my mother. And she is renowned for her salty tongue. She has terrified Jack since he was in short coats.'

'It will be most interesting to meet her,' Alex said, non-committally.

'That is one way of putting it, I suppose. Don't be fooled by her appearance, Alexei Ivanovich. She is elderly, and white-haired and she dresses in the fashions of decades ago, for she maintains stoutly that the current ladies' fashions are indecent. She was some kind of cousin to my grandfather, but I have never dared to probe further, even though she accords me rather more respect than other members of the family. Dukes must not be scolded, it appears. At least, not in public.'

'What? Even a Duke who is a royal doorstop?'

He burst out laughing. 'I knew it was a mistake to say that, the moment the words were out of my mouth. I pray you, Alexandrov, do not repeat that to Miss Penworthy. It will be the talk of London in the wink of an eye.'

'Poor Calder.' She felt sympathy and envy at the same time. Miss Penworthy might be a bit of a trial, but she was yet one more part of the large, loving family that surrounded him. He seemed to take it all for granted. If only he knew how lonely it could be, when there was no loving family to turn to, no one who cared. 'I promise I shall not speak of the doorstop…'

'Thank you.'

'…provided you do not give me cause, by baiting me in front of the lady,' she finished, with a twinkle.

'I?' He was trying to look outraged, as if he was appalled at her suggestion. But then his sense of humour got the better of him and he laughed.

It was the warmth in that laughter which convinced Alex she had made the right decision. Being in company with this man, however painful it might be, was all she had. These would be the memories she would cherish, years in the future, when she was alone again. His friendship and generosity warmed her heart.

And when they laughed together, as now, she wanted to cry her love to the skies.

Alex had spent a great deal of time in front of her looking glass, ensuring that every detail of her dress uniform was exactly right. She tried to convince herself that it was for the Dowager Duchess, who was a very great lady. But that was not true. And she knew it. She wanted to impress the Duke himself, even though he would see her only as a young man, and a temporary friend.

If only she had dared to accept his invitation to spend a month or two here in England. But surrounded by the Duke's family, and the Duke's servants, there would have been a real chance that her secret would be discovered.

Not a chance, but a certainty! Lord Jack would be bound to insist on taking her to Jackson's boxing saloon, or something worse. She had been right to refuse. Her rational mind told her so.

And yet the idea of spending time with Calder, walking with him, talking with him, even in her male guise, was so very enticing. Just the thought of being near him made her heart swell and her pulse race. She could feel her skin starting to burn even now, when she was quite alone. She glanced again at the mirror. Yes, she was blushing. To herself!

She knew now that she was as deep in love as it was possible to be. She must be stark mad!

'Mama, may I present Alexei Ivanovich Alexandrov, Captain in his Imperial Majesty's Mariupol Hussars?'

The Dowager smiled and extended her small gloved hand. Dominic caught a sudden breath on the image. His mother's was a small, lean hand, such as the ones that had invaded his dreams, one with a wine glass, and one with a dagger. So had they both been women's hands, in spite of the sudden violence? What could it possibly mean?

He tried to remember exactly how those hands had looked, but failed. The image had come to him only once, many days ago, and it had not returned. Yet it had seemed, somehow, so real.

Alexandrov lifted the Dowager's hand in his own and kissed it gallantly, much in the manner of his Emperor. For a lad who was, apparently, afraid of women, he was doing extremely well, Dominic had to admit.

It was only as Alexandrov relinquished the Duchess's hand, that Dominic noticed that the young Russian, too, had small, lean hands under his gloves. But Alexandrov's were certainly not lady's hands. His were strong enough to wield a lance and a sabre, strong enough to control a cavalry charger and to fight to the death. Dominic's dim recollection was that the fingers around the wine glass had been much too elegant for such bloodthirsty deeds. Definitely not a soldier's hand.

'I am delighted to meet you at last, Alexei Ivanovich.' The Dowager was speaking French, of course.

Dominic came back to himself with a start. His mother was remarkably observant. He could not afford to let her see the slightest hint that he was anything but his normal, controlled self. He must keep his ghost, and his peculiar dreams, to himself.

But his mother was paying all her attention to her Russian guest. 'You must allow me to present you to my cousin, Miss Harriet Penworthy,' she said. 'I'm sure Dominic is quite capable of looking after our other guests,' she added, with a dismissive wave of her elegant hand.

Dominic turned away, trying to conceal his smile. His mother was definitely one of those ladies who was more than capable of wielding a dagger.

Alex had warmed instantly to the Dowager. Had the Duke reminded her of the use of the Russian form of address? It was very comfortable to have it so, Alex decided. The Aikenhead family was so generous, so welcoming. With each successive encounter, Alex found herself growing more envious of what this family had. Freedom, combined with love. Something it was impossible for a daughter of the nobility to find in Russia, in Alex's experience. Calder little knew how very lucky he was.

The Dowager led Alex across the saloon to where the elderly lady stood by the huge fireplace, in conversation with Lord Jack.

Watching them, Alex quickly corrected herself. It was not a conversation. More of a lecture, to judge by the mutinous look on Lord Jack's face, and the fact that he was not being permitted to say a word.

'You should have known better, Jack. And after all the years when I tried to teach you good *ton*.' Miss Penworthy shook her head in dismay, but she did not even pause for breath. 'How could you be rash enough to be caught in such a low place? In my day, gentlemen chose their whorehouses with more care. Why don't you find yourself a mistress instead? I'm sure Dominic would frank you for the costs and—'

The Dowager cleared her throat ominously, but her eyes were dancing. As for Alex, she bit down hard on the inside of her cheek to prevent herself from smiling. She was not supposed to have understood Miss Penworthy's pithy words.

'Cousin, may I present Captain Alexandrov, of the Russian Hussars?' The Dowager spoke in prettily accented English, rather than French.

Miss Penworthy raised her lorgnette and stared at Alex, starting with her face and then scrutinising every part of her person, right down to her gleaming boots. The Dowager and Lord Jack stood mutely by while she did so. No one moved a muscle, least of all Alex. At last, the old lady raised her head again, extended two fingers and said, in English, 'How de do?'

Alex blinked hard, wondering whether she looked as stupid as she felt. Then she bowed over the fingers, murmuring, *'Enchanté, madame.'*

The Dowager's smile encompassed all three of them. In English, she said quickly, 'I am afraid that Captain Alexandrov does not speak English, Harriet, and so, much as you dislike it, I must ask you to use French this evening.' Her smile broadened then, and she added, 'If you have any difficulty in making yourself understood, I, or one of the boys, will be more than happy to translate for you.'

Alex saw that Lord Jack was struggling to keep his countenance.

'I'll have you know, Amalie,' Miss Penworthy retorted, 'that I have no need of such services. And even if I did, I certainly wouldn't trust Jack here to be my interpreter. He'd probably add all sorts of foul-mouthed oaths to everything I said, just because I rang a peal over him about his choice of brothels. And—'

'Harriet! This is most impolite to our guest. In French, if you please!'

That was altogether too much for Lord Jack, who muttered an excuse and bolted from the room. Alex had not the slightest doubt that he was now doubled up with laughter. It seemed that the Dowager was almost as outrageous as her elderly cousin. Or perhaps it was just that she knew how to call the old lady's bluff?

Miss Penworthy looked at the Duchess with narrowed eyes, but the Duchess had managed to maintain an expression of bland innocence. Alex was very glad that the two ladies were sparring with one another. If either of them looked at Alex, they would know at once that she had understood every word.

Miss Penworthy snorted in a very unladylike fashion and then said, in slightly hesitant but correct French, 'French may be the language of the enemy, as I have said more than once, but one does have the ability to use it when there is no alternative.' She turned to Alex. 'How is it, sir, that you are come to London without having learned our language first? It seems a rather flagrant omission, do you not agree?'

Goodness, she was certainly direct. 'Er…I…I'm afraid that I was only recently attached to the Emperor's staff, ma'am. It was an unexpected honour and so there was no time to—'

'Nonsense. Of course there was. Young army fellows like you have plenty of time to improve yourselves. Unless you were off wasting your substance in gambling dens, like that rascal, Jack.'

Alex felt winded, rather as if she had been punched, but she replied with barely a pause. 'No, ma'am, I was not frequenting gaming houses. As it happens, I was fighting Bonaparte's army.'

The Duchess nodded approvingly at Alex's sally.

Miss Penworthy snorted even more loudly and used her lorgnette to raise the Cross of St George on Alex's jacket. 'I suppose you received this bauble for engaging a troop of French cavalry single-handed, or some such?'

'Nothing so gallant, ma'am. I merely lent my horse to a wounded officer. I was a common soldier at the time.' She was not about to let the old lady goad her into boasting about what she had done.

'Hmmph. I take leave to doubt it was as simple as that. A common soldier, eh? Now that *is* interesting. How comes it that a common soldier receives a commission in the Russian army? Must say you don't sound like a common man.' She looked Alex up and down once more, nodding to herself.

'Thank you, ma'am,' Alex said quietly, with a slight bow.

'Well?' Miss Penworthy tapped Alex twice on the chest with her lorgnette. 'Explain yourself, sir. You don't expect me to accept a story like that without any details, do you?' Her French had become less hesitant all of a sudden.

It seemed it had all become too much for the Duchess. Like her son, she fled, leaving Alex to the mercy of her inquisitor.

There was a glint of mischief in the little old lady's eye. She was relishing this battle of words. Alex, warming to the struggle, decided that she could enjoy it, too. 'You would not expect me to boast of my own exploits, ma'am, I am sure. Just as you taught Lord Jack about good *ton*, so my parents taught me. Suffice it to say that the Cross of St George is the usual reward for a soldier who saves the life of an officer, no matter how mundane the circumstances.'

'That does not explain the commission, however.'

'His Imperial Majesty, Tsar Alexander, commissioned me himself, ma'am.'

'Don't believe it,' she retorted. 'If you were gentleman enough to be commissioned, why were you ever a common soldier in the first place? Sounds damned smoky to me.'

Alex prepared to launch into the story she had repeated many times. 'You are very astute, ma'am,' she began.

The old lady frowned and waved her lorgnette dismissively. But Alex was almost sure her eyes were sparkling with amusement. She was testing Alex. And it was a test Alex was not about to fail. 'The truth is that my father did not wish me to join the army. So I ran away and joined the cavalry as an ordinary trooper.'

'Under an assumed name, I suppose? That was always the way, in my day.' Her tone was gentler, suddenly, and there was a look in her eye that suggested she was thinking of someone else, perhaps a long time ago.

Alex allowed herself to smile. 'Yes, ma'am. I used the name Borisov.'

'But you are a gentleman. How could you reconcile yourself to a trooper's life?'

'I enjoyed it, ma'am. And my comrades helped me greatly. Besides, we were fighting for our Emperor and for our country. What is a little hardship compared with that?'

'Very laudable, I'm sure. But that still doesn't explain the commission.'

She was like a terrier with a bone, but Alex was equal to this. 'A commission is granted only to a man with proof of his nobility, ma'am. I did not have the necessary written proofs, so I could not seek a commission.'

Miss Penworthy raised her lorgnette again, imperatively.

'His Imperial Majesty had learned my identity from… er…sources in my family. He offered me a commission himself.'

'I see. So your parents hadn't totally given up on you, then?'

'No, ma'am. And before you ask, I will admit to being sorry about the pain I caused my father when I ran away. But he refused to understand my longing to join the Hussars. He left me with no choice.'

'Hmmph. Young people! And what about your mother? What about her pain? You do not even mention her. If Jack did such a thing, his mother would—'

'My mother died when I was just a child, ma'am.'

That stopped the old lady in her tracks. But only for a moment. 'Tell me about her,' Miss Penworthy said simply. Now, she smiled encouragingly. It was a smile of understanding. It reminded Alex so much of her own mother's smile.

It was a long time since Alex had spoken of her mother. It could do no harm now, surely? The old lady had a salty tongue, certainly, but she also had a softer side. 'Er…her name was Anne—Anna. I wish I remembered her better than I do. It is only…pieces.'

'What was she like?'

'I remember that she was very beautiful, with dark red hair, and deep blue eyes. Much darker than mine. And I remember her perfume. I have never smelt anything like it since. Never. Yet it was so elusive. I could not describe it to you. And then there was the way she moved. As if she were floating. She danced a reel with the grace of the finest Petersburg ballerina. I could never dance it like that, no matter how much I tried. After she died, there was no one left to teach me. I gave up trying.'

'But I'm sure you do dance, Alexei Ivanovich?'

Alex started at the sound of the Duke's rich voice, just behind her. She had been so absorbed in her own memories that she had not heard his approach. Yet now her skin was tingling and her heart was thumping in her breast, as it always did when he was near. The clean masculine scent of him enfolded her like a velvet wrap. Her whole body was softening, weakening. She must fight that. She was a Hussar!

'My dancing, Calder, is a disgrace,' she announced roundly. 'I'll wager you would laugh if you saw me.'

'So you will not be joining us at the masquerade tomorrow?'

She shook her head, deliberately. It was a lie, but only a small lie. And, to be fair, Captain Alexandrov would not be there; the lady in the *polonaise* costume would be Miss Alexandra McGregor, from Scotland.

'Pity. It promises to be a most entertaining evening. Even without the chance to watch you dance,' he added with a mischievous grin.

'There is no need to roast the poor boy,' Miss Penworthy protested.

At that moment, the butler appeared in the doorway and announced, in a stentorian voice, 'Your Grace, dinner is served!'

The Dowager hurried over to them. 'Would you be so good as to take Miss Penworthy in to dinner, Captain Alexandrov? You will have Lady Malcolm on your other side. She speaks excellent French, as you know.'

'Don't worry, Mama,' the Duke said, smiling broadly. 'Surprising though it may seem, you are not sending Alexandrov into the lion's den. Cousin Harriet has decided to take him under her wing.'

Chapter Nine

Alex had had a headache when she woke on the day of the masquerade. She could not understand it. She never drank enough to suffer from after-effects and last night had been no exception. Perhaps it was because she was anxious about tonight's ordeal?

Her usual early ride in the park soon blew the cobwebs away. It would have to be her last appearance as a man that day, for there was much to do, even before she started applying paint and powder to cover her weather-beaten skin. After breakfast, she warned her comrades not to disturb her. If she was not to disappoint them, she had to prepare. Alone.

She spent several hours walking around her bedchamber in her petticoats and her new shoes. She knew how to walk like a lady, and stand and curtsy like a lady. It had been drilled into her, first by her mother and later by Meg. But she was very much out of practice. Apart from that one day in the disguise of a peasant woman, she had not worn a skirt for years. It felt very odd to have so many yards of material floating around her legs.

Worst of all was the need to be naked from the tops of her silk stockings to her waist. Many ladies wore drawers nowadays, but Alex had not thought to ask Petrov to buy any. And now it was too late. Besides, he would laugh at such a request. No doubt he would advise her to wear her own riding breeches instead, or something of the sort. But there were just too many circumstances in which a lady's petticoats might lift. Miss Alexandra McGregor could not be seen to be wearing a man's breeches under her gown.

The Duke of Calder would be there. He has said as much, last evening. So Alex was not preparing her disguise to please her fellow officers; she was making it as convincing as possible in order to impress the Duke. It was a fiendishly dangerous course to take, but she was leaving London in a few hours and she wanted…she longed to be with him, just once, as a woman. Just once, to see if he would be attracted to her, as she was to him. If he would talk to her, perhaps even dance with her, she would be able to touch him without embarrassment, in a way she could not do in her male guise. She might even be able to flirt with him. She didn't think she was very good at flirting—she had had very little practice—but she had watched many young Russian ladies flirting at parties and dances.

She thought she could remember enough about how it was done. Ah yes, her fan. She picked it up from the heap of clothes and cosmetics on the bed, opened it and stood in front of the glass to practise her moves. She raised it so that it covered most of her face, leaving only her eyes visible, and waved it gently to and fro. A come-hither gesture. Yes, that could be very seductive, especially when the eyes were large and lustrous, and gazing with love on a special gentleman.

Would he guess how she felt?

Her stomach started turning somersaults at the thought. She had intended to be fully in control of this encounter, but what if she were not? What if he saw something that she wished to hide? He was a very perceptive man. Did she dare?

She stared at herself for a full minute. Then she nodded

decisively at her reflection and did a pirouette on the tips of her delicate apple-green shoes. That final move made her feel like a lady, at last. And for tonight, that was exactly what she would be.

'You look…um…dangerous, Dominic,' Jack said.

'Do I?' Dominic glanced down at his costume. He had chosen it simply because it was easy to wear. He was not about to tie himself up in layers of cloth and paint. The ballrooms, when filled with thousands of people and perhaps as many lamps, were like to be as hot as Hades.

'It's probably the effect of that elaborate sash, and the dagger and sabre,' Leo said thoughtfully. 'And the flowing white shirt. No doubt the ladies will be intrigued to know who is hidden under the guise of a corsair.'

Dominic took off his tricorne and swept an extravagant bow. 'Why, thank 'ee, sir.' He grinned. 'At least I shall not have paint dripping off the end of my nose like you, Jack.'

'I say! Coming it a bit strong, brother! I thought it would be a great lark to go as Mr Punch.'

'And so it would be, to an open-air masquerade at Ranelagh Gardens. Indoors, however, you'll find it plaguey hot in all that paint, I fancy.'

'Besides being singularly unattractive to the fair sex,' Leo added. 'You won't be stealing many kisses with that enormous nose.'

Jack seemed to shrink a little as he considered that. But he quickly bounced back. 'And you, Leo, do you expect to do any better dressed as Falstaff? Your false belly is so large that you won't get near anyone, of either sex!'

They all began to laugh. Leo's false belly wobbled so much that Jack was soon doubled up and gasping for breath.

Eventually, Leo managed to say, 'Are we expecting to see Alexandrov tonight? Wonder what he'll come as?'

Dominic shook his head. 'Alexandrov won't be there.'

'Why not? Isn't he supposed to go wherever his Emperor goes?'

'Alexandrov is not on duty tonight. And he chooses not to go to the ball. His excuse is that he does not dance.'

'Afraid of the ladies, more like,' Jack said, with a wink. 'I've always thought there was something…er…virginal about him. As if he—'

'Thank you, Jack,' Dominic said, more sharply than he had intended. He would not allow Alexandrov to be insulted. Even in jest. 'That will do. Remember that Alexandrov is our guest, if you please.'

At that moment, Withering appeared in the open doorway to the library. He totally ignored the strange costumes and addressed himself to the fireplace. 'The carriage is at the door, your Grace.'

'Thank you, Withering. Is there much traffic tonight?'

'All the streets are full, your Grace. I am told that it will probably take several hours to reach Piccadilly.'

'In that case, why don't we go on foot?' Jack suggested, capering around the room and making very strange noises with some kind of squeaker. 'Let Londoners see what the Aikenheads look like when they're out on the spree.'

Dominic exchanged glances with Leo. 'Do you feel up to walking, Sir John? Perhaps we should order a litter for you?'

Leo gave the lie to that by executing a neat little dance. He prodded his huge belly. His fingers made a dent several inches deep. 'Only padding, Dominic. Jack's right. There's nothing worse than sitting cooped up in a carriage for hours. Let's walk.'

'Very well. Withering, send the carriage back to the mews. And fetch me a plain black cloak to cover this costume.' He grimaced. 'I'm perfectly content to walk, but not looking like an actor from a bad melodrama.'

* * *

Along with many of the newly arrived guests, Alex walked slowly through the vast reception rooms, looking from side to side in wonder. She had not realised quite how many people would be attending this masquerade. There must be thousands of them, milling about. Some of the men were in uniform, rather than in costume, but everyone was masked. Alex had assumed, naïvely, that the Duke would be easy to recognise. Now she could see how stupid she had been. He would be wearing costume, since he was not a military man, but what kind of costume? And he would be masked, just as she was. How was she ever to hope to find him, far less approach him?

Ahead of her, she spied a very tall man, dressed in Turkish costume. Of course, Calder would be obvious, even here. He was so much taller than most men. Could he be that Turkish soldier? She made to force her way through, so that she could see better.

'I say, Alexandrov,' said a soft Russian voice in her ear, 'that is a truly splendid rig. If I hadn't known better, I'd have sworn you were a girl.'

She turned round, frowning, to see Petrov with two of the young cavalry officers from the Emperor's suite. They were easy to recognise, in spite of their masks, for they were all in uniform. And all were grinning at her.

This was her first real test. She smiled back at them and sank into an elegant curtsy. 'Gentlemen,' she said in French, 'I am delighted to meet you. Such interesting uniforms, too. You must have gone to *so* much trouble to get them.'

'Well, we spent so much money on *yours*,' Petrov whispered conspiratorially, speaking Russian still, 'that we couldn't afford anything for ourselves. But I dare say it will be worth the investment. I cannot imagine that anyone will discover what you really are.'

'Let us hope not,' she said, with feeling.

'Well, if you should fail, you may summon us to your aid. We will be in the card room until supper.'

Of course they would! She should have guessed. 'I wish you every success at the tables, gentlemen. But now, if you will excuse me, I do not think I should be seen with you.' With a wave of her hand, she slipped through the throng of people and sped away, hoping desperately that she would not see any of them again until the ball was over.

The man in the Turkish costume was talking to a tiny lady dressed as a nun. How could Alex ever have thought he was Calder? Even with his mask, she could tell that his features were coarser. And he was not nearly as broad in the shoulder.

One of the stewards, conspicuous in his light blue domino, was standing not far from the tiny nun, calmly surveying the scene. Alex decided he would prove useful as a test of her English. It was some time since she had used it and she certainly did not want the Duke of Calder to be the first person to whom she spoke. 'Good evening, sir,' she said, fluttering her fan. 'Forgive me, but I am rather lost in this enormous house. Could you tell me where the dancing is taking place?'

He smiled down at her and gave her directions. 'And there will be music in the gardens, too, ma'am, if you care to go out. If I may advise you, I should say that dancing with a cavalier under the stars can be most enjoyable. Especially if one can find a secluded corner in which to be alone with him.'

Alex was blushing under her paint. She would dearly love to do just that with the Duke of Calder. With him, she would—

She pushed her wayward dream to the very back of her mind. First she had to find him. She swept her skirts back to dip a curtsy to the blue domino. 'Thank you kindly, sir. I will think on what you have said.'

'My pleasure, ma'am. May I say that we are delighted you have chosen to come all the way from Scotland for our little entertainment.' He winked at her. 'Perhaps we may meet again one day, without the masks?'

Goodness! He was flirting with her! As if she were truly an attractive woman! She could hardly believe her own success. She spread her fan to hide her mouth and forced a girlish giggle. 'Ah, but then you would have to be able to recognise me, sir, and I have no intention of making that easy for you.' She closed her fan with a snap and hurried off down the corridor, hoping he would not follow her. She was hugely reassured by his interest, but the real triumph was that he had detected a Scottish accent, rather than a foreign one. It seemed she could pass for a native, in spite of her lack of practice.

The ballroom was absolutely enormous. Hundreds of couples seemed to be dancing. Moreover, they were dancing the wicked waltz. She could see that the Emperor himself was on the floor, unmistakable in his uniform. He was dancing with a partner who looked remarkably like Lady Jersey. That was no surprise, since he was known to be much taken with her.

Alex herself was not a particularly good dancer—especially when she was required to take the man's part—but she did know how to waltz. As a lady. Her stepmother had insisted that she learn all the dances that were in fashion at court, for the Emperor was known to be extremely fond of dancing. She stood watching as he swept his partner through the dance with great skill and elegance. It would be wonderful to be held in that way, by a truly special man.

By the man she loved.

But was he even here? She began to search the ballroom, section by section, like a soldier quartering a battlefield. She could not see anyone who looked tall enough to be Calder. Perhaps he had decided not to come at all? Perhaps she would have to spend the evening eavesdropping, as Major Zass wished? That was the last thing she wanted to do.

Alex made her way slowly along the corridor, peeping into

the various reception rooms that she passed. Most were full of gossiping guests. In one smaller room, she came upon a couple kissing in the darkest corner behind the door, their masks dangling from their fingers. Alex backed out quickly, hoping they had not realised they were being observed. She was very hot all of a sudden. Her mask, though it covered only her eyes, felt as if it were cutting into her face.

The next room, surprisingly, was totally empty. It was filled with exotic flowers and foliage and had elegant ottomans dotted about, draped with pale green satin and silver muslin. The room was lit by large ground-glass globes suspended from the ceiling, making the overall effect almost magical. It was also refreshingly cool compared with the other rooms. She decided she would enjoy the restful feeling of this place for just a little while. It would help her to overcome that sudden surge of emotion at the sight of the kissing couple. And then she would continue her search.

She walked further into the room so that she would not be visible from the door, for she did not want that blue domino to happen upon her here, alone. Then she sank on to one of the ottomans, carefully arranging her gown around her. She would never be beautiful, but at least one man had found her attractive. With a sigh, she undid her mask and let it fall into her lap. Then she leaned back a little and closed her eyes, wafting her fan slowly to and fro in the scented air. It was delicious.

'Ah, this will do,' said a voice from the doorway.

'It's your own fault for wearing all that padding, Leo,' said a second voice. 'I did warn you about how hot it would be.'

There was no mistaking that voice. It was Calder's. Alex would have recognised it anywhere. And he was with his brother, Lord Leo. What was she to do? She longed to speak to him, to be with him, but she certainly did not want to be confronted by two of the Aikenhead brothers. That would be twice as dangerous.

Uncertain what to do, she hesitated too long. It was too late to escape. So she simply sat where she was, keeping her eyes closed. Perhaps when they came further into the room and saw that a lady was sitting there alone, they would withdraw, out of courtesy? But Alex didn't want that either! She cursed under her breath. It seemed she really had no idea of what she did want.

'Come and sit down, Leo. If you like, I'll fetch you a— Oh! I beg your pardon, madam. We were not aware that there was anyone else in the room. We will withdraw, of course, and leave you to your reverie.'

That was when she remembered her mask! In an attempt to cover her confusion, she did not open her eyes. She felt for her mask and replaced it as swiftly as she could. She sensed that Calder was standing just in front of her. But she also knew that she was like to blush crimson the moment she set eyes on him. It would be easier to speak while she could not see him. 'Pray do not trouble yourselves on my account, gentlemen,' she said, hiding the lower part of her face behind her fan. 'Like you, I was merely a trifle warm and had found this little retreat. Delightful, is it not?'

'A Scottish lady, if I mistake not,' Lord Leo said.

Alex opened her eyes. Lord Leo seemed to be almost as broad as he was tall, wearing a padded brown velvet doublet and knee breeches. The ruff round his neck looked rather tight and very uncomfortable. A black mask covered his nose, mouth and chin. In his hand, he held a high-crowned hat with a wide brim and a trailing golden feather.

'Sir John Falstaff, I presume?' Alex said smoothly.

He swept her an elegant leg. Or rather, he tried to do so. Unfortunately, his ample padding made bending rather awkward and he almost stumbled.

'He is exactly as you say, madam,' the Duke said, 'but he is having—shall we say?—a little trouble with his *embonpoint*.'

Alex raised her fan again to hide her grin. Ladies neither

grinned nor laughed loudly in company. That had been drummed into her by her stepmother. She managed to produce a discreet tinkle of laughter instead. It was only then that she really looked at the Duke.

Her breath caught at the realisation of just how magnificent he looked. He was dressed as a corsair: loose white shirt, with lace at collar and cuffs, wide black breeches tucked into black knee-boots, a blazing red sash from shoulder to waist, a gold-hilted sabre on his left side and a matching dagger on the right. He had put a black curly wig and a tricorne hat over his own dark hair. And, like his brother, more than half his face was hidden by a mask. But Alex had not the least difficulty in recognising the man beneath. Or in deciding, in a heartbeat, that she would willingly be carried off by *this* corsair.

The Duke gestured towards the ottoman and bowed with all the elegance that his brother had lacked. 'You permit, madam?'

Alex could barely breathe. Unable to speak, she nodded and indicated, with a slightly shaky hand, that he might sit.

'Leo, you look much too hot. Since you can't rid yourself of all that padding, why don't you go and find yourself a cooling drink?'

'What? Oh, yes, very well. Good idea. You don't want—?'

'No, Leo!'

'No, I see that you don't.' Lord Leo bowed, from the neck this time, and left the room extremely quickly.

It was too much. Alex was unable to contain her laughter. 'Fie, sir,' she said, tapping the Duke lightly on the arm with her fan, 'that was not well done of you. Your companion, poor man, had sought refuge here to refresh himself a little, and now you have sent him out into the heat once more. I dare swear that the poor man will faint under all those layers.'

'That poor man, madam, is my brother. And since he was mutton-headed enough to wear the costume I warned him against, he may reap the harvest he has sown. Besides, he was much in need of a drink. I merely sent him off to find one.'

Alex raised an eyebrow at him and blinked slowly, once, twice, conscious that her lashes were catching on the eyeholes of her mask. Then she shook her head, just a little. 'And he would have fetched one for you, too, if you had not given him such a dusty answer.'

'Madam, I do not need the kind of drink that my brother could fetch for me. I should much rather be here, drinking in the beauty of your fine eyes.'

This could not be happening! The Duke of Calder was a rational man. He would not say such things to a lady he had only just met. It was impossible! He must have drunk far too many glasses of champagne. Or could it be that Alex was dreaming?

Now he was smiling down into her eyes. His own were huge and dark, and full of the warmth of admiration. No man had ever looked at her in that way before, and yet she knew exactly what it meant. She understood him. She had known it, almost from the first.

At the sight of her, Dominic's heart had leapt into his throat. His little lady of the stables! He had found her! There was no mistaking that small, pale face, wreathed in curls of grey smoke. She was here! Waiting for him.

Then she had spoken, in English, and he had realised that his mind was playing tricks on him. Again. His overeager imagination had been gulled by a grey wig and white *maquillage*. His mind had seen the object of his desires. Not a real woman at all.

But this real woman, sitting there without her mask, and with her eyes closed as if she were escaping from the whole world, was totally alluring. And yet so innocent, so vulnerable. That recognition came from deep within him. He felt a primitive urge to pick her up and carry her off. To protect her. Why? This woman did not need a protector. She was not weak. He knew that, instinctively. There was a whip-core of steel running through her.

If only she had not replaced her mask. It covered only her eyes, but he so much wanted to be able to see them properly. She had eyes for a man to drown in. And she was a beautiful woman, too. For a second, he wondered how he could possibly know that. Her face was painted and she was wearing a wig, as her old-fashioned costume demanded. She could be anything, underneath all that, could she not?

No. She could not. She was beautiful, hidden behind her costume, and she would be even more beautiful without it. Her voice, with its low, honeyed tone and soft Scottish burr, simply added to her magic. It was the kind of voice that stirred a man's senses. The kind of voice that had been haunting him. But this time, he would not be making a fool of himself by responding to it.

When he spoke, he found himself uttering extravagant compliments to her fine eyes. What on earth was happening to him? He had never done that before, either. And yet…and yet, somehow, he knew it was exactly the right thing to say.

He leaned forward, in an attempt to look into her huge, lustrous eyes. That mask was so frustrating. He wanted to rip it off and catch her in his arms. He wanted to rip her gown off, too, if truth were told. He could not understand these sudden, insane urges. He was Dominic Aikenhead, the man whom Castlereagh had employed because he had the coolest head in the kingdom. Cool? Nothing of the kind! Not with this woman!

'Sir?' Her voice was still low and melodious, but there had been a hint of a shiver in that single word. He was intimidating her.

He sat back a little, giving her space and berating himself. If he frightened her, he might lose her altogether, and then he might never have an opportunity to find out who she was. But he did not succeed in resisting her for very long. After only a minute or so, he reached out and gently took one of her gloved hands, holding it loosely in his own much larger one. She had elegant hands, as attractive as every other part of her fascinating person. But they were strong, too. Like the hands in that confounded dream, the image he had been unable to banish. Perhaps this meeting was meant? She seemed to fulfil so many of his half-acknowledged longings.

He had to say something. Before his emotions betrayed him. 'Are you indeed a Scottish lady?' he managed, in a low voice. 'It seems a very great distance to travel, just to be present at a masquerade.'

'You must decide for yourself, sir, who I may be. But I will gratify your curiosity in this, at least. I have travelled a considerable distance to be here.'

He was quite sure now that her accent was Scottish. There was something about the way she rolled her *R*'s. The two of them sat in silence for what seemed a long time. She had not withdrawn her hand from his. It seemed she was content that they continue to touch, but he had no idea what she might be thinking. Had she felt the same instant attraction?

Don't be a coxcomb, Calder! he scolded himself immediately. *Why should an exquisite little lady be drawn to a great hulking brute like you?*

And yet she had not withdrawn her hand. Encouraged, he raised it to his masked lips and dropped a gentle kiss on to her glove, never taking his gaze from hers. 'Madam, you affect me strangely. I...' Now, he could not find the words. Calder, of all people, was finally at a loss!

She dropped her gaze. She had long dark lashes that fanned out across her white skin like tiny black lances. They were so long that they were catching on the eyeholes of her mask.

'Your mask is uncomfortable, I fancy, madam. Will you not remove it?'

She looked back up at him, in surprise. Then her eyes warmed into something more like mischief. 'Why, sir, that is the best excuse I have ever heard to persuade a lady to unmask. But I fear it does not convince me. Concern for my comfort, forsooth!'

She was suiting her language to her antiquated costume. He smiled down at her, but she could not see that; his own mask covered his mouth. 'It grieves me that you should doubt me, ma'am.' He found himself responding in kind. The elevated language of a bygone era seemed to suit the situation very well. 'I may assure you that I am thinking only of you.'

She pursed her lips and shook her head a little. He was almost certain she was trying not to smile. 'I have no doubt that you are thinking of me, sir. But about my comfort? That I take leave to doubt.'

She was right, of course. He raised her hand to his lips once more, playing for time, trying to think of what to do next. It was as if they were partners in the figures of a complicated dance, a dance whose steps he understood only vaguely. If he put a foot wrong, she might well drop him a neat curtsy and leave him stranded on the floor. For a man who had made love to a great many women, he had to admit that he was making a very poor fist of even stealing a kiss from this one.

'Would you think it too forward of me, madam, if I removed my own mask?' he said at last. Let her decide on the shape of the next figure of this dance.

Slowly, she smiled. Her glorious white shoulders seemed to relax a little, as if she had been waiting for him to make the next move, and was now satisfied. 'I imagine that your mask must be uncomfortable, too, sir. Out of concern for your comfort—and for that reason only—I give you my permission to remove it.'

She had given him his own again. In the cleverest possible way. She was utterly enchanting.

He returned her hand to her lap, reached up under his wig with both hands and untied his mask, letting it fall to the floor. He did not dare to hope that she approved of what she now saw—he was not vain enough to wish for admiration—but he was very impatient for the chance to put his naked lips to her hand. Even through her glove, that would somehow be much more sensual, much more immediate than before. 'If you will not remove your mask for me, madam, will you at least remove your glove?'

She shook her head instantly. He could hardly believe she had reacted so. She had been more than content to allow him to hold her hand, and to kiss it through her glove, but she would not agree to remove it. Why on earth would she—?

At that moment, she reached up and, with her gloved fingers, very slowly began to unfasten her mask. She held his gaze unblinkingly throughout. The movement was as erotic as if she had been stripping herself naked in front of him. As he watched, the strong attraction that he had been feeling for this extraordinary woman intensified inexorably. He did not dare to breathe.

And then, in the moment when the mask loosened and fell away to reveal her perfect oval face, the Duke of Calder found himself consumed with pounding, shattering desire.

Chapter Ten

Dominic took a sharp breath through clenched teeth, and let it out in a long hiss. His body was demanding that he pull her into his arms and make love to her. Now! He forced himself to repress it. He was not a savage. He was a gentleman. And he was in company with a lady. If he wanted to frighten her off, that would certainly be the way to succeed.

She had not moved. The mask was lying in her lap, in her gloved hand. And she was still gazing up at him. Could she detect just how aroused he had become at the sight of her unmasked face?

At that very moment, he had a sudden insane urge to laugh. He had not chosen his corsair's costume with seduction in mind, but the baggy trousers certainly had their advantages.

She had seen something in his face. 'You have had your wish, sir,' she said, in a voice so soft he could barely make out the words. 'Such a pity the result is not to your liking.' She made to replace her mask.

'Stay!' He put his hand quickly over hers, to stop her, all the while cursing himself for a fool. She had seen that spark of amusement in his eyes, and she had assumed—as any woman would—that he was laughing at her, rather than himself. 'I beg you, gentle lady. Do not replace your mask. For you have brought sunlight into this place by removing it. Do you not see that all the flowers are turning towards you, to bask in the warmth and light you bring?' He gestured vaguely in the direction of the greenery that filled the room. 'Flowers die without sunlight. I do not share their beauty, but I, too, will suffer if you cover yourself. Pray do not.' He squeezed her gloved hand. Then, when she made no move to repulse him, he gently extracted the mask from her fingers and tucked it inside his shirt. 'Thank you.' His voice was barely a croak.

Her eyes had followed the movements of his hands, first to her lap, and then to his own body. She now seemed to be blushing a little, under her white *maquillage*. 'Such extravagant words, sir.' It should have been a reproof, but her voice was too low and musical for that. And she had not raised her eyes to his.

'Madam, it is not my wont to shower ladies with extravagant compliments. Pray believe that. But with you, the words come without conscious thought. I say only what I truly believe.'

This time she did look up. He saw that her eyes were wide with astonishment. He could not tell whether or not she believed him. Then, at last, her expression softened. She had made up her mind about him. But what had she decided?

Her lips opened a fraction and she leant forward, as if she were about to speak. But then she stopped, with a tiny nod, probably to herself. Instead of words, she gave him a delicious smile, her face full of warmth, her eyes glowing.

Dominic felt his whole body beginning to smoulder in response. If he did not kiss her soon, he would be in flames. In an attempt to control his primitive urges, he raised her gloved hand to his lips and kissed it, passionately. It was not enough. Those confounded gloves! He could not remove them. Not without her permission. And he knew instinctively that she would not give it. But there were other ways.

Without removing her hand from his lips, he raised his head a little and fixed his eyes on hers. She was not afraid of him. But she was wondering what he was going to do. Holding her gaze, he slowly turned her hand over and bent it back, stretching the fine leather over her wrist. Now he could do exactly what he longed to do—put his lips against her skin.

It was a glorious moment. He touched his mouth to the inside of her elbow and slowly, slowly nuzzled his way down her inner arm. The supple leather folded itself towards her palm, as if it approved of his every move. When, at last, he kissed the inside of her wrist, a fierce shudder ran through him. And he felt an answering shiver run through her. Wild magic had captivated him at the sight of her, and now she, too, was in its thrall. 'Madam,' he breathed against her soft skin, 'I swear you have bewitched me.' He kissed every inch of her bare wrist. It was the sweetest torture. She was so very desirable. With every touch, he wanted more. He could not resist the temptation to touch his tongue to her skin.

She gasped and tried to pull her hand from his.

He held her fast. But only for a second. Then he gentled his grip and returned to merely kissing her wrist.

'You are very bold, sir.' There was still that tiny shiver in her voice. She was trying to sound normal, but she could not. She, too, was aroused by this magical encounter.

He touched his tongue to her skin again. This time, she did not gasp. She sighed. It sounded like a sigh of longing. 'Ah, my sweet lady, if only you could imagine how you make me feel. Like the richest of kings when I touch your skin. Like the poorest beggar when I think how much more there is that I may not have. Your pale cheek, your lustrous eyes, your cherry lips.' She was truly blushing now. 'Your delicate white throat. I would fain kiss them all, lady, and more besides.'

'Sir, you—' Her voice broke. She raised her free hand to his cheek and held it there. Then, with a little groan, she dropped it back into her lap. 'It cannot be.' Her voice sounded like misery itself. And then she made to rise. She was going to leave him.

'No!' All restraint forgotten, he pulled her into his arms and kissed her fiercely. She tried to push him away, but it was only a second before she melted into his embrace, accepting and then returning his kiss with gentle sweetness. First one arm, then a second stole round his neck. Her gloved fingers sought for his hair under the curls of his wig and softly stroked his scalp until it tingled. When he touched his tongue to her closed lips, she opened softly to him, with another long sigh. She tasted exactly as he had known she would—like ambrosia, the food of ancient gods. He could not prevent himself from groaning as he deepened the kiss. She was so very beautiful, so desirable. He was aching for her.

Alex leaned into him, allowing his strength to enfold her. She felt tiny and protected and desired. So very much desired. It was indeed magical. Like living in a dream. It could not continue—she knew that—but she did not want these feelings to end. Not yet. Not so soon. Her whole body was glowing with a fierce, burning heat, longing for fulfilment, for union with this man. And she gloried in it.

But it could not be.

Ignoring the protests of her rational mind, she gave herself up to his kiss. He had put one hand to her back, pulling her closer to his own body, and the other was caressing her cheek, with a touch so gentle that she barely knew his fingers were there. The kiss went on and on, deeper and deeper, until Alex's body was hot and churning with desire, and her head was swimming. If she stood up now, she would surely faint.

But it could not be.

He broke the kiss at last. She heard her own mew of disappointment as his lips left hers. His fingers were still soft against her face, touching and stroking as though he could not get enough of her. His eyes were deep pools, black with desire. And his mouth was only a breath away from hers. He was waiting for her to show him that she wanted more. More of him. More of his touch.

But it could not be.

He must have seen the moment when she took her decision, for he sat back a fraction, silently watching her. He ran his tongue slowly over his lips, as if they were parched. Without conscious thought, Alex did the same, realising what she was doing only when she saw the reaction in his face. He was going to kiss her again. And when he did, she would be lost. She must stop this. Now. For it could not be.

She raised one gloved hand. It was not the hand he had kissed so passionately. The inside of that wrist was still tingling from his caresses, as if his lips and tongue had never ceased to touch her there. That thought troubled her so much that she could not meet his eyes, but she managed to speak with tolerable composure. 'Sir, I must ask you to stop. Such passion between two strangers is…is unseemly. Do you not agree?'

There was pain in his face as he shook his head, very deliberately. 'No, sweet lady, I do not agree. Such passion comes but seldom to man and woman. It is a gift. For both of us. But I can see that it makes you uneasy. For that reason, I will do as you ask.'

'Then I will leave you, sir,' she said, starting to rise.

He caught her hand. 'Ah, no. No. I have said I will curb my passion, lady, but I cannot agree to deprive my poor eyes of the sight of your beauty. That would be too much to ask. Will you not stay by my side, at least for a little? I will do nothing without your consent. I give you my word. But, I pray you, stay.'

There was something in his voice that tore at her heart. Before, she had been glowing with desire; now her heart was weeping. For the passion they dared not share. She knew she should leave him—now—but she could not. 'I take you at your word, sir. Nothing without my consent.'

A harsh smile was twisting the corner of his mouth. 'You may drive me to Bedlam, fair lady, but it shall be as you wish.'

She forced herself to smile back up at him, as if everything were perfectly normal, as if they were two people meeting in a Society drawing room. He seemed to catch her mood, for his smile broadened and lost its edge of bitterness. She smoothed the wrinkled glove back into place over the sensitised skin of her forearm. 'Perhaps we should join some of the other guests?' she suggested, gesturing towards the door.

He stood up and offered his hand to help her rise. She stared at it for a moment, and then looked up at his face. She recognised that the fires of his desire were banked now, but they had not been doused. She shook her head, regretfully. 'I permitted you to take my hand once before, sir. And we both know what happened then.' She rose to her feet without aid. 'For the moment, I think I had best forgo the…er…the…'

'The pleasure of my touch, lady?' He was truly smiling at her now. There was a gleam of real amusement in his eyes.

Alex realised that verbal sparring, with such a man, could be almost as sensuous as touching. But she would not try to avoid it, in spite of all the dangers it brought. She had sacrificed enough already.

'There is surely less risk when we are not alone, would you not agree?'

She nodded, wondering what he might be planning.

'In the ballroom, yonder, hundreds of couples are dancing. Do you dare to take the floor with me, my sweet lady?'

'Perhaps I do not dance, sir.'

He glanced down at her feet, shod in their apple-green buckled shoes. 'Wearing dancing slippers like those, ma'am? I take leave to doubt it. Those shoes, and that gown, were made to be shown on the ballroom floor.' He offered his arm. 'Will you?'

She dropped him a curtsy. 'Yes, sir. I will.' She tapped him twice on the arm with her folded fan. 'And, as soon as we are no longer alone, I will even agree to take your arm.'

'Madam, I should not have thought you so lacking in courage.'

'Sir, I should not have thought you so lacking in guile.'

He laughed then, a low, genuine laugh. It warmed her heart.

They were only a step or two from the door when she remembered. 'Sir, you still have my mask. And you are not wearing your own.'

'You are awake on all suits, ma'am, I am sorry to say.' He reached inside his shirt to retrieve her mask, but held it fast for a moment. 'I had hoped that I might keep this, as a…to remind me of a kiss shared with a most beautiful lady. But since you ask for it…'

She nodded.

'Will you allow me to fasten it for you?'

She nodded again. How could she refuse? He moved to stand behind her and gently, very gently, stroked the mask into place over her eyes, tying its strings over her wig. She felt as if he were somehow claiming her, by tying that knot. He did not need to do so, for she was already his, heart and soul. She swallowed hard. He must never suspect that she was already won. For him, she spelt disaster.

If her anguish showed on her face, he had not seen. He strode back to the ottoman to retrieve his own mask. Standing there with it dangling from his fingers, he raised an eyebrow at her. She shook her head. He wanted her to replace it for him, but she did not dare. Nothing so close. Nothing so intimate.

'I see your courage fails you again, ma'am.'

It was true. She would not deny it. 'My mother taught me long ago, sir, that discretion is the better part of valour. I do believe that tonight—now—it is time that her daughter learned to heed her wise words.'

'Touché.' A wry smile touched his lips, but he tied his mask on himself. Then he returned to her side and took a step into the corridor beyond their green refuge, offering his arm as he did so. 'Madam, will you do me the honour?'

By the time they reached the ballroom, Alex was almost swooning. It was not that she had put her arm through his, that she was touching him. Not this time. It was because of how the warm scent of his body pervaded the mask over her eyes. It made her feel as though her face was cradled against the bare skin of his chest. The picture conjured up by that masculine scent was so powerful, so erotic, that all her senses were tumbling chaotically. When he spoke to her, she was unable to understand or respond to his words. She was floating.

'Are you quite well, madam?' He put his free hand over hers, where it lay loosely on his arm. His voice was filled with concern.

She forced herself back to earth, trying to take only the shallowest of breaths so that his scent would cease to ensnare her traitorous body. 'I…I am a little warm, sir. That is all.'

He pressed her fingers lightly. 'If you will allow, I shall fetch you a cooling drink before we venture on to the dance floor. A glass of champagne, perhaps?'

'No!' The word was torn from her. The thought of champagne, and the risks of losing even more control of her faculties, had brought her back down to earth with a jolt. 'No, thank you, sir,' she said, rather more politely. 'I find that champagne is not refreshing when one is suffering from the heat. I should much prefer lemonade.'

'As you wish.'

She had assumed he would leave her where she stood, at the side of the ballroom, in order to fetch it for her. But he did not.

He nodded in the direction of a side door. 'I believe the refreshment room is through there. Shall we go together?' There was just a hint of a smile at the corners of his eyes. 'Much as I desire to serve you, madam, I am not about to leave you here alone. I have you, and I plan to keep you, at least until you grant me the honour of one dance. You do waltz, I trust?'

The fire in her lower limbs grew white hot. Oh yes, she waltzed. But never yet with a man who could wreak such havoc with all her senses. 'I…I—'

'Excellent. I was not sure that the new fashion had yet reached the north. Do you attend many balls in Scotland?' He was leading her across the floor to the refreshment room as he spoke.

Alex forced herself to concentrate on his words, ignoring the touch, the scent of him. He had been at least as aroused as she. If he could now control his ardour enough to sound like any gentleman at a ball, she should be able to do so, too. 'I have not told you that I come from Scotland, sir. You shall not gull me so easily into betraying my secrets.'

'I see that I must show a great deal more guile if I am to discover what I wish to know. You were right in that.'

'Have you considered simply asking the questions, sir?'

He stopped dead. Then he chuckled. 'No, lady, I had not. However, since you suggest it… Madam, will you be so good as to tell me your name?' Her sharply indrawn breath must have betrayed her shock, but he ignored it. 'I do not ask anything of you that I would not do myself. My name is Dominic.'

'Dominic.' It was the first time she had spoken his name aloud. It was such an intimate thing, a man's given name.

He raised an eyebrow, waiting.

She had no reason to deny him. For what harm could it do? It was only a name. For a fraction of a second, she wondered whether she should give him a false one. No sooner thought than discarded. She wanted—no, she longed to hear her own name on his lips. 'My name, sir, is Alexandra. But my—' She bit her tongue. She must not tell him that her family called her 'Alex'. That was much too close to 'Alexei'. Knowing that she must say something to cover her slip, she added, 'It is something of a mouthful, I fear.'

'No, it is lovely. But unusual, certainly. Are you named for your mother?'

'No. My mother was Anne Catriona. And, before you ask, my father was not Alexander, either. My mother was a student of Greek.'

His eyebrows rose. He was surprised, perhaps even shocked, by the idea of a woman studying Greek. Alex determined to puncture his masculine arrogance.

'My mother was a scholar. Until her marriage, she travelled a great deal, as companion and hostess to her father, who was a diplomat. She planned to name her son Alexander. Unfortunately, her son turned out to be a daughter.'

'It is a beautiful name. Will you permit me to use it?'

She nodded. 'Here, at this masquerade, we are somehow outside Society. It seems that the rules do not apply.' She was looking back across the room at the waltzing couples, some of whom were dancing far, far too close together. One or two of the men could be seen to be whispering in their partners' ears, or nuzzling their necks. It would have been shocking if all had not been masked.

'And you will call me Dominic? Please?'

She looked up into his eyes. 'Yes, Dominic. I will.'

Alexandra was waltzing divinely now. She had been a little hesitant at first, as if she were minding her steps, but she had soon relaxed into the dance, allowing him to whirl her round the floor in such harmony that they might have been practised partners. She fitted beautifully into his arms, in spite of the marked difference in height. She was everything he had glimpsed in his girl of the fire. And yet, she was so much more. For she was a lady, with wit, and poise and presence. She was perfect.

Alexandra. An unusual name. But a fitting choice for this woman. He remembered vaguely that Alexander had been the name of Scottish kings, as well as the name of the great Greek conqueror.

Dominic steered her past a couple who were almost stationary in the middle of the floor, while the gentleman planted kisses on the lady's temple. Dominic longed to do the same. But not here. Not in front of this vast audience. Not in that vulgar way. His Alexandra was a lady. She was not to be treated like a member of the muslin company. Away from the ballroom, however…

He knew a sudden urge to find a secluded spot. Surely there must be one in this vast place?

He waited until the music ended, for it would have been too obvious to take her from the floor in the middle of the dance. 'You look a little warm, Alexandra,' he said, putting an arm behind her back to usher her towards the door. 'There are refreshments in the garden, I believe, and illuminations, too. And no doubt it is much cooler there. Shall we join the throng outdoors and pass an opinion on the merits of the regimental bands?' He hoped he was managing to keep the desire out of his voice, to sound merely polite, and considerate of her comfort.

She was fanning herself enthusiastically. And she was glowing from the effort and the exhilaration of waltzing for what had seemed like hours. Dominic had refused to let her leave the floor, or to dance with any other man. One masked Guards officer had tried to cut Dominic out, but the man had slunk away after receiving a few pithy words of advice about how he might mend his manners. Rather than being shocked, Alexandra had simply laughed at Dominic's caustic wit, melting back into his arms and into the rhythm of the waltz without a murmur of protest. It had been as if they were the only couple on the floor. At least, so it had been for Dominic. Had it felt equally special for Alexandra, too?

She glanced a little anxiously in the direction of the garden. The lights and the people she saw there seemed to reassure her, for she nodded her agreement and strolled down into the grounds at his side. One regimental band was playing quite near the house. There was another, too, in the far distance, playing just loudly enough to make itself heard throughout the garden.

'A pity they are not both playing the same music,' Alexandra said, with a slight frown. 'They provide a most discordant echo, I think.'

'You are fond of music, I collect?'

'Yes, I am, though I must warn you that I do not play any instrument, and my singing voice has been likened to a magpie with a head cold.'

'How…er…unusual. I must make a point of listening out for one of those. But I doubt there will be magpies here this evening. And we already have enough discord with these competing bands. Perhaps we should seek out a listening post where we can enjoy only one of them? There must be somewhere in this vast garden, surely, to protect our ears from this?'

To his surprise, and pleasure, she agreed immediately, tucking her gloved hand confidingly under his arm and smiling up at him. 'Which direction do you suggest we take, Dominic?'

She knew she had been taking a risk in going apart with him, but the temptation had been so very strong. If she had just met him for the first time, she might have been much less inclined to trust him. But she knew the Duke of Calder, man to man. He was a man of honour and integrity. He could be trusted to treat Alex as a lady. Unless his passions overcame him?

They were meandering through the furthest part of the huge garden, arm in arm. The alleyways here were less well lit than those by the house, and the overhanging trees cut out much of the moonlight. Few guests had ventured so far.

Dominic steered her round a corner and into an even

narrower, darker path. There, Alex heard a gasp, followed by a nervous giggle and the low rumble of a man's voice. Somewhere ahead, and to the left of the path, a couple had stolen away from the crowds. She had known it would be so at such a ball. The anonymity provided by the masks encouraged guests to take liberties that would be unthinkable in normal circumstances. Liberties such as dancing waltz after waltz with the same man, as she and Dominic had just done.

That lady's giggle had finally reminded Alex of precisely how her conduct might be viewed. By Society. And by Dominic himself. She might know him well enough to trust him, but he believed they had only just met. As far as he was concerned, his companion was a masked lady who was content to dance for much too long with a total stranger and then to walk alone with him in the gardens. And to respond with passion to his kiss! What could he possibly think of her?

A leaden weight landed in the pit of her stomach. Her comrades had joked that some of the most exclusive courtesans in London would be at this ball, mixing with the Society ladies who normally shunned them. Given the way Alex had responded to Dominic, it was more than possible that he believed her to be one of those—a high-priced whore.

A grey mist of despair settled over her. She shuddered.

'Alexandra?' He had stopped in his tracks. His voice was filled with concern. 'What is wrong, sweet lady?'

Confused, and desperate to leave this place, she blurted out the truth. 'That couple over there. What they are doing is vastly improper. And it was equally improper of me to agree to be here, alone, with you.'

'You wish to return to the house?' There was tension in his voice.

She nodded, unable to say more.

'Then we shall return, of course.' He turned round to lead her back to the broader path. 'But before we do, will you allow me to point out that I have done nothing at all improper since we left the house?'

Now she could feel the blood draining from her face. She had insulted his honour. And he had given her no cause. No cause at all.

Chapter Eleven

The horrified look on her face made Dominic furious. With himself.

He had insulted her. Oh, she had impugned his honour—there could be no doubt of that—but with no malicious intent. She was a lady. She had agreed, quite innocently, he was sure, to walk with him in the garden. And now, the sound of another couple's lovemaking had brought home to her just how much risk she was taking. After all, she had no knowledge of who he was or whether he could be trusted. He might be the worst rakehell in London. He was certainly strong enough to overpower a lady like Alexandra. And ravish her, too, if he chose.

She was afraid. And no wonder.

For several seconds, he stood stock-still, gazing at her expressive face. He had not the first idea of how to retrieve the situation, to undo the hurt he had caused. He cudgelled his brain for the right words, but they would not come.

'I…I beg your pardon, sir,' she whispered at last, breaking the strained silence that stretched between them. She was staring at the ground beneath her apple-green slippers. 'I did not mean— Pray accept my apologies. I should not have spoken as I did.'

He had insulted her, but *she* was apologising to him! He felt an overpowering desire to take her in his arms, to stroke away the frown from her brow, and to protect her from a hateful world that contained the sort of men who could inspire her fear. He was just lucid enough, however, to realise that he must do no such thing, for it would provide proof of everything she feared. He put his left hand on his sword hilt, gripping it hard, and clutched his dagger with the other. He must not touch her!

The taut silence continued. She was waiting for him to say something.

'Madam,' he tried gently. Still she did not raise her head. 'Alexandra,' he said, the words coming out in a rush, 'you have no need to apologize to me. You expressed your perfectly reasonable concern about being here, alone, with a man you barely know. Whereas my reply was exactly the sort of arrogant, top-lofty remark I would deplore in anyone else. I humbly ask your pardon. Will you forgive me?'

She raised her head then. It was difficult to be sure in the half-light, but he thought her eyes were glistening. Oh, he had been a brute!

'I think perhaps we should forgive each other. Both of us spoke insulting words that we did not intend. Might we agree that they shall all be forgot?'

He let out a long breath. 'You are generous. Thank you.' But he was clutching his dagger more tightly than ever. He wanted to touch her so very much.

'So be it. We are at one. And now, Dominic,' she said, gently pulling his elbow from his side and tucking her arm through his, 'shall we see what we might discover at the end of this path?' With her free hand, she pointed down a path that ran at right angles to the one with the noisy lovers. 'I do believe I can see some kind of light down there. And the sound of the first band is definitely fading. We may find our musical refuge at last.'

It was as if her gloved hand were a magic wand, casting a spell over him. The moment her fingers touched his arm, longing flooded him all over again. His whole body was burning for her.

He hurried her down the path towards the light, hoping that they would no longer be alone. In front of witnesses, his rational mind would remain in control of his raging desire. Probably. But if he spent much longer alone in the dark with her, he might not be answerable for his actions.

Alex could feel the tension in his arm muscles through the fine lawn of his shirt. She could feel the warmth of him, too. It made her fingers tingle, even through her gloves. She wanted to touch his skin with her bare hand, to stroke it, to transfer the scent of him to her own body, where she could wear it like the rarest perfume. Here, where it was almost dark, she could take off a glove, surely, and lay her hand over his? Just for a second?

It was too late. He had brought her to the end of the alley where there was a small, circular seating area, surrounded by scented roses. Lighted globes hung from the trees and from the wooden archways between the seats. To Alex's surprise, this pretty grotto was quite empty of people. Where were they all? She did not care. She was determined that she would not allow her missish fears to overpower her again. This was Dominic, the man she loved. And this was the only night she would ever have with him. Every second was to be savoured.

The music was very clear now. They must be quite close to one of the bands, even though she could see no one. No one but Dominic.

The band began to play a waltz.

Dominic groaned.

That sound told her everything. He was fighting his desire. He was determined to behave as a gentleman should. If she allowed him to, he would succeed.

She turned her back on him, gazing up into the overhanging branches so that he would not be able to see her smile. 'I wonder how they managed to put the globes so very high up,' she murmured matter-of-factly, pointing.

'Devoted servants, I expect. And ladders.'

The strain was in his voice again. Alex found she was really rather pleased. When she turned back to him, she could see it in his face, too, in spite of the mask. This was her moment. 'We are alone here. There is no need for me to remain masked.' She was deliberately allowing herself to sound quite irritable. Reaching up, she untied the strings of her mask and removed it, allowing it to dangle from her hand. 'I had not realised before just how uncomfortable a mask could be.'

She waited. Hopefully.

He sighed as he removed his mask. 'We should not, Alexandra. What if someone were to happen upon us? To recognise us? Your reputation—'

She shook her head quickly. 'I am not known in London. No one will recognise me, particularly in this wig and paint.' That was not true. The Russians could recognise her, and it would spell disaster if they found her with Dominic. She offered up a fervent prayer that they would not go beyond the card room and the supper room. And then she decided to ignore the threat they represented. She had only this one night.

She looked Dominic up and down, assessingly. 'You may be at greater risk than I am. I dare say you are well known in these parts?'

'I…er…I do live in London for some months of the year. So I might be recognised without my mask. But for a man, that is no risk. They would just say that the D—that Dominic was following in his brother's footsteps.'

'Would those be the footsteps of Sir John Falstaff, by any chance?'

'Mmm. My younger brother. He has a reputation as something of a rake, I fear. He spends far too much time gambling. And he has—um—a roving eye.'

'And you do not?'

'Ah. There you have me, madam. What can I say without incriminating myself even further?'

He was almost blushing. It was a sweet victory to have brought him to this. She reached up to lay her left hand on his right shoulder. 'Dominic,' she said in a low murmur, 'they are still playing a waltz. And we are wasting it.'

That was enough. He pulled her into his arms, and they began to dance, around and between the wooden benches, and through the graceful arches of roses. Their perfume filled the air, but Alex wanted only to inhale the clean, masculine scent of Dominic Aikenhead, to fix it in her memory for ever.

'You dance so beautifully, Alexandra. You are as light as thistledown. I feel as if you might float away if I were not holding you safe in my arms.'

She did feel safe in his embrace. Safe, and protected. And desired. But she did not dare to say so. She barely dared to admit it to herself. Her treacherous body was trying to betray her again, her insides burning like a furnace, and the heat transferring to every last inch of her skin. Could he not feel it? Did he not know?

The music ended. Dominic spun her to a halt. 'Dancing with you, Alexandra, is like dancing with a bewitching spirit. I cannot be sure that you are really here with me. You might be only a beautiful apparition, sent to haunt me. Are you?'

She put her hands to his cheeks and pulled his mouth down to hers. She touched her lips to his, hesitantly at first, but soon more boldly.

The fire exploded between them. There were no more words. Dominic crushed Alex to him, and plundered her mouth with an urgency she could barely comprehend, until she, too, was caught up in it. She wrapped her arms around his neck, but it was not enough. She needed to touch him. This time, she must!

She pushed aside the wide collar of his shirt and laid her gloved hand on his bare chest. Not enough! Still not enough! She tore her lips from his, ignoring his groan of disappointment. Then she laid a single, gloved finger across his mouth and dipped her head to his chest. The moment she began to kiss his skin, his whole body stilled and tensed. He seemed to have stopped breathing altogether.

Alex was revelling in the taste of him. Strong, and clean and with hints of sandalwood and salt. Greatly daring, she stretched up to put her tongue into the hollow of his collarbone and lapped. He groaned, from deep in his chest. She trailed the tip of her tongue slowly along the bone, from his shoulder to the centre of his neck. There, at the small round hollow at the base of his neck, she paused. 'I wonder,' she murmured. 'Mmm. Yes, I think that will do.' And then she kissed his skin there, as passionately as if it had been his mouth.

He ground out her name. His voice sounded raw. 'My beautiful witch. You torture me.' With that, he caught her up in his arms and carried her to one of the wooden benches. The moment he had settled her on his lap, he began to visit retribution on her. It was torture, indeed.

It was glorious.

He kissed her temples and her eyes. He kissed the line of her jaw. And just when she was sure he must come back to her parched lips, he began to feather tiny kisses down the side of her neck, from the lobe of her ear to her collarbone. And beyond.

His mouth was on the globe of her breast above the low neckline of her gown. And the fingers of his free hand were trying to mould the breast beneath, through the silk and the stays. It seemed to be swelling to fit his hand, straining to escape from the confines of its prison. She wanted him to touch her. Even there. Her whole body was longing for his touch. Everywhere.

She groaned.

He stilled instantly. Raising his head, he said hoarsely, 'You want me to stop.'

'No.' Her voice was so strained that she barely recognised it. Words were not what she needed. Not now. She touched her hand to the back of his neck and pressed his mouth to her breast. Where it belonged. And she groaned again at the pleasure of it.

Even that was not enough. He pushed long fingers down between her skin and her chemise so that he had her nipple under his hand, rubbing it back and forth until it rose, hard as a pebble, against his flesh. Then, at last, he brought his mouth back to hers, kissing and teasing with his lips and tongue, and nipping at her lower lip with his teeth. Emboldened, Alex began to return his kiss with even greater passion, touching her own tongue to the soft inner surface of his lips, advancing and retreating, tempting and tantalising, just as he had done. Such welcome, fearful torment. Her whole being was filled with the joy of this moment, and with her love for this man.

'Oh, Alexandra, no. We cannot. Not here.'

He had put her from him, only a little way, but enough. For several moments, Alex could not remember where she was. Her eyes could barely focus. Her head was swimming.

He rose with her in his arms and set her gently on her feet. Then he held out a hand, waiting.

Without hesitation, she put her hand in his and allowed him to lead her away from the light.

Dominic knew it was wrong. He should be taking her back to the house, or, at least, to the areas of the garden where there were plenty of other people. But his desire for her was so all-consuming that he found himself unable to gainsay it. He told himself that he was doing so only because her own passion was at least as strong as his. She had responded to him with such amazing fervour that his own body was reacting more like that of a schoolboy than a grown man. That urgency was intensified by a drumming voice in his head, reminding him constantly that this might be his only time with this woman, that she, too, might disappear from his life at any moment, like a wraith. Overwhelmed by his own need, he refused to heed the tiny nagging voice of conscience. He forced it behind a stout door at the back of his mind, and led Alexandra down the dark winding path, to where they might be totally alone together.

She seemed to be fully aware of what he was about. When they were still just within sight of the illuminated arbour where they had kissed, she said, in a slightly unsteady voice, 'Where are you taking me, sir?'

'Dominic,' he said firmly. It felt immensely important, for some unfathomable reason, that she should use his given name.

'Dominic,' she repeated softly. 'Dominic. Where are you taking me?'

'Nowhere that you do not want to go, Alexandra,' he said, after a pause. Passion was certainly driving him, but he would do nothing without her consent.

By the time they reached the end of the narrow walk, it was completely dark around them. The moon had disappeared behind a cloud and the starlight was barely enough to allow them to see their way. Dominic found himself hoping that the darkness would encourage Alexandra to forget her inhibitions. He so much wanted to be able to touch her beautiful body, to kiss his way from her lips to the core of her. Would she permit him to do so? He did not know.

There was a small stone seat, set back from a bend in the path and partly screened by tangled shrubs. He noticed it only because the moon reappeared for a second and caught the corner of its pale stone with a shaft of silver light. He picked his way through the mass of plants at the edge of the path, leading Alexandra by the hand. The seat was just big enough to accommodate two persons. Provided they sat very close together.

The fleeting shaft of moonlight had gone again. They were alone together in the velvet darkness.

Dominic sat down at one end of the seat, pushing his sword impatiently out of the way. He drew Alexandra down to sit at his side, even though he would have preferred to take her on to his lap. But he had to be sure that she was willing. 'Ah, my sweet lady,' he murmured, taking her hand. 'My sweet, beautiful Alexandra. Will you permit me to kiss you again?'

Her response was instantaneous. She slid her arms around his neck and put her lips to his. She was more than willing. The mutual desire that had been damped down while they walked had risen again, even more strongly. They kissed passionately for so long that Dominic lost track of time, or of where he was. He could think only of the beautiful woman in his arms. He found himself wanting desperately to run his fingers through her hair, but he managed to restrain the impulse. She was wearing a wig. Her own hair would certainly be tied up tightly beneath it. He was just rational enough to remember that no lady would thank a man for exposing her like that. She would be intensely embarrassed. She might even flee from him.

He returned instead to exploring her delectable body. He had been surprised to discover how attractive he had found her outmoded costume. The tightly boned bodice emphasised her tiny waist, and the voluminous looped overdress swayed beautifully when she walked, or danced, emphasizing the feminine grace of her carriage. It had made her so very alluring.

It was quite otherwise when they were making love, however. Now he was ready to curse the gown. The bodice was so tight that it was impossible to free her breasts for his kisses. He had explored the swell of her slight breasts above the neckline of her gown but that was as far as his lips could reach. His frustration was growing by the second.

He ran a hand down the front of her gown to the waist, seeking for the free ends of the laces that bound the sides together. They were hidden, tucked under the boned point of her bodice, and tied in a fiendishly difficult knot. Taking his arms from around her, he applied both hands to the task of undoing it, even though he could barely see what he was trying to do. After several minutes of futile tussle, he was almost ready to explode. This was impossible!

There was a simpler solution, one that would solve the dilemma for both of them. He drew his dagger.

'No!' she gasped, grabbing his wrist. 'No, Dominic, you must not. Would you shame me?'

She was right. If he slit her laces, he would certainly gain access to the glories of her body, but she would be unable to make her gown presentable again afterwards. Anyone who saw her would know exactly what she had been doing.

He returned the dagger to its scabbard, with a growl of reluctant acceptance.

'Wait,' she said softly. She quickly stripped off her fine kid gloves and put her fingers to her bodice. In a trice the knot was undone.

'Alexandra,' he breathed, afraid to move.

She said nothing, simply drawing on her gloves once more. But then, lifting her face to his, she took a very deep breath. The two sections of her bodice parted a little as the laces eased under the pressure of her expanding ribcage. She was offering herself to him, waiting to see how he would react to her gift.

He wanted to rip the gown from her body and bury himself in her enticing warmth. But he must not do anything so crude. Such a gift had to be approached slowly, and relished. He bowed his head and feathered a kiss on to the hollow now exposed between her breasts. She shivered. She smelled of citrus, with a woody undertone he could not place. Her skin was so delicate and fine that he feared he might bruise her with his rough male caresses. He must go slowly. He must treat her with care, like a fragile work of art.

She breathed his name. She was waiting. Waiting.

A mischievous thought prompted him to take out his dagger once more. He heard her tiny gasp of surprise, but this time she did nothing else. She was still waiting. He tucked the point of his dagger into the lowest cross of the laces and gradually pulled it loose, smiling wickedly as he did so. The twisted silk rubbed slowly through the eyelet, the only sound in the taut silence. 'More, my lady?' Her answering intake of breath told him what he needed to know. He slid the dagger beneath the next lace and slowly pulled it free. And another. And then another. By the time her bodice had been fully loosened, her breathing had become very shallow indeed.

And his own control was slipping.

There was still the barrier of her corset, laced over her fine chemise. He swore softly. It was more than he could stand. This time, he truly would slit the laces with his dagger. He could not wait any longer to put his mouth to her breast.

There was no need. His questing fingers discovered that her corset was already loose. She must have untied it herself when she had undone the knot of her bodice. She truly did want him!

He was too impatient to unlace it fully. He pushed it aside so that he could cup her breast and put his lips to her skin. The touch of her was like a blessing. She tasted—he circled the skin around her nipple with the tip of his tongue—she tasted like perfumed wine. He groaned with the pleasure of it. He felt her hand on the back of his head, pushing him closer, urging him on. He took her nipple in his mouth, sucking so strongly that the hard round pebble lengthened under his caress. Satisfied, he moved to roll it between finger and thumb, while he transferred his attentions to the other breast, kissing and teasing until the second nipple swelled and rose into his mouth.

'Kiss me, Dominic. Please.' Her voice was a strained whisper.

He pushed the pieces of her bodice back together and raised his head to hers once more. Her lips were slightly open, and still swollen from his kisses. He could not resist her plea. She was absolutely delectable. So very, very desirable. He touched his lips to hers, and their passion sparked even higher, and hotter.

He lifted her on to his lap. That brought them satisfyingly closer, almost close enough, were it not for the barrier of her remaining clothing.

Lifting her had caused her gown to gather around her hips. The overdress had fallen back and the quilted underdress now reached only to her knees. The temptation of her silk-clad calves was impossible to resist. He touched his free hand to her neat ankle. The silk was deliciously smooth, as her skin must be, beneath it.

He waited. He was kissing her fiercely still, waiting to learn whether she would reject his bolder caresses.

She did not. She moaned a little under his mouth and used one arm to pull him closer, while the fingers of her free hand were again exploring the bare skin of his neck. It seemed impossible to deepen their passionate kiss, but they did. Dominic slowly brushed his fingers up the side of her leg until they found the garter, just above her knee. It was a slight, lacy affair, barely robust enough to support even her fine silk stocking. He explored it hesitantly. When his fingers reached the inside of her thigh, he allowed his little finger to stray upwards, on to her bare skin. It was so soft and delicate that it made the silk of her stocking seem coarse by comparison. She wriggled a little in his lap. Her passion was increasing. She was trying to make it easier for him to touch her. And the more she moved, the more urgent his desire became. She must be able to feel how aroused he was, even through the layers of petticoats.

She groaned out his name. Unsure, he stopped, but she raised her hips to urge him on. 'Touch me, Dominic. Please,' she moaned, her voice fathoms deeper than before.

He did as he was bid. But slowly, slowly. He stroked his way gently towards the core of her, then retreated. Once, twice, and again, until she was almost writhing with need in his arms. Then, at last, he touched her. Her whole body seemed to stiffen. Her tensions rose even more as his fingers teased and stroked. She was so hot, so ready for him. She wanted him to take her now.

He could not do it.

She was a true lady, not a wanton. She trusted him.

He could not do it.

He pulled her closer, so that her hand on his chest was trapped between them, so close that he was leaving her barely space to breathe. He could feel the tension mounting in her body with every stroke of his fingers. He would give her this, denying his own need for release.

Her breathing was even faster now. And faster. Her whole body tensed and then melted again, as she moaned against his mouth. He let his fingers lie still against her heated flesh, waiting until the spasms subsided, satisfied that her release was compensation for the lack of his own. With this woman, his own pleasure had ceased to be his prime concern. If she felt the joy of sated passion, it was enough.

With infinite tenderness, he stroked his fingers down her leg and replaced her skirts. Then he tightened the laces of her bodice. The moon came out again, as if to bathe his actions in a silver glow of approval. Alexandra lay still against his body. She had not moved to help him. Her expression was otherworldly, as if she were floating. Her eyes were wide and impossibly dark. Her skin, in spite of her face paint, was blooming. Dominic did not dare to speak. He gazed at her, and waited.

At first, she said nothing. She simply raised a gloved hand

to his cheek and held it there. 'I…I have never felt—' She stopped short. The skin above her breasts was turning a delicate shade of blush pink. Then she buried her face against his shirt.

Dominic put his arms around her, holding her protectively. He was not absolutely sure what she was feeling, but his own emotions were absolutely clear to him. What he felt was pride. He had given her fulfilment, without betraying her honour. It occurred to him that she might never have experienced such fulfilment before. She might even be a complete innocent. Was that possible?

He did not know. And he could never ask.

Chapter Twelve

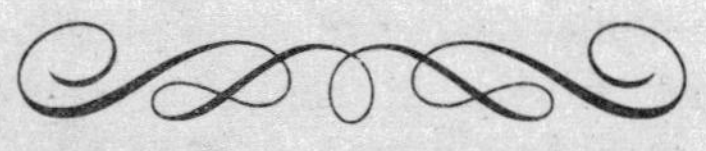

Why on earth had he been stupid enough to let her out of his sight for even a single second? He should have known the risks. Yet he had done it. And now she was gone. Alexandra. His Alexandra. Gone.

Dominic swore, long and fluently. It did not help.

He ripped off his mask, seized the bumper of brandy and downed it in a single swallow. It did not help.

'Drowning your sorrows, brother?'

Dominic frowned forbiddingly. He was in no mood to bandy words with Leo.

'Lady abandoned you, has she? An entertaining little piece, too. She—'

Dominic seized his brother by his ruff and twisted it mercilessly until Leo began to turn purple. 'Do not mention her. Do not dare. If you value your life, brother mine, you will mind your tongue where that lady is concerned.'

Leo had put his hands to his throat, trying to loosen Dominic's choke-hold. 'For God's sake, Dominic,' he croaked in a strangled voice.

Dominic let him go, like a cat dropping a dead rat. 'Heed my warning, Leo. I mean it.'

Leo was pulling at his ruff, trying to free his neck from its knotted folds. His face was still an alarming shade of crimson. He backed a step or two away and said, shaking his head, 'Never seen you act so over a woman—er—over a lady, Dominic. Not even your wife. I'd say you've got it badly.'

Dominic turned on his heel and stalked off. He did not trust himself to say another word. The last thing he needed now was to quarrel with Leo.

He made another desperate round of all the public rooms and then of the gardens. Alexandra was nowhere to be found. Unless she was hiding in the ladies' withdrawing room, she had gone. She had covered his face with passionate kisses, she had welcomed his touch on her body, she had allowed him to bring her to fulfilment and revelled in it. And then she had fled from him.

In desperation, he made his way to the entrance hall and questioned the servants. He must be sure that she had really left the ball.

It seemed that she had. One of the old retainers described the little lady in the *polonaise* gown and matching green slippers. She had left more than an hour before. Dominic stood motionless, feeling as if some evil genie were filling his boots with lead. It was finished. There was nothing he could do. He had found his perfect woman. The real one, this time. And she had melted away, just like the other. He was cursed.

A hand clapped him on the shoulder. 'What? All alone, Dom?'

Dominic turned. It was Jack, in his Mr Punch costume.

'Leo said you had found yourself a delectable little lady, just the thing for an evening's entertainment at a masquerade. What have you done with her? Or has she found a better bargain?'

Dominic scowled. 'She has gone,' he grunted.

Jack made a noise somewhere between a whistle and a squeak. 'Run off, has she? Well, well, well. And from the great

Duke of Calder, too. Or perhaps she did not know who you were?'

'I will thank you to let the subject drop, Jack.'

'Oh, very well. Just wondering, however. She didn't abandon a slipper on the staircase as she ran, by any chance?'

'What?'

'Oh, dear me, Dominic. Where is your education? Cinderella.'

'Go and squeak somewhere else, Jack,' he snarled.

It was impossible to see Jack's reaction under his Mr Punch mask, but he made an extravagant leg and ambled off in the direction of the supper room. Dominic was alone in the entrance hall, surrounded only by servants. He was sorely tempted to draw his sabre and cut the nearest inanimate object to pieces.

His Alexandra—his Cinderella—had vanished. But this Cinderella had left not a single clue as to who she was or where she might be found.

At last, she was safe.

Alex bolted the door of her bedchamber and leaned against it, waiting for her panicky breathing to slow. None of the revellers had seen her leave. Dominic would have no idea where to look for her. She had abandoned him without a word of farewell. But what choice had she had? In order to become Alexandrov once more, Alex had had to run from the man she loved.

She let her fan drop to the floor. Her wig followed it. The moment it was gone, she discovered that her head was itching abominably. She almost wanted to rip her hair out. Instead, she peeled off her gloves and began to run her fingers through her cropped hair, massaging her scalp for relief.

Catching sight of herself in the glass, she could not help but laugh, though it was a sound devoid of mirth. Without the long wig, she looked exactly what she was, a would-be man in paint and powder, hiding behind her old-fashioned woman's garb. She started to fumble with the laces of her gown, but her sure touch had deserted her. She could not begin to undo them. She struggled for a little but then, almost weeping with frustration, she seized her own dagger and slit the bodice open from top to bottom.

He wanted to do that. He longed to do that. And, out of concern for your honour, he stayed his hand.

She swore, and tore off the overgown, ripping a sleeve in the process. She had to be rid of this thing. She pulled apart the ties of the quilted satin petticoat and let it drop. The other petticoats followed it to the floor. At last, she stood in front of the glass in her chemise and a badly laced corset.

She reached for her dagger, but something in her own reflection made her hesitate. For one night, she had been a woman; she had been with the man she loved. She had not imagined it could hurt so much to end it. Retrieving the wig from the floor, she replaced it, settling the long curls over her shoulder as they had been when he first saw her. Then she picked up the dagger and applied the point to her laces, loop by loop, pulling them loose from waist to bosom, just as he had done, listening for the rasp of the cord through the eyelets, just as he had done. It did not take long before the corset sagged and fell away from her body. It had not been like that before. With him. It was not the same. Impatiently, she slit the rest of the laces and cast the corset aside. The fine chemise followed.

Alex gazed at her reflection, at the naked body of a woman bereft, a woman dressed only in silk stockings, green buckled shoes, and a grey powdered wig.

She looked different. She had never needed to use any artifice to conceal her breasts, but now they seemed to have swollen to twice their normal size. The nipples stood rosy and proud, as if to proclaim the loving attention that had been lavished on them. And there were tiny red marks there, too, where his sharp teeth had nipped her skin. If only they would remain for ever, as proof of the passion between them. They would fade, in time, as his memories of her would fade. But she—? No, Alex would not allow her memory to fade. She would nurse it, and nourish it, until it filled her consciousness, so that she could cherish it for ever.

It was all she would ever have.

'Good morning, Duke.' Major Zass looked flustered. No doubt the stresses of moving his royal master's household were playing on his nerves.

'Good morning, Major.' Dominic sounded much calmer than he felt. He had had barely two hours' sleep and had spent most of that time tossing and turning in his bed, dreaming about what had been, and what might have been, if he had not acted so foolishly by letting her go. 'Is the Emperor still abed?'

The Emperor had still been dancing at five in the morning, much of the time with Lady Jersey, with whom he seemed to be well-nigh besotted. Dominic had seen them standing together in a shadowy alcove in the small hours of the morning, talking in soft intimate voices. Before he left her, the Emperor had bent to plant a passionate kiss on the inside of her bare arm, above the elbow. It had been one more thing for Dominic to report to the Foreign Secretary.

'His Majesty paused only to change his dress, Duke. He is at present out riding. We shall be setting off for the Earl of Liverpool's seat at Coombe Wood as soon as we may. It waits only for certain Russian nobles to take their farewells of his Majesty. Do you accompany us, Duke?'

'Of course. My role as liaison officer continues until his Imperial Majesty leaves our shores.'

'Excellent. The visit has gone exceedingly smoothly in my view, and much of that is due to your assistance. I'm sure that his Imperial Majesty will wish to thank you personally, but I should like to do so, too, on behalf of his Majesty's suite.'

Dominic bowed.

'Did you enjoy the masquerade last night?' Zass had adopted a lighter tone now that the formal exchanges were over.

'Indeed I did.' Dominic lied. But it was not really a lie. He had enjoyed it immensely, until the moment he lost her.

'Most of my young officers are suffering this morning, though I fancy the main cause is not lack of sleep.' Zass nodded meaningfully in the direction of the decanters on the sideboard. 'Alexandrov is the exception. He has gone riding with the Tsar this morning, but I expect them to return presently. May we offer you some refreshment, Duke?'

Dominic shook his head, rather more vehemently than was wise. 'No refreshment, thank you.' His head was still suffering the after-effects of too much consolatory brandy. He was in a foul mood. But it was not Zass's fault, or the Emperor's, or Alexandrov's. He should not take his bad temper out on them.

With a quiet word of apology, Major Zass bustled away. Alone in the reception room, Dominic picked up a newspaper from the octagonal lacquered table and sat down to read. But he could not concentrate. And he had no desire to read sensational reports about the behaviour of the Regent and his illustrious guests. He had seen quite enough of that for himself.

His mind was drifting off into might-have-beens, all over again. The touch of her skin, the taste of her… Just thinking about her made his body ache with longing. He needed to—

The door opened. Emperor Alexander strode in, followed by Alexandrov and two other young officers. Dominic sprang to his feet, and bowed. The Emperor greeted him with a few words in English, before reverting to his normal French. He looked remarkably spry for a man who had had no sleep. The younger officers, however, were looking much the worse for wear. Even Alexandrov, Dominic noticed with some surprise. Perhaps he had not had a quiet evening after all?

Once the Emperor had left the room, Alexandrov sat down

quietly in one corner. The other two young men began to discuss the masquerade ball, and the various wagers they had laid at the tables. Ignoring their inane chatter, Dominic took his seat alongside Alexandrov. 'Your comrades seem to think that you missed a splendid event, Alexei Ivanovich.'

'Yes. I have heard nothing else from them all morning.' The young man sounded almost as bad-tempered as Dominic himself. For some reason, that made Dominic feel a fraction better. The rapport was still there. At least he had not lost that, along with so much else.

'Well, I have no desire to recite tales of the masquerade to you, or to tell you about every finely turned ankle.' He forced a smile. 'You are safe with me.'

Alexandrov did not respond. The silence was so unexpected that Dominic turned in his seat to look at the young Russian. He seemed to be thunderstruck. But why?

Dominic knew he could not ask. 'Tell me instead, Alexandrov, how you passed the hours last evening. I imagine you had a deal more sleep than the rest of us.'

'I— Well, yes. Though I had to oversee the arrangements for our departure today. Are you to accompany us?'

'Yes. The Prime Minister has kindly offered me his hospitality.'

'Then we may ride together, perhaps?'

Dominic nodded. Under normal circumstances, he would have sought to avoid company altogether when he was feeling as sulky as a bear. But it seemed that Alexandrov was not in the mood for inconsequential chatter either. They would be able to ride together, in companionable silence. It might even be enjoyable. He certainly needed something—or someone—to divert his mind from the cruel memories that were haunting him.

So she was not leaving him behind in London. She was to have him by her for five more days. A blessing. A torment.

Mechanically, Alex fastened the gold frogging of her tight blue dolman jacket and settled her fur-trimmed pelisse across her left shoulder. She stared at herself in the glass for a long time before buckling on her sabre. She was a Hussar officer, blooded in battle. And she looked it. She did not look in the least like a woman, especially not one who could attract the attentions of a duke.

But he had called her beautiful.

She gazed at her reflection, this time trying to see herself with a lover's eye. She had a neat enough figure, though her breasts were small and completely invisible under the uniform jacket. She had a fine ankle, too, when it was not hidden by military boots. But her face was not beautiful. Of that she was quite sure. Her features were regular enough, and her blue eyes were quite large, but that was all. He had called her beautiful, because he desired her. That must be the reason. He would probably say the same to any woman rash enough to follow him into a secluded arbour.

She ran her hands through her reddish-brown hair. It had been trimmed just before she left Russia and it still felt too short, even for a cavalry officer. What a shock Dominic would have had if he had removed her wig! Would he have recognised who she was? Possibly. She had been so very close to discovery, throughout that magical tête-à-tête. And she did not regret one moment of it.

Alex took one last look around her chamber, tucked her shako under her right arm, and marched out and down the stairs to join the Tsar's escort. She was trying very hard not to think about the fact that Dominic—Calder—would be there, at her side. Every word from him, and certainly every touch, was going to bring back memories that would be difficult to control. That was bad enough, but she must now stop thinking of him by his given name. Last night, he had become Dominic to her. There was no going back from that warming intimacy. But if she made a mistake over his name, he was bound to suspect her. Earlier, she had been so concerned that it might slip out, that she had forced herself to call him nothing at all. Had he thought her ill bred for that?

It could not be helped. Better to be thought lacking in manners than to be suspected as the woman with whom he had dallied.

Major Zass was in the hallway. 'You're late, Alexandrov,' he growled.

Alex snapped to attention, but said nothing. Zass was a fair man, but he had been most displeased to learn that her evening at the masquerade had produced not a scrap of information.

'You and the Duke are to ride behind his Majesty's carriage. The Duke is already waiting, so make haste. His Majesty will be down at any minute.'

Alex donned her shako, saluted smartly, and hurried out. Dominic was already mounted on his raking black stallion. She was pleased to see that her horse was the one she had ridden on several occasions now. Then she remembered, with a slight shudder, that she had got into the habit of whispering to it, in English. Well, today, the animal would have to learn that his rider was mute, in English at least. She repeated the instruction to herself twice. It was absolutely vital that she remained in control of her tongue during this journey. It would be so very tempting to start conversing with Dominic, in their old easy way, and to make the kind of mistake that could ruin her life. Silence, even apparently ill-bred silence, was the better option. If he questioned her, she could say that she was suffering the after-effects of overindulgence the previous evening.

It would have the added merit of being true!

Chapter Thirteen

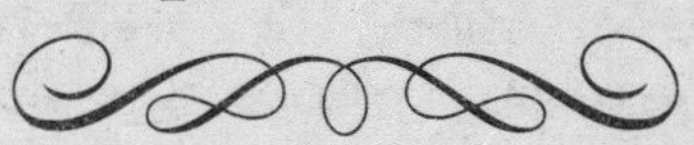

Alex was gazing out of the window of Commissioner Grey's residence, in Portsmouth dockyard. How was she going to continue to avoid Dominic? She had succeeded in doing so for three days, even at Lord Liverpool's seat, because Dominic had been in no mood for company. At times, he had even appeared to be brooding.

A tiny voice had whispered to her, more than once, that he might perhaps be thinking about her, about Alexandra. Was he mourning the loss of his Scottish lady? That notion had helped to comfort her, a little, for her own loss. It had not encouraged her to seek out his company, however. That was too dangerous. Yet she longed to know what he really thought about her.

Some of the other officers had been roasting him about being blue-devilled. She had overheard them, quite without meaning to do so. He had laughed it off, blaming his mood on too much brandy, or too many sleepless nights. Maybe that was true.

'I must congratulate you, Alexandrov.'

She started violently. Yet again she had not heard his approach. She swallowed hard, forced her shaky hands to her sides, and turned round to face him. 'Me, Duke?' Her voice came out as something of a croak.

'Major Zass tells me that you spent the whole of yesterday on board the *Impregnable* without being in the least unwell. You are obviously becoming used to the motion.'

Alex grimaced. 'You may have noticed that the sea was amazingly calm yesterday. And the *Impregnable* was at anchor throughout.'

He grinned. His good humour was returning at last. In her company.

'Forgive me. I should not tease you on such a tender subject.'

'Indeed you should not,' she replied, with renewed spirit, determined to keep him in this mood, if she possibly could. It was one more memory to cherish. 'You must be aware that we shall spend almost the whole day aboard her again, and that today she will *not* be at anchor.'

'You could perhaps try the rum. The sailors reckon it's more effective than any other remedy. Even my ginger tisane.'

She grunted and frowned up at him. From the twinkle in his eyes, she could see that he was teasing her again, even though he had just said he would not. He seemed more like his old self. It warmed her heart to think that he viewed her as a friend, and an equal. But, at the same time, it hurt that he would never have a chance, now, to see her as anything but a friend. She desired so much more.

'However, just in case the rum should be…er…not to your liking, I have arranged with Captain Wood that there will be a supply of my tisane for you, as well.' He pulled his watch out of his pocket and checked the time. 'And now, Alexei Ivanovich, we had best be off. His Imperial Majesty will be arriving back from his visit to the shipyards very soon, I imagine.'

Chatting almost as easily as they had in the early days of their acquaintance, they made their way down to the King's Stairs and on to the waiting barge. This time, there was a strong wind blowing and the sea was not calm at all, but Alex managed to reach the huge warship without disgracing herself. From its deck, they could see the fleet stretching for miles against the background of the Isle of Wight. As soon as the Emperor came on board, a royal salute echoed across the water. Then, with the Regent's yacht, *Royal Sovereign,* leading the way, the fleet of ships slipped their cables and made for the open sea.

The Emperor, who seemed to have remarkably good sea legs, soon disappeared below to continue his exploration of the ship, begun on the previous day. His curiosity about military matters appeared to be insatiable.

'Stay on deck, Alexei Ivanovich,' Major Zass said, as he made to follow the Tsar. 'One of the others can take over your duties for the moment.'

'Thank you, sir,' Alex said, with real gratitude.

'Will you join us, Duke?' the Major continued. 'His Majesty may have need of your language skills. It is not always easy to understand the accents of the common sailors.'

She watched them go with relief. So far, she was managing well enough. Staying on deck, with the fresh breeze in her face, certainly seemed to help. She leaned on the smooth wooden rail and gazed out across the grey sea, focusing on the distant ships rather than on the heaving swell, and thinking about her strange predicament. It seemed that Dominic was determined to be as friendly as ever to Captain Alexandrov. With less than two more days in his company, she could not bring herself to do anything that would undermine their friendship. She might try to avoid him, if she could do so without raising eyebrows, but that was all. She wanted him to think well of Captain Alexandrov after her departure.

She would certainly think well of the Duke of Calder.

The thought of him was too tempting to resist. No one was going to speak to her here for at least half an hour. She had time to indulge her memories, for just a little while. She closed her eyes, letting her mind drift. The warm darkness of the masquerade garden surrounded her again, filled with the smells of freshly turned soil and burning oil lamps. She was on his lap, in his arms. His mouth was at her breast, kissing and sucking so strongly that her belly was contracting in the same passionate rhythm. Her whole body was yearning for him.

It still did. That strange heavy burning had started again, here on the deck of a British warship. Her legs were beginning to tremble. She must not let this self-indulgence continue. Someone would see!

She opened her eyes quickly. Too quickly. At the sight of the heaving sea, her head began to spin and her stomach turned to water. She clutched the rail in desperation, praying that she would not be ill again. Not here in front of everyone.

'Are you feeling unwell, Captain?' It was Captain Wood.

She could not speak. She swallowed desperately, trying to keep her throat closed, and managed a slight nod.

'I will send for something to help you.' The Captain summoned a midshipman and ordered him to procure some of 'the Duke of Calder's special remedy' for their guest. 'Walk up and down with me, Alexandrov,' Captain Wood said kindly. 'Keep your eyes on the horizon, if you can, rather than the sea.'

Anything was better than standing there by the rail, torn between erotic memories of the Duke of Calder and the embarrassing demands of her rebellious insides. Alex took her place beside the Captain, matching her stride to his and staring unblinkingly at the distant horizon, as he had advised.

Surprisingly, it did seem to help. Alex even managed, eventually, to say a few complimentary words about the ship. Captain Wood was clearly pleased by that, and began to talk at length about the *Impregnable*'s many fine qualities. Alex nodded, whenever she thought it was appropriate, and the pair continued to pace.

'Ah, here is your tisane, Alexandrov,' Captain Wood said,

gesturing towards the companionway. A sailor appeared from below, bringing her a tin mug.

Behind him was the unmistakable figure of the Duke of Calder!

Alex turned away and forced herself to focus on the tisane. She gripped the hot mug in both hands and sipped gratefully, welcoming the feel of the steam on her face and the ginger scent in her nostrils.

'How do you feel now, Alexandrov?' Dominic's voice was just by Alex's ear. He was standing behind her.

She concentrated on sipping her hot tisane. 'Mmm. Improving by the minute, I think. Thank you for your concern. But are you not needed below? What is his Majesty doing?'

'Your Emperor is viewing the gun deck. I think there is about to be a rather noisy demonstration of the *Impregnable*'s fire power. There is no need for me to be there. I could not make myself heard, in any case.'

Alex managed a rather wan smile, even though she wished him away. But there was no opportunity to say anything more, for at that moment the roar of the cannon began. It was like being back on the battlefield, except that she did not have solid ground beneath her feet. Here, when the broadside fired, the whole ship seemed to move sideways in recoil.

'Impressive, is it not?' Dominic asked, as soon as there was a lull in the firing. There was a definite hint of pride in his voice.

Alex was feeling almost normal now. The effect of the tisane, coupled with pacing the deck, was miraculous. She nodded in response and began to pace once more, for the firing had begun again, making conversation impossible. She was glad of it, since it gave her a chance to reflect on the new ideas that were starting to whirl around her mind. There was something about being here, in the alien surroundings of this huge warship, so far from home. She understood now, more clearly than before, why the Royal

Navy was master of the seas. It was no wonder that the Emperor was trying to stop the match between the Regent's daughter and the Prince of Orange. England was already strong enough at sea, without adding the power of the Dutch fleet to its Navy. It had to be curbed, for the sake of the Russian Empire. Except—

Except that half of Alex belonged to this powerful little country, as Meg, her Scottish nurse, had reminded her, over and over. Should she not have a care for it, too, as well as for Mother Russia? Until now, Alex had never given a moment's thought to such an idea. It would have seemed like a betrayal. She had devoted her life to the Tsar and to Russia; she was more than prepared to die in their service. But now that she was here, in England, and in love with an English Duke, it all seemed to be so much more complicated. Could she ever love the Regent as she loved the Tsar? No, impossible. The Regent inspired more mirth than love. Men such as Dominic were well aware of his many faults. They even made jokes at the Regent's expense. No one would ever make jokes about the Tsar.

Of course not. Making jokes about the Tsar could lead a man to prison, or the gallows. Alex could almost hear old Meg's voice saying so. She had always counselled Alex against such blind, uncritical love. In Meg's view, the ability to laugh at their rulers made the British stronger than their enemies. Alex had never believed it, but now she was beginning to think that it might be true.

'Do the people hate the Regent?' She had blurted out the words before she realised. How could she had said something so incredibly boorish, particularly to Dominic? 'Oh, forgive me. I did not mean—'

He waved aside her apology. 'They love the King. And the Queen.' He looked suddenly very serious. 'It is not that they hate the monarchy, you must understand, Alexei Ivanovich. But they hate some of the things that the Regent does, especially his treatment of his wife.' He stopped pacing and looked at Alex. 'May I ask what prompted your question?' he asked silkily.

'I…I am not sure. I think I may have been contrasting the power of the Royal Navy, as demonstrated today, with the caricatures I have seen in the print shops. And the way the Regent was hissed by the crowd. In most countries, such behaviour would not be tolerated.'

He smiled rather knowingly, Alex thought. 'It is like trying to control a fiercely boiling cauldron. If you push the lid a little to one side, some of the steam may escape without doing any harm, and the contents do not boil over. If, on the other hand, you are determined that all of the steam must be controlled within the cauldron, then you fasten the lid tightly to keep it in. That will succeed, but not for ever. Eventually, the lid will be blown off and the contents will explode all over the fire. That was the French way, and look how it ended for them. We British prefer a little bit of escaping steam to a full-blown revolution.'

Alex could not deny that he was right about France. He might even be right about England. But Russia was different. There would be no explosion in Russia.

'You are silent, Alexei Ivanovich. You do not approve?'

'It is not for me, a foreigner, to pass an opinion, Duke. I say only that I do not think the English way could be successfully adopted in any other country of my acquaintance.'

He nodded. They both began to pace again, in thoughtful silence.

The ship recoiled under another huge broadside. Alex clutched at the rail in a vain attempt to stop herself from falling. She was losing her balance and was about to end up as an undignified heap on the deck. At the same moment, Dominic seized her by the arm and took her weight. His unexpected touch was like being struck by a bolt of lightning. She completely forgot where she was. Her whole body shuddered, from head to toe, and she cried out.

Dominic ignored it. He simply grabbed her by her upper arms and set her solidly on her feet. Once he was sure she had regained her balance, he let her go, as if the whole episode had been the most normal thing in the world.

She could not speak. Had she betrayed her feelings for him? She looked anxiously up into his face, wondering whether she would see signs of distaste or even scorn there. Nothing. His face was a blank.

'You have become a little too sure of yourself, Alexandrov,' he said.

She felt herself blushing bright red.

'You thought you had found your sea legs, and the *Impregnable* decided otherwise,' he added.

Alex gulped. Her body was still tingling all over. She felt sure he must be able to see it. Did she look as hot as she felt? She reached for the support of the rail and tried to straighten her back. She was a Hussar officer, not a weak-willed woman! With an effort, she forced her limbs back under control. 'Thank you, Calder,' she managed at last, in a remarkably normal voice.

'I think we are safe from now on. The firing has finished. I understand there is to be an entertainment below. And a splendid cold collation.'

Alex's stomach heaved at the very thought of food.

'But I'm sure you will be excused from that.' He put a friendly hand on Alex's shoulder.

This time, her reaction was even stronger than before. She groaned in distress, the sound torn from her tormented body. It had begun to shake as if she were in a fever. She fought desperately for control. It took a long time, but eventually the shivering stopped. Dominic had long since removed his hand. He was standing by her side, waiting for her to come to herself again.

She did not dare look up at his face. Instead, she hugged her belly with both hands and muttered grimly, 'Forgive me,

Calder. The mention of food is like to undo all the good from your tisane. Pray excuse me.' She moved along the deck, as far away as she could, and stood there alone, gripping the rail with one hand and clutching her middle with the other. She stared out at the horizon, praying for rescue. Her only hope was that he might come to believe her peculiar actions were caused by seasickness.

Strange. Most strange. Dominic stood for a long time, watching Alexandrov intently. No doubt he was a fine young man, but there was something extremely odd about his behaviour. He claimed to be suffering from *mal de mer*, and he had certainly done so on the voyage to Dover, but he had seemed much improved, these last two days. He had even coped with the swell today when the fleet sailed out from Portsmouth. Yet he had lost his balance so easily. And the slightest allusion to food had produced an extreme reaction.

No. That was not quite the way of it. Alexandrov had certainly turned a little green at the mention of food, but his strange shivering had not begun until the moment Dominic placed a hand on his shoulder. Dear God, was that the cause of the lad's malady?

A dull shiver ran down Dominic's spine. He began to pace the deck, keeping well away from where Alexandrov stood, by the far rail. There had been such affinity between them. He had treated the Russian like a friend, almost like a younger brother. Had that been unwise? Alexandrov certainly avoided the company of ladies. Was there more to be read into that than mere shyness? Dominic fervently hoped not. He would be infinitely sorry for the lad if it were so.

However, what mattered now was action. It would be painful. But he was becoming used to pain. For the next two days, until the Tsar left England, Dominic would need to be rather more circumspect. He must continue to be perfectly friendly and polite—that went without saying—but he would not seek Alexandrov's company if it could possibly be avoided. And there must be no more touching. Of any kind.

Dominic glanced round swiftly. Alexandrov's stance, by the rail, was telling. His posture betrayed more mortification than sickness. How was it that Dominic had not noticed the signs before? Stupid! From now on, for the lad's sake, Dominic must be very, very careful.

Captain Wood came to join him. He nodded in the direction of Alexandrov. 'Poor lad. But I'm afraid we have no time to look to his ailments. The Regent and the King of Prussia will be with us shortly.' He pointed to where the *Royal Sovereign* was rapidly approaching the *Impregnable*. 'By the bye, Calder, I'm not like to be kissed when the Emperor disembarks, am I?'

'What makes you ask that?'

'One of Clarence's men said that the Emperor had embraced all sorts of men before he left London.'

'True, Captain, but they were all Russians. I understand it is their custom. As an Englishman, you can be confident that you will be spared.'

'Thank God for that! I would never live it down, otherwise.'

Dominic laughed, glad of the change of mood. Side by side, the two of them made their way across the deck to await the arrival of the Regent and his guests.

Alex had seen enough. She had caught that scornful look on Dominic's face. He knew. She was sure he knew that her reaction was not just another attack of *mal de mer.* And if he knew that, he thought that Captain Alexandrov had developed a very unhealthy regard for the Duke of Calder.

She groaned aloud. She had wanted him to think well of her, and now he believed *that*. She would never be able to look him in the eye again.

There was absolutely no way of remedying the situation. Either he believed she was an unnatural man; or she told him the truth, that she was an unnatural woman. The first was a repulsive idea; the second was ruinous. There was nothing at all that she could do, except to bear the consequences as best she might. In two more days, she would be gone from England. She would not have to suffer the shame after that. She would not have to see the loathing on his face when he looked on her.

She would be able to remember the joys of their one night, as man and woman together, and to bury every other hideous memory far beyond recall.

Chapter Fourteen

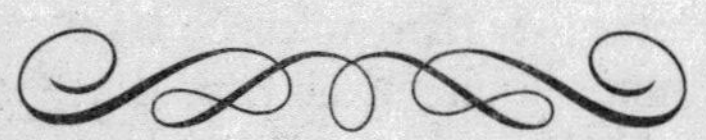

The sea in Dover harbour had been remarkably calm. Perhaps tomorrow's crossing to Calais would not be so rough, after all?

Alex closed her bedroom window and turned away. Tomorrow, she would finally say farewell to Dominic Aikenhead. And she still had not decided what she was going to do. He would probably expect her to salute, perhaps to shake hands, and then simply to march up the gangplank and leave. Could she really do that? Would her body obey her if she tried? She did not know.

These last two days had been torture. Dominic had certainly been avoiding her. On the royal party's return to Portsmouth, the welcome had been tumultuous. And then, to cap it all, the Duke of Wellington had arrived. Amid all the cheering and celebrating, the increasing coldness between the Duke of Calder and Captain Alexandrov had gone unnoticed.

Yesterday and today, they had spent many hours travelling. The aides-de-camp had been rushing to and fro all day long, each with a dozen different duties to perform. But now they were here in Dover. It had all changed. Everything was tense, holding its breath, waiting.

It was well after midnight. The thunder of the welcoming

cannon had long since ceased, and the townsfolk had gone home to bed. If only Alex could do the same.

Automatically, she finished fastening the ties of her bedgown. But sleep was impossible. She knew that. If she dared to close her eyes, she would see that look on his face—disgust, and scorn.

Now he was just a few yards away from her. She pictured him sleeping, his dark head against the white pillows, his powerful body relaxed. How would it be if she, Alexandra, crept in beside him, slipping in between the sheets and sliding into his embrace? He would welcome her. She was sure he would. And together, they would—

Berating herself for a besotted fool, she told herself to go to bed. But her body ignored its instructions. Instead, her hand quietly opened her chamber door. The corridor was empty, and silent. Her solitary candle gave just enough light to make out Dominic's door, diagonally opposite her own. He was there, behind that door! So close, so alive!

She stepped out into the corridor, her bare feet making no sound on the floor boards, and set her ear to his door. Silence. No, something. The low sound of slow, measured breathing. He must be asleep.

Without further thought, she tried the handle, expecting the door to be locked. But it was not. The door opened silently under her hand. It was a sign! She slipped inside and pushed the door behind her, leaning her back against it to survey the room. Dominic's bedchamber.

He lay there, almost exactly as she had imagined him. He was asleep. But now no longer relaxed. While she watched, he threw off most of the bedclothes and began to thrash about, almost as if he had a fever. She moved a few steps closer, lifting her candle. There was a sheen of sweat on his bare torso. His face had become contorted and his neck muscles stood out like knotted ropes. He was suffering. He moaned, deep in his chest. It echoed the anguish in Alex's own heart.

One more step, just one, and she was beside his writhing body. She did not want to remember him like this. He must be strong, and at peace.

Alex offered him the only remedy she had. She laid a gentle hand on his forehead, smoothing away his ferocious frown. 'Rest easy, Dominic,' she said softly. 'Sleep now.'

He stilled almost at once, and Alex allowed herself a few seconds to gaze down at his sleeping form, relaxed once more. This was how she would remember him. Strong, but vulnerable. To her.

After tomorrow, they would never see each other again, but he was hers. She knew that. Just as she belonged to him.

A sudden draught sent her candle flickering. Harsh reality intruded like a chill winter blast. She dare not wake him. It would spell ruin. And she must not be discovered here. If her candle were to go out…

She permitted herself one long loving look and then crept quickly back the way she had come. In the open doorway, she paused for one last second, her candle held aloft, her gaze fixed on the figure in the bed. 'Farewell, Dominic,' she whispered. And then she closed the door on the man she loved.

'No! Not farewell! Stay!'

Dominic found he was sitting up in bed. Most of the bedclothes seemed to be on the floor. And there was a faint whiff of candle wax in the air.

He couldn't have lit a candle, could he? And then extinguished it again, all without waking up? And those words echoing in his mind. Were they real? Had he cried out for her to stay?

He must have been imagining things. Or dreaming. The sooner he was back at Aikenhead Park and properly rested, the better it would be. Then these strange haunting memories might cease to plague him.

Dear God! It had been the little *bourgeoise* this time, still in her white bedgown and cropped hair. She had touched his face with soft, gentle fingers. Soothing fingers. And she had spoken, too. Words of farewell.

What on earth did it mean? Was he going mad?

He groped for his tinder box and lit a candle. The bed looked as though teams of wrestlers had been fighting for possession of the sheets. Had he done all that by himself? Possibly. Of late, his sleep had often been disturbed. Too often, he seemed to be trying to chase Alexandra, fighting his way to her through strange obstacles. And watching her vanish.

But why, this time, had it been the little *bourgeoise*? It was the Scottish lady Dominic wanted now, not the Frenchwoman, brave though she was. He had not thought about her even once since the masquerade, he was certain. And yet, now he was dreaming of her. And talking to her in his sleep. It was unfathomable.

He dragged the bedclothes back into some kind of order, snuffed the candle, and settled down once more. This time, he intended to sleep peacefully. He would not dream, not of Alexandra, nor of the little *bourgeoise*, nor even of poor benighted Alexandrov and his misplaced affections. He would simply sleep.

He closed his eyes and let his thoughts drift where they would. When he was just on the edge of sleep, a question began to form—something about candle wax—but it was too late to catch it. It was swallowed in the fog of sleep.

Calmer now, Alex took her candle to the little table by the window where paper and fresh ink had been provided. She dipped the quill in the standish and wrote the first thing that came into her head. *Dominic Aikenhead, Duke of Calder.* The words, stark and black, screamed at her from the paper. And provided a kind of answer, at last.

She should write to him. That was the solution. She would write to him, and tell him the truth. Then he would know—What would he know? That he had dallied at the masquerade with a half-Russian woman who had wilfully deceived him about her ability to speak English and who was deceiving the whole of the Russian army about her sex?

She dropped her head into her hands. Impossible! Such a confession would be so devastating that the paper might burst into flames of its own accord. Better to leave things as they were. For a second or two, she felt the beginnings of despair.

Alex jumped up and began to pace the floor. Two days ago she had thought she could bear his disdain. But the truth was that she could not. She loved him. She was going to leave him for ever, and she needed, desperately, to have him think well of her.

She would write. She would find a way of telling him some of what she needed him to know. The letter would be delivered after she had gone, so she would not see his reaction to it. But she was sure, in her heart, that Dominic would understand what she was trying to say, no matter how obliquely she had to phrase it. They had been at one, in London, when they clung to each other, with desire racking their bodies. And their minds had been as one.

He would understand. He would.

Dominic had awoken surprisingly refreshed. His first good night's sleep in weeks. Though he had vaguely recollected some kind of odd dream, something to do with candle wax. He couldn't remember any more. But it didn't matter in any case. It was only a dream.

He glanced out of the window. It was still raining; the Emperor and his suite were all stuck here in the hotel. Everyone was impatient to leave, but no one could, until the evening tide.

He looked at his watch again. It was time he returned to his duty station. For the last time. No doubt the Emperor would be profuse in his thanks for the work of the British liaison officer. Dominic chuckled to himself. He would certainly get greater thanks from the Emperor than from Castlereagh. By now, the Foreign Secretary would have been on the receiving end of the Regent's anger over his daughter's broken betrothal and her flirtations with the German princes presented to her by the Emperor's meddlesome sister.

He made his way down to the main reception room. The Emperor himself was not there. Nor was his sister. As a result, the young officers were relaxing, gossiping as usual, and wagering on anything and everything.

Major Zass appeared from the door to the withdrawing room. 'Ah, Duke. I am delighted that you are here. His Imperial Majesty wishes to bid you farewell, and to thank you. Will you come this way?'

Dominic bowed and followed the Major into the side-room. The Emperor was seated on a large imposing chair by the fireplace, his sister at his side. At Dominic's entrance, they both rose. That was a singular mark of distinction, Dominic knew. He paused in the doorway to bow, first to the Emperor, and then to the Grand Duchess.

The Emperor beckoned him forward. 'I must tell you, Duke, that it has been my privilege to visit England, the land which has saved us all. And such a reception! The people of your country are so warm, so welcoming. I must also thank you for your own good offices. Your help with my inadequate English has been invaluable. You will allow me to salute you, in the Russian way?'

Before Dominic could utter a word, the Emperor stepped forward and embraced him, kissing him on both cheeks. Dominic was so taken aback that he did not move a muscle.

'I will pray for blessings to rain upon England. And also upon you, Duke.'

Dominic bowed. There was nothing else he could do. 'Thank you, your Majesty,' he murmured. He started to back away.

'I, too, should like to thank you, Duke.' The Grand Duchess took a pace forward. Was she going to embrace him also? Surely ladies did not embrace gentlemen in that way? She was smiling magnanimously. Dominic fancied he spied a twinkle in her eye. Had she read his mind?

Perhaps she had, for she extended her ungloved hand. Dominic breathed a sigh of relief and kissed it dutifully. But then, just as he made to straighten and step back, she dropped a kiss on his forehead. It was such a shock that he could not suppress a gasp.

She looked down at him in a very superior fashion and said, quietly, 'It is our way, Duke.' She said it with an absolutely straight face, but Dominic was sure that she was laughing at him.

He released the Grand Duchess's hand and straightened. Both the Emperor and his sister were now waiting for him to withdraw. Since he had no choice in the matter, he bowed low to the Emperor and followed Major Zass out of the room.

All he could think of, as the door closed behind him, was Captain Wood's comment when they had been talking together on the deck of the *Impregnable*. Dominic had been so sure that no Russian would ever force an embrace on an Englishman. Fool! Wood had had the right of it, too. If this extraordinary episode ever became known, Dominic would never live it down.

When Dominic emerged from his audience with the Tsar, his face was like thunder. Alex could not begin to imagine what might have happened. Had he received some insult? It seemed very unlikely, for the Emperor's manners were impeccable. Besides, Major Zass was looking totally unconcerned. Whatever had happened, it related to Dominic alone. And he was having great difficulty in keeping his temper.

Major Zass looked around the room, commanding instant attention without saying a word. All the young men were on their feet in a trice. 'Gentlemen, his Imperial Majesty and her Imperial Highness have been graciously pleased to take a formal farewell of the Duke of Calder. We all know how much we owe him for the success of this visit. It behoves us to offer the Duke the same courtesy.'

Alex saw the momentary flash of recognition in Dominic's face. His eyes widened and his mouth opened to protest, just as Major Zass seized him by the shoulders and kissed him, twice. Oh, so that was what had happened. The stiff-necked Englishman, always proud of his ability to betray no emotion in public, had been made to feel a fool by a simple Russian custom. Alex bit her lip. She loved him, but she very much wanted to laugh aloud. Dominic had been looking down his long nose at her for two solid days. And the Emperor had given him his own again. It was priceless. A moment she would treasure.

She had to admire his sangfroid, however. When Zass embraced him, Dominic stood stock-still, not raising his arms or moving his head even a fraction. The embrace was all on Zass's side. By the time the Major stepped back, Dominic's face had become a blank mask, though Alex fancied she could see a faint tinge of red on his cheekbones. As the farewells continued with Zass's senior colleagues, she was sure of it. Dominic was becoming more and more embarrassed with each successive embrace and his body had become increasingly rigid and unresponsive.

She was standing among the little group of junior aides-de-camp, trying hard not to laugh aloud. It was cruel of her, perhaps, but he had spent the last two days avoiding coming anywhere near her. She might have done the same thing in his place, but that did not prevent her from feeling perversely glad that he, too, was being made to suffer from embarrassment.

She might even make mention of it in her farewell letter to him, if she ever succeeded in finishing it.

At last, the salutations were over. Dominic would be leaving now. She fixed her eyes on him, drinking in the image of him that would be her last. She ignored the slight flush on his face. She wanted to remember the man she loved, and admired and valued. She wanted to remember the powerful figure, so strong and yet—with her—so tender, so passionate.

Major Zass put a hand on Dominic's shoulder. 'Of course, the junior officers are also much beholden to you, Duke. Will you not bid farewell to them, too?' The Major ushered the Duke towards Alex's group.

Oh, no! Zass was determined that Dominic should be embraced by every last one of the aides-de-camp. That included even the most junior—Captain Alexandrov. In full view of everyone! Dominic would never submit to that, surely? Not when he thought that she was a—

Her whole body stiffened. She could feel that doom-laden weight in her gut. What could she possibly do? Dominic was now being embraced by the young captain who stood three away from Alex. In moments, he would be here. She would be expected to reach out and embrace him, as all the others were doing.

What if she did not? Could she step back, and just offer her hand, in the English fashion? Dominic might be glad of that, but the Major would be insulted. And her comrades would detect something very smoky in her refusal to behave like a normal Russian officer. No, she would have to offer the embrace. The handshake, however attractive, was not an option.

She could feel the blood sinking to her feet. She knew she had probably turned deathly pale. She, the most junior, would be the last. She waited. She did not dare to close her eyes. She was going to have to embrace Dominic, here in front of them all. Not just touching him, but holding him, setting her mouth to his cheek. She prayed that her rebellious body would not betray her again when he touched her. Please, not here. Not now. Please. Her future depended on the good opinion of these men, her comrades. If she blushed, or flinched, they would see it. And the gossip would begin, gossip which could finish her career.

She swallowed several times, trying to force her emotions back under control, and telling her body that it must not, *not* betray what she felt for this man. He was only a couple of feet from her now. He was being embraced by Petrov at Alex's side. She took a deep breath, and held it.

'And, finally, Captain Alexandrov,' Major Zass said, 'who owes you a great deal, I believe, Duke, particularly in the matter of *mal de mer*.'

Alex thought she heard a slight snigger from Petrov. She forced her back to straighten. The moment of her trial was now!

Dominic took a sideways step and came to stand directly in front of her. She took another deep breath, telling her arms to grasp his shoulders. Her arms seemed to have mutinied.

A tiny twitch of a smile touched the corner of Dominic's mouth. 'I am afraid that we English are not in the habit of embracing, as you Russians do. Not embracing men, at least.'

Out of the corner of her eye, Alex glimpsed a broadening smile on Major Zass's face.

'I think it is time that I learned how it is done. Do not you, Alexei Ivanovich?' Without waiting for her reply, he laid his hands lightly on her shoulders, bent down, and kissed the air by each of her cheeks in turn. The moment he straightened again, he dropped his hands. As if she were diseased. His touch on her body had lasted no more than a second or two.

Alex was mortified. The skin of her shoulders was ablaze from that briefest of contacts. Her face, she knew, must be burning too, even though his lips had come nowhere near her cheeks. She opened her mouth to speak, but her throat was so tight that no words at all came out.

Major Zass laughed genially. 'Well, Duke, that was not *quite* how we Russians do it, but I thank you for your courtesy in having tried.' As if on cue, the other officers began to laugh, too. The tension was broken. Even Dominic was laughing.

Alex tried to do the same. She willed herself to ignore the burning and prickling in her shoulders where his hands had rested for the last time. She willed her trembling legs to remain upright. She willed her cheeks to lose their betraying blush.

Dominic appeared to be completely at his ease, laughing along with Major Zass but, from something in his stance, Alex knew it was not the case. He believed he had unnerved her, and for some reason that was a matter of concern to him. Then she saw the truth. He pitied her! Damn him! She would not allow that!

'Perhaps, Major,' she began, with spirit, 'we should demonstrate to the Duke that we can adopt his English ways just as well as he does our Russian ones?' She held out her hand. By force of willpower alone, it was rock steady. 'Will you shake hands, Calder, as we say our thanks and our farewells?'

He hesitated. It seemed he was truly unwilling to touch the man-woman he had befriended and who now disgusted him. But Alex was determined that she would part from the Duke of Calder as an equal. She stood motionless, hand outstretched, waiting.

It was no contest. In front of all the Emperor's suite, Dominic could not possibly refuse to shake Alex's hand. He took it, and they shook.

'I bid you farewell, Calder,' Alex said, with much more confidence than she had been feeling just moments before. 'I thank you for all your kindness to me, and for the services you have rendered to our beloved Emperor.'

As their hands dropped apart, Alex snapped both arms to

her sides, clicked her heels together and bowed from the neck, in the Prussian fashion.

'Bravo, Alexei Ivanovich,' Dominic said, with more than a hint of admiration in his voice. 'It seems that you have mastered the customs of *all* the Allies. One day, when you cease to be a bloodthirsty Hussar, you will doubtless make an excellent diplomat.'

It appeared to be getting dark. It couldn't be so, of course, not in June, not at this time of the evening. It must be the effect of the constant rain. It was making everything grey, and bleak.

Alex stood by the rail, alone, watching. She told herself she could still see the tall, imposing figure of the Duke of Calder standing on the quayside, but it might be just a trick of the light. Dover receded gradually into the mist. Eventually, she could see nothing at all, but still she could not bring herself to move. There was not a great deal of wind, and the crossing was going to be slow. For Alex, that was rather a blessing. A slower, calmer voyage was less likely to make her ill. Especially if she continued to stand on deck, in the fresh air. That was what Dominic had said she should do. On that topic, at least, his advice had been sound.

A barefooted sailor brought her a steaming mug. She had not asked for it, but she recognised the characteristic aroma of hot ginger and took it gratefully. No doubt the Duke of Calder had given instructions that his tisane was to be provided to Captain Alexandrov during the crossing. It was typical of his thoughtfulness. 'Thank you,' she said in English. Well, why not? They had left England and she was most unlikely ever to return. It did not matter now if anyone suspected that she spoke the language.

She heartily wished that she had not had to deceive Dominic. On so many fronts. It made her feel ungentlemanly, dishonourable, even soiled. And what had it achieved?

Nothing of note. Her understanding of the English language had yielded precious little by way of useful information. Some snippets about the Prince Regent, and his relationship with his daughter. Those might be of use, she supposed, since the Tsar was particularly interested in Princess Charlotte's potential marriage partners. But he could probably have discovered just as much, or more, from his own intimate discussions with Lady Jersey. For there had been many. It had been clear that he admired her greatly.

Alex frowned at that memory. The Tsar was not a good husband. No matter how much Alex revered him, she could not overlook the fact that he was a philanderer. He heartily disliked his wife, even though she was beautiful, and sweet-tempered. By all accounts, the Prince Regent had had cause for his dislike of the Princess of Wales, but it was much more difficult to justify the Tsar's conduct. Everyone knew that his mistress had borne him several children. That must be a cruel humiliation for the Tsarina. Alex found that she was truly sorry for the Empress.

What on earth had made Alex start to think in such a way? She had never in her life voiced any criticism of the 'Little Father'. She could not remember that she had ever thought of such things, either. When old Meg had been arguing with Alex about the wickedness of serfdom, Alex had defended the Tsar. Would she argue the same way now?

What was it that Dominic had said? Something about letting a little steam out of the boiling pot. Just like Meg, he seemed to approve of the way the popular prints made sport of the Regent, and his mistresses, and his extravagance. The English had cut off the head of one of their kings. Now they made them into objects of ridicule. Was that progress?

Alex was not at all sure. But she did know that her visit to England had changed her. She was no longer able to accept everything in the Russian system without question. The Tsar was not perfect. He was her sovereign, she owed him her duty and, if needs be, her life, but she had come to see that he had shortcomings.

By comparison with Dominic Aikenhead, Duke of Calder, Tsar Alexander was very much a man with flaws.

Alex put the mug down on to the rail with a sharp click, appalled at what she had just been thinking. Dominic must have bewitched her. He was far from perfect either. He was not even as good-looking as the Tsar. Dominic's features were much too serious, too austere.

Except when he laughed. Or when he was about to kiss a woman. When his deep blue eyes became soft and filled with desire, and his lips were seeking hers, he was the handsomest man on earth.

She shook her head and took another sip of the now lukewarm tisane. The taste of ginger would always remind her of Dominic, she decided. She loved him, and he would always be with her. His image would outshine that of all other men, even the Tsar. And his generous way of thinking would affect her opinions, too. She had been narrow-minded and unquestioning of many things. From now on…

Alexei Ivanovich Alexandrov would be returning from England a very different man.

Chapter Fifteen

Dominic was bone weary but, on reaching London, he drove straight to the Foreign Office. It was very late indeed, but Castlereagh was waiting for him. He received Dominic's report in silence, until Dominic made a slightly unflattering comment about the Emperor's sister and her political meddling. 'The Regent was grateful for your reports about his daughter's male visitors,' he said. 'Without your information, we should not have known what the Grand Duchess was plotting there. It has been dealt with. Thank you.'

Dominic expected nothing more. He rose to leave.

'One other thing. The Prime Minister may have questions to put to you. You will be in London for several days yet, I hope?'

Dominic was not best pleased by that request. What he needed was a few weeks' rest at Aikenhead Park. What he wanted… Ah, that was very different. What he wanted was an opportunity to discover more about the mysterious Alexandra of the masquerade. In Scotland, perhaps? It did not matter. He would happily forgo his time at the Park for any chance to unravel the intrigue that seemed to surround her.

However, that would now have to wait. He could not refuse Castlereagh's request. It was a matter of duty.

'As you wish, sir. You may reach me at my London house for the next week.'

Dominic awoke to darkness. Where was he? For a moment he was confused. And then he remembered. He stretched lazily and put his arms behind his head, staring up into the gloom. He was in his own bed, in London, and he must have slept for hours and hours. Leo and Jack would be in whoops over this. *Old men do need their sleep.* He could hear them already.

He had been dreaming again about Alexandra. His body tensed anew at the mere idea of her, but he forced himself to think carefully and rationally. Lust was a pretty poor compass when it came to deciding on where to go or what to do. In his years as a spy, he had learned the importance of careful planning and weighing the odds.

He cudgelled his brains for information. He had her name—part of it. He had her appearance—part of it, again. And he had what little information she had let slip. She had spoken of her mother, a scholar who spoke Greek, whose name was Anne Catriona. Until her marriage, she had travelled with her own father, who had been a diplomat. That was some kind of a clue. And Dominic had enough contacts in Whitehall to be able to follow it up. A diplomatic daughter, Scottish, much travelled, and a student of Greek. There could not have been too many such. But how old would she be? Hmm. If Alexandra was the eldest child, then the marriage would probably not be much older than she was. Alexandra was no green girl. She had poise and maturity. She knew her own mind. Twenty-five, perhaps? So, in tracking down the mother, Dominic was looking for a lady who had travelled with her diplomatic father and who had married some twenty-five years ago.

He nodded to himself. He had a start. He would send his ferrets into Whitehall.

She had worn a very elaborate and expensive costume for the masquerade. Might that provide some clues? Those green buckled shoes were certainly out of the common way. If he could find the maker, he might be able to bribe his way to the name, or the delivery address, of the buyer. Yes, that was a promising lead. The same might also be said for the long powdered wig.

Dominic relaxed back into his pillows. He was beginning to feel a little hopeful. But the lady herself…why had she run from him? And where on earth had she gone?

The answer to the first question was not far to seek. Her passion had overwhelmed her. In the dark intimacy of their loveseat, she had responded to him without restraint. In the mundane surroundings of the ladies' withdrawing room, she had no doubt been overcome by embarrassment at having behaved in such a way with a total stranger. And so she had fled, rather than face him again.

There must have been clues, there at the masquerade. He should have sought them out, there and then. But desire had been driving him, desire followed by despair. He should have questioned the doorman much more closely. A lady could not just vanish. There must have been a carriage, a coachman, a destination. Why had he not asked about those?

Because he was besotted. And driven by passion. Raging, unsatisfied passion. His body was stirring even now at the thought of what he had shared with her in that secluded bower. He quelled the reaction ruthlessly. It had caused him to fail once before. He would not do so again. He forced himself to focus on his search. Yes, if the doorman's palm were greased enough, his memory might return. After all, there had been only one lady at the masquerade in a pale green *polonaise* and buckled shoes.

Who to send? He could not do this task himself. The doorman might remember him as the man who asked after that particular lady on the night itself. That could put the price up, which he could afford, but it might also start rumours about the Duke of Calder, which he could not. Better to send a trusted agent.

After a moment's reflection, he decided on Leo. Jack could be trusted, just as much as Leo. They would both be close-mouthed. But Jack's reputation was that of a gambler and a choice spirit. He was not yet much of a womaniser. He did not keep mistresses. Leo, on the other hand, was known as an out-and-out rake. Gambling certainly, but women most of all. He prided himself on his success in seducing Society ladies. No one would raise an eyebrow at reports that Lord Leo Aikenhead was enquiring after a missing lady.

What time was it? How long had he slept? It was all very well to lie here making plans, but it was time for some action. His hand reached out and automatically found the bell-pull hanging over the nightstand.

Seconds later, Cooper appeared from the dressing room, carrying a branch of candles. He must have been waiting there for just such a summons.

'You rang, your Grace?'

'Very prompt, Cooper. What time is it?'

The valet grinned. 'It wants but ten minutes to ten o'clock, your Grace. I suspicioned that you'd be awake soon.'

'Did you now? I shall have to remember that you read minds.' He swung his legs to the floor and stood up. He had slept naked, as was his wont, and the slight evening breeze from the open window prickled his skin. Cooper held up his black silk dressing gown, and Dominic slipped his arms into it. It slithered over his skin in a most disconcerting way, reminding him uncomfortably of the touch of Alexandra's silken *polonaise*. To distract his unruly thoughts, he said, 'Is Lord Leo at home?'

'No, your Grace. Her Grace asked for his escort to Lady Morrissey's soirée. They left about fifteen minutes ago.'

'And Lord Jack?'

Cooper could not quite meet his master's eye. 'Lord Jack has not yet returned, your Grace.'

'Not at all?'

'Not since last evening, when he and Lord Leo went out together.'

Oh, hell! Jack must be out on one of his extended gambling sprees, wasting his substance yet again. Damn the boy!

'I expect he will return soon enough,' Dominic said, adopting a light tone to cover his concern, 'if only to change his clothes. He may still be fit for a gaming house, but I doubt he would be received anywhere else.'

Dominic was almost half-way through his heap of correspondence. It was amazing how it had piled up in only a few days. Most of it was routine, bills and invitations to the most eligible man in London. But it all had to be dealt with.

To his surprise, there was a letter from Alexandrov. He scanned it quickly, wondering why the lad had bothered to write when he had already expressed his thanks in person, more than once. It was not a long letter. The style was rather more flowery than Dominic would have expected. Perhaps it was the Russian way. He would think about that later. When he had more time. He cast it aside and turned his attention to the rest of the pile.

He had just finished writing the last of his responses when the library door opened. This time, it was Leo. 'I did not hear you arrive.'

Leo grinned. 'Why should you? We spies have to be able to slip in unnoticed, you know.'

Dominic pushed his chair back from the desk, trying to

appear relaxed and unconcerned. Leo sauntered across and dropped into the chair opposite him. He leaned back, clasped his hands across his middle and closed his eyes. 'If it's sleep you want, brother, there's an excellent bed upstairs,' Dominic said, rather testily.

Leo opened one lazy eye and swivelled it to look at his brother. 'Impatient, are we?' The corner of his mouth twitched into a half-smile.

'Damn you, Leo! You know perfectly well that I should not have sent you if it were not important. Now, tell me what you have discovered.'

Leo opened both eyes and sat up a little straighter, stretching out his booted feet. 'Discovered nothing about a carriage or a coachman. The lady left alone, and on foot.'

'Are you certain?'

'Doorman was sure of it. Once I had put half a guinea into his hand. He had no reason to lie, Dominic.'

'No, I suppose not. But it would have been dangerous, surely, for a lady to walk through the streets of London, alone, and at that time of night? Did she wear a cloak, do you know?'

'Apparently not, which made the rest of my mission easier to fulfil.'

'You *have* discovered something.'

'Well, perhaps. But it is very puzzling. Found a crossing sweeper, near the entrance. Young urchin, but well meaning. He remembered her, too. He had swept the crossing for her and she gave him sixpence.'

'Did he see where she went?'

'Yes. That is the puzzling part of this story. He says he saw her go into the Pulteney Hotel.'

'The Pulteney? But the whole hotel was taken for the Emperor's suite. I don't think there was room for any other guests.'

'I thought the same, Dominic. But, just to be sure, I questioned some of the staff at the hotel. They denied that any lady matching that description had ever been there.'

'The crossing sweeper must have been mistaken. Perhaps she went into one of the other entrances on Piccadilly.'

'Do you want me to go back and make enquiries?'

'No, Leo. That would be a very strange thing for Lord Leo Aikenhead to do.'

'So what shall you do now?'

'I shall send some of my ferrets to enquire at the various houses on Piccadilly. And perhaps to question your crossing sweeper again, also. He may remember something more. It's possible, I suppose.'

'This matters to you, Dominic, doesn't it?' For once, Leo's voice was low-pitched and serious.

Dominic looked into his brother's face. He probably trusted Leo more than any other man on earth, but this was too private to share. Especially when it seemed that he had lost her again. Instead of replying, he said only, 'Thank you for trying, Leo. I'll let you know if my ferrets discover anything more.' Then he walked over to the window and stood there, staring out. A moment later, the soft click of the latch told him he was alone.

Why had she left on foot? Even if she had no carriage of her own, she could have called for a hackney. And to walk along Piccadilly, alone, in that gown and those shoes... It was a wonder she had not been accosted. Or worse. It did not bear thinking about.

Frustrated, he went back to his desk and started leafing through his letters. He needed something to occupy his mind. Tomorrow he could set wheels in motion, but for now there was absolutely nothing he could do. Alexandrov's letter was somewhere among the others. Since the boy had taken the trouble to write, Dominic should at least do him the courtesy of reading his letter properly.

Once he had found it, he sat down and leaned back in his chair to read. At the third sentence, his whole body stiffened. The hairs on the back of his neck were standing on end. 'You took me to places of wonder,' the letter said.

Dominic's gorge rose. The boy must be mad to commit such words to paper. What a risk to take! Dominic made to crumple the letter with both hands. It needed to be burnt. He took a deep breath and rose.

He was back in the masquerade garden. It was her scent. There, on the paper. Citrus with that unusual dark undertone. He could not be mistaken. It was Alexandra's scent. He smoothed out the single sheet and forced himself to read the words, slowly, slowly. 'You took me to places of wonder. I shall treasure the experiences we shared.' It couldn't be true. It could not!

A little voice whispered that it would certainly explain how she came to have disappeared into the Pulteney Hotel. But it *must* be impossible. Alexandrov had spent years serving in the Hussars. He had fought in battles. He was decorated for his bravery in the face of the enemy. He could not possibly be a woman. It was unthinkable.

Dominic sat down at his desk once more and read Alexandrov's letter for the third time. Alexandrov's letter. Alexandra's letter? 'You took me to places of wonder.' No man could ever write that to another. Not unless he harboured unnatural feelings for him. Was that the meaning of Alexandrov's letter? But it would not explain why Alexandra had disappeared into the Pulteney. It would not explain her scent. He inhaled again, deeply. There could be no mistake.

Dominic tried to remember exactly what had happened at the masquerade. He was looking for clues that Alexandra, and Alexandrov, were one and the same. The names were almost identical, of course, but Alexandra had spoken English like a native. Alexandrov spoke none.

No, that was not true. Alexandrov had *said* he spoke no English.

If they were the same person, her costume for the masquerade had been cleverly chosen to disguise her without arousing suspicion. A wig to cover Alexandrov's cropped hair and *maquillage* to hide his weather-beaten skin. Of course! Those gloves! The gloves that Alexandra would not remove. No wonder. Alexandrov's hands were as brown as his cheeks. He—she could never have passed for a lady with hands like those.

He remembered, then, that she had removed her gloves, just once, for long enough to undo the knotted laces of her gown and her corset. It had happened when there was not enough light for Dominic to see the colour of her skin. She had drawn on her gloves again, even as he was removing her gown! That was very odd behaviour. Yes, it must be so. Alexandrov must be Alexandra.

She had returned to Russia with her Emperor. No doubt to continue her extraordinary career as a cavalry officer. Dominic could not begin to understand how she could have done it. Or why she would have taken such a perilous path in life. But he was now sure—almost sure—that she had.

If it was true, she had made a complete fool of him. And of the whole of the Russian army, too. He ought to be furious with her, ready to wring her neck. But, strangely, he was not. What he wanted to do to her involved intimacy, not violence.

What a coil! He had admired her courage as Alexandrov, but as Alexandra it was breathtaking. What an amazing woman she was.

It must be true.

He poured himself a glass of Madeira and sipped it slowly, savouring its richness. There was no doubt in his mind about what he was going to do. There was only one way of proving that Alexandrov truly was Alexandra. He must follow her to Russia and confront her with what he knew. He would force her to tell him the whole. And if it turned out that he was wrong, that Alexandrov was indeed a man with an unhealthy interest in Dominic Aikenhead, he would have to apologize and retreat as best he might. But it would not happen. He was sure of that. Alexandrov was Alexandra.

Why had she donned a woman's garb to go to the masquerade? Any of her fellow officers might have seen her. Her position in the Russian army might have been fatally compromised. What on earth had made her take such a risk? Perhaps she wanted a little time as a woman again, after so many years as a man? Or perhaps…

He shook his head, trying to prevent the thought from surfacing, but it was determined to be out in the light. For he was desperate to believe it. That she had dressed as a woman because she wanted to show herself, in her female guise, to Dominic Aikenhead.

Chapter Sixteen

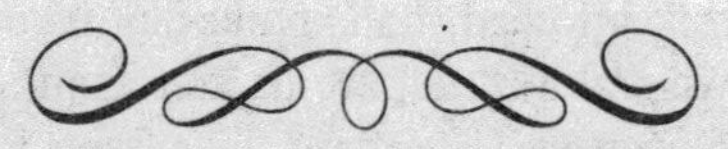

'How long will you be gone?'

It was late and the brothers were sitting in the small bookroom of Dominic's hunting box after a long day out riding. There was little else for them to do, since the shooting season had not yet begun. Castlereagh was sending Dominic to Russia, to discover the Emperor's intentions for the Congress of Vienna, but even the Foreign Secretary could not organise a speedy departure. The Russians had their own ways of doing things.

'I don't know, Leo. In spite of Castlereagh's urgency, I still don't have any papers, so I can't even set out. I've ordered the yacht to be made ready. I'm sure it's better than attempting the journey over land. With a fair wind, I should be able to make it to Cronstadt in less than three weeks. St Petersburg is only a day's travel from there, I understand.'

'And what will you do when you do get there?' Leo was staring out of the window. His voice was quiet, even a little tentative, as if he knew he was treading on dangerous ground. Leo might suspect, but he would not probe into a wound he knew to be raw.

'I shall present myself to the Emperor and find out what I can about his intentions. That is why Castlereagh is sending me.'

Leo sat silent. Waiting.

'Some of the Emperor's aides-de-camp will probably be there. With Europe at peace again, I doubt their regiments will have recalled them. They are probably all enjoying court life.'

'Well, if you should happen upon Alexandrov, give him my compliments. And Jack's. We were both sorry that he did not accept your invitation to stay in England for a while.'

Dominic swallowed, conscious that he must have gone pale. But Leo was still gazing fixedly at the garden. He had missed his vocation. He should have been a diplomat, not a spy. 'Yes, I will. If I should happen to see him. Now, while I am away, Leo, I need you to hold the fort here.'

Leo swung round in his chair. His eyes were dancing.

'I mean as far as the Foreign Office is concerned. If any new missions are required, you must take charge.'

'Do you expect something to happen?'

'No. At least, not immediately. Bonaparte is safely settled on Elba so we can forget about him. The major concern at the moment seems to be the Congress at Vienna. All the powers of Europe will be there. Indeed, with this interminable delay, I shall be lucky to arrive in Russia before the Emperor leaves. Castlereagh is going to Vienna himself. I think he may want to send us there, too, as a kind of quiet back-up, to skulk around the backstairs as usual.'

'You want me to go?'

'If I am not back from Russia, you will have to use your own judgement about what should be done. Take Jack and Ben, if you think you'll need them.'

'If there's a chance of a jaunt to Vienna, there will be no holding Jack.' Leo grinned. 'Ben, too, probably.'

Dominic laughed softly. The two youngest members of the Aikenhead Honours were irrepressible. It needed only a whiff of possible adventure and they were off on the scent like a couple of hunting dogs. 'You're right, of course. But it will do no harm.'

Leo yawned and hauled himself out of his chair. 'Think I'll have an early night. I'm devilish sleepy. Must have been all that fresh air and exercise.' He made his way to the door. 'Night, Dominic.' The door opened before he could put his hand to it.

'Good evening, Dominic. Leo.'

'Cousin Harriet! Why, I thought you and Mama had gone to bed hours ago.'

'When you get to my age, Dominic, you don't need much sleep. But I can see that Leo still needs his.' She reached up and patted Leo's cheek, as if he were still a child. 'Good night, Leo. Sleep well.'

Leo grunted. 'Don't worry, Coz. I can take a hint. Good night.' He went out, closing the door quietly behind him.

Dominic pushed a chair forward for Miss Penworthy. 'May I offer you something, ma'am?'

'I'll take some of your brandy, Dominic. If you two haven't drunk it all.'

Turning his back to hide his smile, Dominic poured her a generous measure. Why had she come? She wanted something. Information, possibly. The trouble was that she knew him too well. And unlike Leo, she was no diplomat. If she suspected something smoky was afoot, she would not rest until she discovered what it was. However, he was not at liberty to share Castlereagh's secrets. And he did not wish to share his own.

'Hear you're going to Russia. Is that right?'

'Yes. But I cannot leave until the official papers arrive. Once they do, I shall be off.'

'Why Russia?'

Typical Harriet. Such a bald question. 'It's a matter of duty, ma'am,' he said after a moment. 'I can't say more than that, even to you.'

'Hmmph. Don't trust me to keep my own counsel, eh? No, don't shake your head at me, Dominic. I know what you're thinking. And I do understand that you can't discuss your secret business with me.' She took a long swallow of her brandy, smiled down into her glass and then looked Dominic straight in the eye. 'I take it you will be seeing young Alexandrov while you're there?' Without giving Dominic a chance to speak, she continued, 'Interesting young man, I thought. He's another man with secrets, just like you, Dominic. Must say I wasn't surprised that he refused to stay on in England.'

Harriet was trying to play him like a trout on a line. She had information, that was almost certain. And Dominic was going to have to humour her in order to get it. 'What have you been up to, Cousin?' he said indulgently. 'I thought you spent only one evening in his company.'

'Aye, and so I did.' She swallowed the remains of her brandy and held out her glass for a refill.

He fetched the decanter obediently but paused with his hand on the stopper. She shook her empty glass impatiently, but he ignored it. 'Why do you think he refused my invitation?'

'My glass is empty, Dominic.'

He gave in and poured her brandy. Then he sat down opposite her and waited.

'Oh, very well. But you may not like what I say. I think he would not stay because he was worried that his secrets might be discovered here.'

Dominic had come to exactly the same conclusion himself, once he knew the secret of the letter. Did Harriet know something that he did not? Every scrap of information about Alexandra was vital. His heart had begun to pound. It sounded like thunder in his ears.

'You think me a brain-addled old biddy, I know that.'

'Nothing of the sort,' he replied, glad that his voice sounded almost normal. 'You're as sharp as a tack. And you know things about Alexandrov, don't you?'

'Well… I believe he lied to you about not being able to speak English.'

'Are you certain?'

'Judge for yourself, Dominic. He overheard a conversation I was having with Jack. At your dinner party. He referred to it later, just in passing, you understand, but it was clear that he had understood it. Jack and I were speaking in *English*, Dominic.'

He nodded slowly, waiting for his heart to slow. It fitted with the rest of the evidence he had. Alexandrov was Alexandra.

'What's more, I fancy his mother was Scottish. The colouring would certainly fit: he said she had auburn hair and blue eyes. And she taught him to dance reels.'

'That would explain his understanding of English, certainly. But, are you sure, ma'am? Might you not be mistaken?'

'I am not in my dotage yet, Dominic. Remember, he sat alongside me throughout dinner that evening. And I made sure I probed further, especially when he had had a few glasses of wine.'

'But Alexandrov never allows himself more than one glass. I have seen it myself, more than once.'

'Ah.' She would not meet his eyes. There was even a tinge of red on her neck. 'I did not know that. I just assumed— I'm afraid I have a small confession to make, Dominic. I arranged with Withering to top up the boy's glass, surreptitiously you know, every time his head was turned. Must say that Withering was very good at it. Just the merest drop each time. Never enough to be noticed. And so Alexandrov may have drunk… er…slightly more than he intended.'

He swore under his breath. 'Harriet Penworthy, you are a—'

'I am an aged relative who does not take kindly to being

insulted by a young whippersnapper like you, Dominic Aikenhead, duke or no duke!'

He burst out laughing. 'I would not dare, ma'am. I meant to say only that you are…shall we say, inventive? And I'd wager that you discovered a great deal more about young Alexandrov in the course of that dinner. Am I right?'

'Perhaps,' she said coyly.

'Tell me what else you found out, ma'am. I will happily praise your abilities to the skies, even to Jack, but tell me what you know.'

Suddenly, the twinkle disappeared from her sharp old eyes and she looked hard into his. 'This really matters to you, Dominic. I am right, am I not?'

Peacetime duty was frustrating in the extreme. Interminable guard duties and far too many inspections. She would have much preferred to be on exercise with her men. Lance drill and sabre drill and riding practice were all useful. The precise set of a plume in a shako was not.

Today, for the first time in a week, she was not on duty. It ought to have been possible to ride Pegasus out into the countryside around St Petersburg, to enjoy the peace and the fine summer weather. Unfortunately, even her free time was being regimented. Her Colonel had bidden her to spend the day with his family. He meant it kindly, no doubt, but it would not have been Alex's choice.

She stood for a long time in front of the mirror, adjusting tiny details of her dress uniform. She really did look like a man. She began to draw on her gloves.

Gloves! She threw them down and turned to open the topmost drawer of her chest. Yes, they were still there, wrapped in tissue and nestling under piles of male linen. Suddenly, she did not care if she was going to be late arriving at the Colonel's house. She took out the parcel and carefully unwrapped the green kid gloves. She could not put them on without removing her uniform jacket. Instead, she stroked them gently with the back of her fingers. Then she raised them to her face and breathed deeply. She was almost sure that there was still a faint scent of Dominic on them. Memories came flooding back. His mouth on her inner arm, nuzzling the skin down to her wrist, her fingers pushing into his hair, his—

The knock on her door made her jump.

'What is it?'

'The Colonel's carriage has arrived, your Honour.'

Alex began to rewrap the gloves in their tissue. 'I shall be down presently,' she said loudly. Carefully, she restored the gloves to their hiding-place at the bottom of the drawer. If only she had kept the gown, or the slippers. But her fellow officers had demanded them back, to sell, in hopes of recovering some of their outlay. The apple-green gloves were the only memento she had.

'Look here, Alexei Ivanovich. Is this not the most wonderful thing?' The Colonel's elder daughter was pointing to a huge golden ornament, studded with precious stones. 'This is much more interesting than all those pictures you keep staring at. What's the point of coming to the Hermitage just to look at the pictures? It would take months to go round them all. And they're so boring.'

Alex glanced at the jewel. It was hideous, but good manners required her to appear to consider it for a moment. 'Your mother seems to be beckoning to you,' Alex said, pointing. It was almost true. The Colonel's wife was certainly looking in their direction. 'Perhaps she would be interested in the jewels you admire so much?' Alex bowed. 'But if you will excuse me, I shall return to the paintings.'

Alex made her way to the painting that she had been staring at earlier, a portrait that seemed to have been painted in

England. Its subject was an unnamed man, dressed in the full-bottomed wig and elaborate velvet coat of a century before. The clothes did not matter a whit. It was the eyes. They could have been Dominic's eyes. And they seemed to be looking straight into Alex's. She felt as if she could reach out and touch him. As if the man in the painting was about to speak to her. With Dominic's voice.

'Alexandrov, is it not?'

Alex started, and turned. It was Prince Volkonsky, the Emperor's Court Minister, and the one other person who knew Captain Alexandrov's real identity. She snapped to attention. 'Your Excellency. Good evening.'

'Yes, I thought I recognised you. I was minded to send for you. There is something I wish to discuss with you. Shall we walk together?' Volkonsky led Alex into an empty side-room where they might talk without fear of being overheard. 'I am delighted to have this opportunity of speaking privately to you, Alexandrov,' the Prince said with a genial smile. 'We have corresponded, of course, over financial and other matters.'

Alex felt her skin reddening. She had never been completely easy about the fact that the Tsar himself supplied all the money she needed for her day-to-day expenses.

Volkonsky must have noticed her embarrassment, for he put a hand on her shoulder and said, 'Do not be concerned. His Majesty is more than content to frank you. The money is precious little recompense for the outstanding bravery you have shown in his service.'

Alex swallowed. 'Thank you, your Excellency. You are very good.'

'I understand from Major Zass that you used your knowledge of English to good effect during his Majesty's visit to London.'

Alex began to protest. She had discovered almost nothing.

'That is not the point, young man,' Volkonsky said sharply.

'You discovered little because there was little to discover. That in itself was valuable. No one else could have done it.'

'Thank you, your Excellency.'

'But that is not the issue I wanted to discuss with you. I hope you will not be offended, Alexei Ivanovich, but I know that I speak for the Emperor himself when I say that we are concerned about the rift between you and your family. We know how it arose, of course—and we remain immensely grateful for your service—but the Emperor would like to see a reconciliation between you and your father.'

'His Majesty means to send me home? To my petticoats?'

'No, no. His Majesty has given you, with his own hand, a commission in the Mariupol. His Majesty is content that you continue to serve as a man. But he would very much like to see a reconciliation. I am instructed to write to your father and to ask him, in the Emperor's name, to receive you as Alexei Ivanovich Alexandrov, Captain of Hussars. I shall not do so, of course, without your permission.'

That was a momentous offer. And from the Emperor himself! Alex hesitated. She needed time to consider this. 'I am truly grateful to his Majesty, and to your Excellency, for the offer, but— Forgive me, I do not feel able to give my answer immediately. It would be such a great change in my life.' She shook her head a little, trying to clear her thoughts. 'May I ask if your Excellency truly believes that my father would be prepared to receive me as I am?' She indicated her Hussar officer's uniform.

'I cannot say for certain, of course,' Volkonsky said, 'but I know, from various sources, that your father has been most anxious about you. I have no doubt that he loves you, Alexandrov, as a father should. I think there must be a good chance that he would agree to receive you. And that he would not insist on your resuming your petticoats.'

Alex nodded thoughtfully.

'Do not answer me now, Alexei Ivanovich. I completely understand that you need time to think about this. My wife has arranged a small gathering at our house tomorrow evening. Some of the guests will be people you know. And there will be music which, I seem to recall, is one of your passions.'

Alex nodded again.

'Why not join us? I will make sure that we have a moment for a private word during the course of the evening. You can give me your decision then.'

Alex worried at her lower lip. Soon her carriage would be at Volkonsky's door. She had yet to decide whether she would accept the Prince's offer of mediation with her father. It was very tempting. She missed him sorely. They had been so close when she was younger, when they and Alex's mother had lived in the army camp and, later, after her mother's death, when Alex had been at her father's right hand, riding out around the estate and learning all the skills he would have taught to a son. She knew that her flight had given him pain. He must have been afraid for her, too. So many Russian officers had been killed on campaign, or gravely wounded. But Volkonsky had ensured that her father knew she was alive and well. And now that Europe was at peace, the danger was past.

Did she dare to visit him, to kneel at his feet as a daughter should, and to ask for his blessing? She was not sure. Perhaps the scandal over her ruined betrothal would have been forgotten, after so many years? He might even be prepared to accept her as she was. The difficulty was that Alex's stepmother almost certainly would not do so. For her, Alex's behaviour was a denial of everything that a dutiful Russian daughter should be.

Alex took a deep breath and sighed it out. Perhaps her situation was more straightforward than she imagined. The decision lay not with her, but with her father. If he accepted Volkonsky's invitation to arrange a reconciliation, then Alex would agree to it. If he was still so very much influenced by his wife, he would refuse. The situation would be no worse than before. Better, in some ways, since he would know that Alex had tried for a reconciliation.

The carriage drew up. Alex gathered her thoughts and stepped down, remembering that Prince Volkonsky had promised that she would know some of the guests. She climbed the steps to the magnificent entrance of the Prince's residence, wondering who those guests might be.

It was a much larger gathering than Alex had expected, full of prominent and influential people. But Alex would not allow herself to be daunted. As a cavalry officer of considerable experience, and a one-time member of the Emperor's personal staff, she had as much right to be there as any of them.

'Alexandrov! How good to see you.' Major Zass was beaming at her. They embraced heartily and the Major clapped Alex on the shoulder. 'Some of the others from our London trip are here also.' He looked round. 'Can't see any of them just at the moment. They have probably sneaked off to play cards, as usual.' He shook his head sorrowfully. 'Don't know where they find the money, myself.'

'Nor do I, Major. I've never had the money to play, even if I wanted to. Which I don't.'

'Very wise. Champagne?' Zass summoned a waiter.

Alex caught up a half-full glass from the tray. She would not drink it all, and then she would be able to have another half-glass with supper. She must not appear to be unwilling to join in the gaiety.

'Since you do not wish to play cards, do come and meet my wife.' Zass began to usher Alex across the room. 'I have told her all about you, and she is eager to make your acquaintance.'

'I would be honoured, Major.'

'And I have a surprise for you, too, Alexei Ivanovich.'

'Really?'

'Yes.' He tapped a finger against the side of his nose. 'But it would not be a surprise if I said anything more. Come.' He led Alex across the room and out through the double doors on the far side. In the room beyond, he looked around in puzzlement. It appeared that his wife was not where he expected her to be. 'Confound it! Where on earth has she gone?'

Behind them, a voice said, in immaculate French, 'If you are seeking your wife, Major, she has tasked me to tell you that she is taking the air in the garden. May I bring you to her?'

That voice was unmistakable. It was the voice that had haunted Alex's dreams since the day she sailed from Dover, the voice she had longed to hear just once more. He was here! And now, when she could turn and face him, turn and see his beloved face, she was not really sure that she dared. Her body was telling her to run. But that was impossible. Courage! Face him, as you faced the enemy!

She forced her feet to move and her mouth to smile. 'Why, good evening, Duke. What a pleasant surprise to find you here in St Petersburg. To what do we owe the honour?'

'Good evening, Alexei Ivanovich. Well met.' He was smiling down at her in a very odd way. And then, without warning, he pulled her into his embrace and kissed her soundly on both cheeks.

This time, his kisses were all too real.

Chapter Seventeen

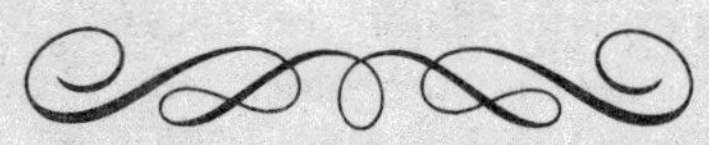

Poor Alexandra. She had not been prepared to find him at Volkonsky's party. And his embrace had rendered her totally speechless. He smiled to himself at the thought of it. He had never been able to feel really angry with her for making a fool of him, but, if she deserved punishment, she had certainly had it now. For her, his embrace had been a shock. For Dominic, it had been a revelation. Knowing he was embracing a woman—the most desirable woman he had ever met—had made the moment more exciting than he could have imagined. Here, at last, he was back in control. And this time, he would not let her escape from him.

All things considered, she had carried it off very well, he decided. Even though she had blushed bright red at first. Strange that he had never made that connection before. She had always had a tendency to blush. Like everyone else, Dominic had been prepared to accept that Alexandrov was a rather shy young man who was easily embarrassed, even though he blushed more than any other young man Dominic had ever met. The fact that Alexandrov was a girl—and Dominic was now ever more sure of that—explained it all. But it must have been plaguey inconvenient for her while she was playing the part of an army officer. She had done amazingly well to carry it off for years. But then, she was an amazing woman.

So far, they had exchanged only polite nothings. She had been introduced to Madame Zass. They had talked about her duties in St Petersburg and about her recent visit to the Hermitage. Thoroughly frustrated, Dominic had been just on the point of proposing that Alexandrov take a walk around the garden with him when Prince Volkonsky himself had appeared and taken her away for a private word.

Dominic wondered, idly, what sort of matters Alexandra might have to discuss with the Emperor's Court Minister. Perhaps he wished to set her to spy on the Duke of Calder all over again? Well, it would not matter. There would have to be a degree of mutual confession. Soon. Dominic fancied that confession—followed by reconciliation—could be very pleasurable indeed. He was ostensibly in St Petersburg to spy for the British Government, but he had no intention of actively doing so. If useful information fell into his lap, he would have to relay it to the British Ambassador. But he was not about to go looking for it. His quarry, this time, was not the Tsar, or Russia's plotting. His quarry was the mysterious, and delectable, Alexandra.

'I was surprised to see the Duke of Calder here, your Excellency. Might I enquire what has brought him to St Petersburg?' Alex had just about regained her composure. Having a closed door between her and the Duke most definitely helped.

The Prince was searching among the piles of papers on his vast mahogany desk. He looked up. 'An excellent question, Alexei Ivanovich. The Duke says that he is merely accepting the Emperor's invitation to visit. Could be true, of course. But I am not altogether sure that it is simply a pleasure trip.'

Alex frowned. Dominic's objective was probably the same as before—to spy. Why else would he have come?

Prince Volkonsky had finally found the papers he was searching for. He turned back to Alex, and said, in a fatherly way, 'Have you made up your mind, Alexei Ivanovich?'

'Yes, your Excellency. Since his Majesty, and your Excellency, are generous enough to try to effect a reconciliation with my father, it would be churlish of me to refuse. I accept. Gladly.'

'Splendid, splendid! I felt sure you would see the sense in doing so. I have taken the liberty of arranging three months' leave for you from your regiment. You will have ample time to journey to your father's house and to enjoy a long stay there. I have all the papers you will need: passes, requisitions for horses, and so on. Here.' He handed Alex a large sheaf of papers, many bearing official seals.

'You are most generous, your Excellency. But my father may decide not to receive me. He may not wish to accept the invitation.'

'I take leave to doubt that, Alexei Ivanovich. The suggestion comes from the Emperor himself, and your father will be more than happy to accede to it. I shall send the letter tonight. I am sure there is no need for you to wait for a response. Your leave begins tomorrow. So you may start your journey as soon as you wish.'

Damn the man! Why could he not accept a simple *no*?

'And our amiable host tells me that you have leave from your regiment. So there can be no difficulty at all.'

Dominic beamed at Alex with that particular kind of self-satisfied male arrogance that always made her want to start wielding her sabre. He was not going to be content with anything other than an acceptance. Well, she would see about that. She would accept his invitation but, when his carriage arrived to collect her, she would be long gone. It was the only safe way of dealing with him. She could not be alone in his company. One more embrace, one more touch, and she was like to dissolve into a pool of palpitating desire.

'Very well, Calder. I accept.' She gave him her direction in St Petersburg.

'Splendid. I will call for you at half past nine tomorrow. I look forward to hearing your opinion on this country house I have hired. It is quite small, considering how much I have had to pay to rent it, but the view of the river is extremely pleasant and there is excellent riding to be had in the area. There are horses in the stable, but you might prefer to bring your own.'

'Pegasus? Yes, I probably shall. He is getting old now, but he has carried me faithfully for years. I owe him a gentle retirement.'

'Pegasus? The winged steed. A splendid name. Does he fly?'

Alex smiled fondly. 'He is a Circassian. He goes like the wind, Calder. And he is afraid of nothing.'

'Hmm. I look forward to making his acquaintance then. He sounds to be a considerable improvement on the nags that my landlord has provided.'

Alex laughed. She could not help it. 'You are a foreign visitor in our country, Calder. I am afraid you must expect to be gulled. Even we Russians suffer that way, you know.'

'Really? I shall remember that. By the bye, I had forgot to thank you for your most generous farewell letter.'

Alex flushed bright crimson. She had been so obsessed with gazing at him that she had forgotten her incriminating letter. Had she really dared to write those revealing words? And to add that touch of the scent she had worn? It had been an irresistible temptation to smear a tiny drop on the paper, in hopes…in hopes of what? That he would make the connection between Alexandrov and Alexandra? He would never do that. He would never believe for a moment that Captain Alexandrov of the Mariupol Hussars could be a woman. A little voice whispered that he was perhaps more astute than she imagined. Perhaps he had travelled to Russia expressly to find her? No. That was impossible. He was here to spy. It was all too simple.

'You do not dance, Duke.' Prince Volkonsky had appeared from nowhere. 'Nor you, Alexandrov. What can you both be thinking of, standing here in the corner, gossiping like a pair of women.' He shook his head, smiling. 'Come.' He tucked his arm through Calder's. 'Let me introduce you to some of my guests. You will agree, I hope, that they are very beautiful.'

Dominic allowed himself to be led away.

Alone at last, Alex leaned a shoulder against the panelling and ran a slightly trembling hand across her forehead. Without Prince Volkonsky's intervention, that exchange could so easily have become a disaster.

From her vantage point, she watched Volkonsky introduce Dominic to a number of beautiful and high-ranking Russian ladies. Dominic bowed to them with exquisite grace. He was a consummate courtier. After speaking to the ladies for a few moments, Dominic led one of them out on to the floor.

For a waltz! Alex's heart sank to her boots. The thought of Dominic waltzing with another woman in his arms was painful in the extreme. They were gliding around the floor, Dominic guiding his lady with masterly skill. Alex remembered how it had been. In his arms, she had felt she was floating. And now she would never do it again. Never.

She could not bear to watch. She must leave. Now.

She quickly sought out her host and his wife, to explain that she must reluctantly leave the party since she was due to set off from St Petersburg at first light next day. Volkonsky was genial. 'Quite right. Quite right. You have a long journey ahead of you, Alexandrov. And you need to be fresh when you arrive at your destination, eh? Well, I wish you a good journey. And an even better journey's end.'

'Thank you, your Excellency.' Alex bowed to the Prince

and then to his wife. The waltz was about to end. She must go! With a final word of farewell, she hurried out.

She was safe now, sitting at her desk in her own bedchamber. Dominic could not reach her here. She had seen him for the last time.

And she had never felt more desolate.

She gazed out into the darkness beyond her window. It was as if she could still see him against the gloom. She would try to remember that image of him, dancing the waltz, but in her imagination, the woman in his arms would be Scottish Alexandra, not a Russian countess. She would hold fast to the memory. What else did she have?

She had his embrace.

Why had he done that? What did it mean? He had been so careful, in Dover, not to touch her at all. His embrace then had been so cold it was almost icy. But this evening's had been warm. He had put his mouth against each cheek in turn. He had kissed her soundly. Suddenly seeing him, being embraced by him, had been such a shock that she had frozen. She was now heartily glad of that, for her body's natural response would have been to cling to him, and to press her lips to his. That would truly have created a scandal. But why had he kissed her? Was it possible that he had guessed the truth? She had included so many hints in that mad, reckless letter.

She had to leave another letter for Dominic, explaining that she had been called away on urgent family business and that she was therefore unable to keep her appointment with him. This time, it must be quite straightforward. There could be no hidden messages. And no scent.

She quickly scribbled three lines of polite nothings and signed her name. It was but a moment's work to fold and seal the sheet. She wrote his name on the outside of the folded paper and propped it up against the inkstand. The name was beckoning to her.

'Shall you be wanting to take these, your Honour?' Her orderly was holding up the overalls that Hussars wore when going into action.

'No,' she said curtly. 'I am going to the country, on a family visit. I have no need of battle dress. Pack my normal uniforms.'

The orderly nodded and busied himself with Alex's linen.

'Make sure my boxes are corded and carried downstairs. The carriage is ordered for first light. Nothing is to delay my departure.'

'Yes, your Honour.'

Alex looked round at the disorder in the room. She would have no peace until the packing was complete. She certainly had no desire to indulge in small talk with her orderly. She had to keep busy. 'I am going down to the stables. I need to ensure that my horses will be well cared for during my absence. Finish up here, and lay out my second-best uniform for the journey.' Without waiting for his reply, she left the room and clattered down the stairs to the courtyard where the stables lay.

Pegasus was in one of the open stalls nearest the entrance. At the sight of Alex, he whinnied a greeting and tossed his head. 'You've had too many oats, old fellow. I can see that.' She stroked his glossy neck and laid her cheek against it. 'Poor old Pegasus. You are going to feel yourself abandoned. Again. And I am afraid there is no help for it. You cannot come with me to my father's house. It is much too long a journey. I shall have to change horses frequently on the way. You are strong, Pegasus, and your endurance is matchless, but even you could not go so far without rest.'

He tossed his head again, as if he understood and was far from content.

'Yes, yes, I know. And I am sorry.' She glanced quickly round the stable. It was deserted, save for the horses. There was no one to eavesdrop. 'I have to get away from Petersburg, Pegasus. I have to get away from *him*. I cannot continue on my own any more. I need something, or someone, to lean on. Someone to take my side, as old Meg always does.' She straightened and began to stroke the horse's velvet muzzle. 'If only you could talk, Pegasus. Then perhaps you could tell me what to do. If I do not leave Petersburg, I am like to do something I will regret. Like confessing everything to him. When I look into his face, Pegasus, I am lost. I can think only of how much I desire to put my arms about him, to kiss his mouth, to touch his skin.'

Pegasus did not seem to be impressed. He raised his top lip and bared his teeth. Then he began to nuzzle Alex's pockets, searching for treats.

It made her laugh, in spite of her misery. 'And I called you matchless, you old fraud.' She delved into her pocket for the sugar she always carried. 'Cupboard love.' She clapped his neck. 'Well, you shall receive your just deserts. One of the grooms shall exercise you until I return. And you won't like that, will you?'

He whinnied and began to investigate her other pockets.

'No, no. I have nothing more. And you will grow fat if you eat so much sugar.'

He raised a hoof and brought it down on her booted foot.

'Thank you, Pegasus.' She pushed him off easily enough, for he had not put his weight on it. 'I take your point. And I am truly sorry you cannot come with me.' She smoothed his ears and laid her cheek against his. 'You do understand, don't you, fellow? I love him, you see. And I am afraid of how I may react if I am with him. So my only choice is to flee. If my father welcomes me, I shall send for you, Pegasus. You shall be brought to me in easy stages. And you shall have the finest oats to eat and the lushest fields to live in. You have earned nothing less. The rest of your days shall be easy, I promise.'

But the rest of Alex's days would be a loveless desert.

* * *

Dominic had danced with two beautiful countesses, one after the other. His mind was elsewhere. The woman he most wanted to waltz with was denied him, for he had left her standing at the side of the ballroom, dressed as a man. He would have given a great deal to see her there in her pale green *polonaise* and buckled shoes. Instead, he was expected to do the pretty by even more Russian ladies.

Volkonsky ensured that Dominic circulated among his important guests for the best part of two hours. And in all that time, Dominic did not set eyes on Alexandrov. He was probably bored to tears, since he did not dance. No, that was not true. Dominic's Alexandra danced divinely. It was Captain Alexandrov who preferred not to take the floor. On reflection, Dominic could understand that. Such close proximity to another lady could be dangerous. Female intuition was sometimes acute, and always unpredictable. Alexandra would not be foolish enough to take the risk.

When supper was announced, Dominic decided that he could at last seek out his friend, Captain Alexandrov, without exciting any suspicions. But Alexandrov was nowhere to be found. After spending some minutes searching the various rooms, Dominic was forced to conclude that he had left long before the other guests. Why on earth would he have done so? And what excuse could he possibly have made to Prince Volkonsky for such rudeness?

Volkonsky was standing by the entrance to the supper room, chatting to various guests as they sauntered through and acting as a most attentive host. 'A splendid party, Prince,' Dominic said. 'I am most grateful for your hospitality, especially as it gave me an opportunity to renew my acquaintance with some of the officers I met in London. Major Zass, for example. And young Alexandrov, too. Where is he, by the way? I did not see him on the dance floor.'

'Ah, no, Duke, you would not. Captain Alexandrov took his leave some little while ago. I understand he is planning to make an early start tomorrow.'

'Oh, indeed? I see.' But Dominic did not see. An early start? Their arrangement was to meet at half past nine. Hardly early for a cavalryman who was used to rising with the dawn. Alexandra did not need to leave the Volkonsky party early for that. There was something smoky going on here. His gut began to tie itself in knots all over again. He had been so sure she could not escape him again. Not without a reckoning between them. He had to discover what she intended.

Dominic passed through into the supper room. One of his earlier dancing partners waved an invitation to join her, but he bowed a polite refusal. She was not the quarry he sought. Eventually, he found the Princess Volkonsky, seated with three of her elderly female friends. 'May I join you, ladies?'

'Why, Duke! Of course you may.' The Princess was almost simpering. These elderly ladies might not have flirted with a gentleman for some time, but they still remembered the way of it.

Supper was almost finished by the time Dominic found an opportunity to bring the conversation round to the topic of Alexandrov. 'I am sorry that Alexandrov was unable to stay for supper.'

'As am I, Duke,' replied Princess Volkonsky. 'But I could not deny him. He has such a long journey tomorrow and I believe he plans to start at first light. But he is an exceptional young man and I shall certainly invite him again, when he eventually returns to us.'

'You are all that is generous, Princess.' Dominic smiled down into her lined face. He knew all he needed to know. She planned to flee. He could not let that happen. Not again. But what was he going to do to stop her?

Chapter Eighteen

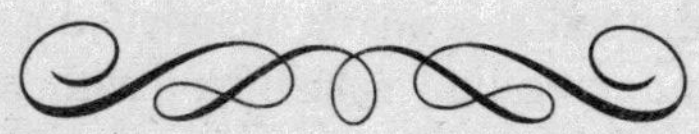

It was still dark when Alex's orderly arrived to wake her. He set down a lighted candle and a glass of tea on her nightstand, and a ewer of hot water in the basin. Then he left without a word. He was used to her requirements for privacy. She allowed herself a few seconds of peace, staring up at the ceiling and listening to the silence. There was not even a hint of birdsong yet.

She rose, then washed and dressed quickly, for she was determined to leave before the sun was up. It would be some hours yet before Dominic arrived to collect her. But she knew it was imperative for her to put as much distance as possible between them. If she had only just left when he appeared, he might even decide to come after her. If she was long gone, however, there would be no point. Even a man as determined as Dominic Aikenhead would surely give up.

Once dressed, she stood by the window to finish her tea. The sky outside was just beginning to lighten. Forcing herself to concentrate on the journey ahead, she buckled on her sabre, set her shako on her head and drew on her leather gloves. She had everything she needed for the journey. If her father was prepared to forgive her, she would not return here for three months.

She snuffed the candle, marched across the room, threw open the door and descended the stairs. By now, her orderly should have loaded her boxes into the carriage. All she had to do was take her seat and give the order to be off.

Strangely, her orderly was not waiting at the foot of the staircase as she had expected. And her boxes were still neatly piled against the wall. Her man must be out in the courtyard, seeing to the carriage. Perhaps it had arrived late.

She pulled open the heavy wooden door and stepped through, to find her orderly standing alone in the middle of the courtyard. Damnation! The carriage should have been here. 'What the hell is going on?' she said testily.

Her orderly, who had been gazing abstractedly in the direction of the gate, turned to face her. He looked shaken. 'Your Honour's carriage… That is to say…'

Alex heard the sound of horses' hooves on the cobbles of the yard. It came from beyond the corner of the building. The orderly looked towards the sound, goggle-eyed and open-mouthed.

'Where the hell is my carriage?' she repeated.

A large bay horse walked slowly into her line of vision. 'Good morning, Alexei Ivanovich.' It was the Duke of Calder. He was smiling down at her as if this encounter was the most normal thing in the world. 'It is such a beautiful day that I was sure you would prefer to ride than to travel to my estate in a hot, uncomfortable carriage. So I took the liberty of sending it away. Your orderly was just about to saddle Pegasus when you appeared.'

Alex could not move. She was staring at him, and she knew that her mouth was open. How could he be here? It was hours yet until their appointment. She dare not spend time with him. She had to get away. She had to.

Dominic was ignoring her. He had turned his attention to the orderly, frowning blackly and indicating with his hand that the man should get about his business.

Alex wanted to swear again. How dare he give instructions to her orderly? 'A moment—' Her throat was so tight that the words were inaudible. She coughed and forced herself to step forward.

'Forgive me, Alexei Ivanovich,' Dominic said, dismounting and drawing the reins over his horse's head. 'I have no place to be giving orders to your servants. But he was looking at me as though I had horns. And, to be frank, I did not want him eavesdropping on our conversation.' He stopped, almost in mid-sentence. 'Or perhaps he has no French?' He chuckled, shaking his head at the new thought. 'No matter. He has gone now. I do hope you slept well?'

Damn him! He was reminding her that she had run away from Volkonsky's house last night, run away from *him*.

'Luckily,' he continued smoothly, 'I am also an early riser. As you know, I like to exercise my horses well before breakfast.'

'Duke, I fear I cannot keep to our agreement.' Would he detect that slight tremor in her voice?

'Oh?' He raised an eyebrow. 'Forgive me, I must have misunderstood you last evening. You did not say that you were promised to another party.'

Alex could not meet his eyes. He knew that she had three months of leave ahead of her. She therefore had no excuse, other than a dire emergency, for breaking her engagement with him. But he had mentioned a party. That must mean there would be other guests! If she would not be alone with him, she might be able to come through this.

She was still hesitating when her orderly emerged from the stables, leading Pegasus. He whinnied joyfully and tossed his head several times at the sight of her. As ever, he was eager to be off. How could she be hard-hearted enough to send her dear old horse back to the stables? And for a three-month separation, too? She told herself that she could not do it, that she owed this to Pegasus. She would ride with

Dominic to his hired house, spend a few hours with him and his guests—though as far away as possible from the man himself—and then return here to begin her journey. It was the correct, the polite solution. Her previous plan had been rank cowardice.

Dominic was admiring her horse and stroking his neck. 'I can see why you named him as you did, Alexei Ivanovich. He is a remarkable animal.' Pegasus began snuffling around Dominic's gloved hand. 'No, no, I have nothing for you,' he said, laughing, 'but you shall have an apple when we reach our destination.'

Pegasus was not normally so friendly to strangers, but he had decided that Dominic Aikenhead was worthy of his trust. Just one more reason for loving the man, if she had needed any.

She gathered her wits enough to summon her orderly into the hallway and give him new instructions. 'I am going to ride out with the Duke of Calder. I…I had forgotten that I was engaged to meet him. However, my journey cannot be put off beyond today. Order the carriage to be here at four o'clock. I shall return by then, or shortly after. I must cover a goodly distance before it is dark. Is that clear?'

'Yes, your Honour.'

'Good.' Alex strode back out into the courtyard and mounted. She had regained her self-possession now. She was sure of that. She was going riding with the Duke of Calder. Nothing more. They would talk of last night's entertainment and she would tell him about Russia and Russian customs. She would be able to carry it off with no difficulty. His Russian servants would ensure that dinner was served to his guests at the normal early hour. And so she would certainly be able to return by four o'clock as she planned. At four o'clock, she would have said her final farewell to him, and she would be on her way to meet her father, for the first time in more than five years.

* * *

Dominic had managed to relax enough to enjoy the ride from the barracks to his hired house. For now, at least, she had abandoned her plans to flee. And, as long as they were together, there was a chance that they might regain the understanding they had had in England. And at the masquerade. She was an amazing woman. It was a pleasure to watch how she handled her magnificent stallion. He had rarely seen a man who could match her skill, and certainly no woman who could. By the time they had been riding together for half an hour, she had begun to relax and enjoy the exercise, perhaps because he was taking the greatest care to say and do nothing to unsettle her. He had done enough of that by turning up, unannounced, and dismissing her carriage. He had been right to do so, of course. His instincts had been telling him she was about to flee. And his instincts had been right.

'Ah, here we are. What do you think, Alexei Ivanovich?'

The red-gold rays of the rising sun were touching the front of a small country house faced with light-coloured stone. It looked absolutely beautiful as they rode up the drive. She turned to him, her eyes sparkling. 'It is splendid, Calder. And in this light, quite beautiful.'

'Hmm. Yes. It might even be worth what I'm paying for it.'

Her laughter rang out through the still morning air. Captivated by the sound, Dominic gazed at her for a second, vowing silently to capture the moment. The joy in her voice had warmed his heart. It was that same voice that had first captivated him, on the quay at Boulogne.

A groom appeared just as they dismounted. Dominic ordered the man to give Pegasus an apple, but he did not appear to understand. 'Not everyone in Russia speaks French, you know, Calder,' she said with a delighted grin, giving the groom some instructions in Russian. He nodded and led the horses away to the stables. 'Are all your servants Russian?' she asked. 'How on earth do you manage?'

Dominic shook his head. At that moment, the main entrance was thrown open. 'I have some of my own servants here.' He indicated the man holding the door. 'This is my valet, Cooper. I have left it to him, and his colleagues, to resolve the language problem.' He grinned mischievously. Cooper was trying to keep a straight face. He was finding it difficult.

'Breakfast is ready, I hope, Cooper?' In deference to his guest, Dominic had not lapsed into English. Most of his servants had very little French, but Cooper's was more than passable.

'Yes, your Grace. I have set it out in the small parlour.'

'Excellent. Lead the way, if you please.'

Alex did not really expect to find any other guests in the breakfast parlour. It was much too early in the day. She and Dominic would be eating alone together. She could feel her skin heating at the thought of it and her pulse beginning to race. She told herself she was being ridiculous. His servants would be present. What could possibly happen between them at this hour of the morning?

The table was laid with only two places, one at each end. He waved her to the seat facing the garden and cast a critical eye over the sideboard, on which there was an array of silver chafing dishes and a number of pots with steam rising from their spouts. 'Fresh coffee, tea and chocolate, your Grace,' Cooper said. 'And everything else exactly as you ordered.'

'Good. Thank you, Cooper.'

To Alex's consternation, the valet then left the room. They were alone!

'This will be breakfast in the English style, Alexei Ivanovich. We serve ourselves. The English have a profound dislike of hovering servants at breakfast.'

She managed a nod.

'Would you care to come and help yourself? You must be devilish sharp set after our ride. I know that I am.'

There was nothing she could do but comply. And try to eat.

'More coffee?'

They seemed to have been lingering over breakfast for hours. Alex had done her best to eat, very, very slowly, in hopes that, by the time they had finished, Dominic's other guests would have arrived. Her stomach had been churning so much that she had, in fact, eaten very little. She fervently hoped he had not noticed. A cavalry officer was expected to have a good appetite.

'More coffee, Alexandrov?' he said again.

That brought her out of her reverie. The coffee must be cold by now. If she asked for more, he would have to send for a servant to bring a fresh pot. 'Yes, please, Calder. I should enjoy another cup.' She thought she saw a flicker of impatience cross his face, but he said nothing. He rose and pulled the bell. It was a long time before Cooper appeared.

'Another pot of coffee, if you please, Cooper.'

'Yes, your Grace.' The valet picked up the pot. 'Would your Grace be wishing for anything else? More chocolate, perhaps?'

Dominic raised an eyebrow at Alex. She racked her brains for ideas, for any way of filling the time. Then she remembered. 'If it would not be too much trouble, Duke, I find I have a great fancy for toast and honey this morning.'

Dominic's eyes widened a fraction and then became hooded. He turned to give the instruction to his valet, but there was no need.

'Fresh coffee, your Grace, and toast and honey for Captain Alexandrov. At once, your Grace.' He bowed and quickly withdrew.

'Toast and honey? That does not sound very Russian to me.'

'No, it is not. I used to have it—' She stopped. Good God,

she had nearly betrayed herself again! 'I acquired the taste for it when we were in…in London.'

'Really? Always thought of it as nursery food, myself.' He drained the last of his coffee.

Alex gazed down at her plate. Yes, it was nursery food. Prepared by Meg and, on very special occasions, eaten by Alex and her mother, sitting together by the fire. For a few minutes, an awkward silence reigned. But Alex did not dare to allow it to continue. 'How did you happen upon this house, Calder? Have you taken a long lease on it?'

Dominic leaned back in his chair and began to tell her about his arrival in Russia and the difficulties he had encountered with the interminable bureaucracy. 'It is only a short lease,' he concluded. 'Six months.'

'Six months? You are prepared to endure the Russian winter? That is brave, Duke. Remember what it did to Bonaparte.'

Cooper entered with the pot of fresh coffee and Alex's toast and honey.

'I do not expect to have Cossacks nipping at my heels, Alexei Ivanovich. And I am sure that the house will be comfortable, even in a Russian winter.'

Cooper finished filling Alex's coffee cup and placed the pot at Dominic's elbow. At his master's nod, he bowed and left the room. They were alone again. Alex busied herself with spreading the golden honey to the very edges of a slice of toast. She took a tiny bite and sighed. Then she closed her eyes. It was like being back in the warm cocoon of the nursery.

'I shall have to visit the Pulteney Hotel for breakfast. Their toast and honey is obviously something quite remarkable.'

Alex started. The clear irony in his tone had reminded her of where she was, and the danger she was in. 'We…I have a confession to make, Calder. When I was a child, there was always honey in the pantry. I loved the taste, even then. I am afraid I used to steal it, quite often.'

'Ah. That would account for the far-away look on your face. Were you remembering the taste, or the whipping you received when you were caught?'

She gulped. Lies had a habit of becoming more and more entangled. 'The taste,' she said at last. 'It always reminds me of my childhood.' That was the truth.

'Well, do enjoy it. I can always send for more, if Cooper has not brought enough. Take your time. We are in no hurry.'

She touched her napkin to her lips. 'At what time are your other guests expected? Are you planning a dinner in the Russian style?'

He was no longer looking at her. As she spoke, he had half turned away and was gazing rather abstractedly into the garden. 'I beg your pardon, Alexandrov,' he said after a long pause. 'No, I do not plan a dinner in the Russian style. It requires far too many servants. Dinner will be laid out at two o'clock, in deference to the Russian custom, but it will be a cold collation. You do not object, I hope?'

She could not object. She shook her head and took another bite of her honey-smeared toast. 'Though how I shall eat again so soon, after all this—' she waved a hand in the direction of the chafing dishes '—I do not know.' She wiped her mouth for the last time and threw down her napkin. 'I am sorry, Calder. Much as I should like to, I cannot eat another bite.'

He laughed and rose. 'Well, if you should wish for toast and honey at dinner, I am sure Cooper will be happy to oblige. Would you like to come out on to the terrace? The view down to the river is splendid. And there are some fine shady walks we might explore. It is already too hot to be walking out in the open, I think.' He opened the French doors on to the terrace and led the way into the garden.

Alex hesitated on the threshold. 'Should we not wait until your other guests have arrived?'

He turned back. The look on his face was an odd mixture

of satisfaction and chagrin, like a child caught out in mischief who knows that he will receive no punishment from an indulgent parent. 'I ask your pardon if I have misled you, Alexandrov. I am expecting no other guests today.'

By two o'clock, they had exhausted the diversions of the garden. They had strolled down to the river and admired the views. They had visited the shrubbery, and the kitchen garden. And Alex had told him so much about life in Russia that she was running out of things to say.

He broke the awkward silence by inviting her to return to the house for the promised cold collation.

This time, there were bound to be servants. She would not have to endure any more hours alone in his company. It had been so difficult to keep her distance from him, to resist the urge to touch him. She resolved that, after the meal, she would insist on riding back to the barracks. Alone.

Cooper was waiting for them in the hallway. 'This way, your Grace, Captain.' He led them down the corridor to a room Alex had not entered before. The valet opened the door, standing back to let them pass through.

'Is everything prepared, Cooper?'

'Yes, your Grace.'

'Thank you. We shall not need you.'

Alex looked around the room in wonderment. And sudden concern. This was not at all what she had expected. There was no dining table in the middle of the room, and no dining chairs. On the far side, there was a long table draped in white linen and laden with a huge selection of the finest meats and fruits. There were decanters of wine, and crystal glasses and bottles of champagne in a wine cooler. But, apart from those, the room contained only a long sofa and a two small occasional tables.

Dominic opened a bottle of champagne and poured two

glasses, handing one to her. 'A toast, I think. To friendship.' He touched his glass to hers and waited.

'To friendship,' she whispered, taking a tiny sip. Then she frowned up at him. 'This is a very unusual dining room, Duke. Is this another of your strange English customs?'

'No.' His voice sounded abnormally deep. With careful deliberation, he removed her glass and set it down, alongside his own. 'No. It is desperation.' With a long groan, he pulled Alex into his arms and began to kiss her so fiercely that she could barely catch her breath.

She managed a strangled cry at last. 'Dominic, no! We must not!'

He raised his head from hers and drew away a little. His eyes were black, and unfocused. 'No?' It sounded more like a groan than a word.

'There are servants here. And I…' She indicated her masculine uniform.

He laid his palms against her cheeks. 'There is only one servant in the house. My valet. He will not disturb us. We are quite alone. And as for your military garb…' He put his hands to her waist and unbuckled her sword belt. Then he laid both belt and sabre carefully on the sofa. Her fur-trimmed pelisse followed. 'Better,' he said in a low voice that shuddered all the way down to the toes of her boots.

From the moment he had laid his hands on her cheeks, she had been quite unable to move. He wanted her, completely, desperately. As he had wanted her once before, at the masquerade. Then, he had denied himself, in order to safeguard her. Now he wanted to make her his. She stood still, waiting for him to return to her. She wanted this too. It would be their one day together, for all their lives. It was right for both of them.

'Alexandra?' He sounded a little uncertain. He must have seen something in her face. She smiled and held out her arms to him, but he shook his head, smiling a little wistfully back at her. He lifted her hand and kissed it. 'Not here, my lady.' His voice was barely a whisper. 'Will you permit me?' She nodded and allowed herself to be led out of the room and up the stairs to a vast bedchamber on the floor above.

He kicked the door closed and dragged her into his arms. 'Oh, my sweet. How I have longed for this moment.' His mouth sought hers. His fingers were desperately fumbling with the buttons and frogging of her jacket, but he was too careful of her honour to rip the jacket from her body. It was just as it had been in the masquerade garden. Her own practised fingers must do this.

She pushed away from him. Holding his gaze unwaveringly, she slowly began to undo the buttons, starting at her throat. First one, then a second, a third. He watched, transfixed. There were so many tiny buttons. And she refused to be hurried. He would be made to wait. For the prize would be all the sweeter. For both of them. Like the finest golden honey.

She ran her tongue over her lower lip. He shuddered. His fists were clenched and his neck muscles were corded with the strain he was under. But he made no move towards her.

Another tiny button. And another. Her fingers were becoming clumsy under his fixed, desperate stare. As she undid the final button, his control snapped. He lunged forward and dragged the jacket down her arms. Then he dipped his mouth to her breast, pushing aside the fine linen shirt.

It was too much to bear. 'You! You, too,' she moaned, pulling at his cravat and trying to push his jacket from his shoulders. 'I want to see you, Dominic. All of you.'

'It shall be as you wish, my lady.' Quickly, he peeled off his jacket and dropped it to the floor. His cravat followed, his waistcoat, and then his shirt.

Alex gasped at the sight of his half-naked body. He was magnificent.

'Now you,' he said, nodding at her, his eyes intent.

She felt no shame. She wanted him to admire her body as she admired his. Slowly, very slowly, holding his gaze once again, she undid the buttons of her shirt until it hung loose on her shoulders, exposing her throat and the cleft between her breasts. Now was the moment. She relaxed her shoulders and arms so that the shirt slipped to the floor. She stood fully exposed before him. And proud. She saw him swallow and lick his lips. His breathing was laboured now. He put his hands to the waistband of his breeches. Then he looked across at her and waited.

Very deliberately, she did the same.

He raised a hand. It was not quite steady. 'Wait. Let me remove your boots.' He took a step forward and knelt at her feet, pulling off her boots one by one. She made to do the same for him, but he swung her into his arms instead. 'Please, Alexandra. No more. You are tormenting me beyond endurance.' He carried her across to the bed and laid her down on it.

'Would you like to do the rest yourself?' she said, marvelling at her own shamelessness. She loved this man. She wanted him. Nothing else mattered.

He undid the fastenings of her breeches and slowly rolled them down her body, baring her secrets to his hungry gaze. She barely heard the sound as the last of her clothing fell to the floor. She lay back on the soft pillows, luxuriating in her own wantonness, waiting.

He dragged off his own boots and the rest of his clothing. And then he came to her. It was everything she had been dreaming about, everything she had longed for in the days and weeks since she had discovered her love for him. He kissed, he teased, he touched, until her skin was aflame and her body was crying out for his possession. Still he waited, now sucking at her breast, now nuzzling at the tender skin of her belly, down, down towards the core of her.

'Dominic, please.' The low cry seemed to be dragged from her throat, without conscious thought. It had to be now.

He sighed out a long, warm breath against her belly and slowly raised his body so that he was looming over her, his eyes gazing down into hers. He touched a hand to the inside of her thigh. He was still waiting, still unsure. She bucked her hips against his body. She needed him. Desperately.

Putting his lips to hers, he entered her in one long powerful thrust.

Her cry was not of pain, but of joy at their union. Her love was overflowing. It seemed to surround them both as the rhythm of their love-making caught them and carried them beyond thought and beyond reason. Fulfilment beckoned and burst upon them like a summer dawn.

Chapter Nineteen

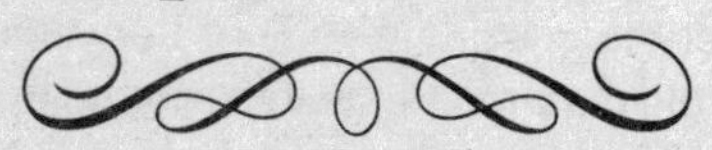

It was so odd to be lying in bed in broad daylight.

The thought came to Alex unbidden, as soon as she awoke. On its heels came the realisation of where she was, and what she had done. She had allowed her passion for Dominic to overcome her reason. And now she faced ruin, for he did not love her. Even if he did, he would never make her his wife. An English Duke did not marry a woman who had spent years serving as a man in the Russian army.

Dominic was still asleep, one bare arm thrown out across the coverlet, the other next to her cheek. She could feel the warmth of his breath on her skin. She gazed at his beloved face, relaxed in sleep, and still so close to hers. There was a tiny frown between his eyebrows. She wanted to reach out and smooth it away, as she had done once before. She wanted… but she could not have.

Carefully, she eased her body away from his and slipped out of the bed. Her uniform still lay where it had been dropped, in a trail from the door to the bed. She picked up the pieces one by one, trying to shut out the memories of how they had been removed. She must not think about him, about how it had been between them. He had found out her secret, and taken her virtue. If she were honest, she would have to admit that she had surrendered it gladly. But she could not bear the thought that he might now despise her, as a soiled, fallen woman. She pushed that despairing thought out of her mind. For now, the only imperative was to get away from this house without being caught.

She tiptoed out of the bedchamber and into the dressing room where she hurriedly donned her clothes. Her fingers were clumsier than usual, in spite of her years of practice at dressing on cold dark mornings, ready to go into battle. Eventually it was done. Carrying her boots, she stole downstairs to retrieve her pelisse, and her sword belt.

Were there servants about? She must not be seen like this, creeping about in her stockinged feet. She paused on the half-landing, listening intently. There was no sound at all.

She padded down the last flight of stairs and made her way to the dining room where it had all begun. The food and wine was exactly as they had left it. The part-filled champagne glasses still stood on the little table. The froth and the bubbles were long gone. The champagne was flat and dull.

Like your hopes, Alex.

She refused to heed that voice, though she knew it was her own guilty conscience. Instead, she busied herself with pulling on her boots and buckling her sabre belt. She draped her pelisse over her shoulder and caught up her shako. It had all taken just a couple of minutes. Surely there had not yet been time for Dominic to discover that she had gone?

It seemed not, for when she peeped out of the room, there was still no sound in the house. She stole down the corridor to the hall, cursing silently every time one of her spurs clinked or her boot scraped on the floor. At last she reached the main door. She opened it, praying that it would not creak. Then she was out, into the sunshine, and the door had been closed behind her. It was now safe to run.

A few yards from the stables, she slowed to a brisk walk. The groom must not be allowed to see her running, lest he suspect something. She set her shako on her head and marched into the stables. 'Where are you, groom?' she called in her best military voice.

He appeared from the back of one of the empty stalls. From the look of him, he had been asleep, but he was speedy enough when she ordered him to saddle Pegasus. Just a few minutes more, and she would be away!

She deliberately made to mount and then paused, taking her boot back out of the stirrup. 'Ah, yes. I had almost forgot.' She turned back to the groom. 'I have a message from the Duke. He asked me to convey his orders, since he has no Russian. You are to—' She shrugged theatrically. 'It's extremely strange. But, of course, he is a foreigner. And foreign ways are often most odd.' She proceeded to tell him exactly what he was required to do.

His eyes grew rounder and rounder as she spoke. 'Are you sure, your Honour? There is no mistake?'

'There is no mistake,' she snapped. 'It is not for you to question his orders. And I should warn you that the English are very fierce with servants who disobey.' The groom was cringing now. 'Do exactly as he bids you. He is the master here now.' She passed him a couple of small coins.

The groom stowed them quickly in his pocket and bowed very low. 'Yes, Excellency. At once.'

Alex mounted and walked Pegasus out into the yard. As she looked back, she noted that the groom was gathering up an armful of tack. The man was now too frightened of his strange foreign master to disobey. Good. She touched her heel to her horse's flank and galloped off towards St Petersburg.

Alex stood in front of the glass, assessing her reflection. Was it really only a day ago that she had stood here, congratulating herself on looking just like a man? She looked different now. So much had changed.

She ran a hand down her right side, over her rib-cage, her waist, her thigh. Her waist seemed narrower, her hips rounder, more womanly than before. The breast of her jacket seemed tighter, and fuller. Her lean, masculine shape seemed to have changed in the space of a single day. She put her hand to her belly and pressed, wondering fearfully, and somehow a little hopefully, if new life could be stirring there. She should never have allowed it to happen. And yet, it had been the most fulfilling moment of her whole life. She had been at one with the man she loved. For that, she might have to sacrifice everything. And she would do it again.

If there was a child…? Dominic's child. She had a fleeting vision of a tousle-haired little boy crawling around at her feet. The child looked up at her, with Dominic's deep blue eyes. If only—

'Your Honour.' Her orderly had appeared in the doorway.

Alex quickly removed her hand from her belly and began to rearrange the set of her sword belt.

'Your Honour, the carriage is waiting below. Everything is prepared.'

'Good. I shall be down presently.' She set her shako on her head and adjusted her sabre. She had a long, long journey ahead of her. Her object now must be a reconciliation with her father. She must try to forget everything that had happened, these past twenty-four hours, to forget that he was here in Russia, to forget how much she loved him. She needed to be accepted back into her father's house, now more than ever. For, if she were carrying Dominic's child, she would have nowhere else to go.

'Alex?' Dominic murmured her pet name in a haze of sleepy contentment and nuzzled his cheek more deeply into the pillow. But it was not enough, not now that he was awake, and remembering. He needed to feel her softness against his naked body. He rolled over and reached for her. The bed was empty, and cold.

For a second, he lay totally still, unable to focus. What on earth—? He threw the covers aside and sprang up. The situation was clear at a glance. His own clothes were strewn around the room where they had fallen during that blissful entanglement, but there was not a single stitch of Alex's uniform to be seen. A knot of pain formed in his gut. She could not have fled! Not again! He prayed that he would be in time to catch her.

Grabbing his dressing gown, he raced out of the room, struggling to force his arms into the sleeves as he went. Out on the landing, the house was eerily silent. 'Cooper!' he yelled. No answer. Idiot! Of course, there was no answer. He himself had ordered Cooper to take himself off down to the kitchens, and not to dare to show his face again unless he was summoned. The other servants would not yet be returned from their day out. The house was empty. Just as he had ordered it to be. And Alex had gone. He had lost her, yet again. What a fool he was! He thumped his clenched fist against the baluster rail and cursed till his words echoed back from the walls. It achieved nothing. He was losing precious time.

He raced back into his bedchamber and hurriedly threw on his clothes. He would ride after her. She must have gone back to St Petersburg, to the barracks. She could not have so great a start on him, but if he did not catch her there, he would surely be able to come up with her on the road? She had been planning a journey by carriage. A determined man, on a good horse, could certainly overhaul a carriage. He would be able to find her before the day was out.

He forced his feet into his riding boots, totally ignoring the fact that his hands were bare. Cooper would ring a peal over him for getting finger marks on the glossy leather. Well,

Cooper could set himself to restoring the shine from scratch. If the man had had the sense to prevent Alex's flight, none of this would have happened.

Dominic clattered down the staircase to the entrance hall. He was being unfair to Cooper, and he knew it, but, just at this moment, he was so frustrated that he would happily have strangled anyone who crossed his path. He wrenched the door open and ran round to the stables.

'Ho, there!' he shouted, running into the stables. There was no answer. The stables were completely empty. All the horses were gone.

Dominic skidded to a halt on the flagged stone floor. It was impossible! Horses could not just disappear!

He strode out to the courtyard and looked about him. No sign. He ran round to the back of the stable block. Nothing. Then back to the terrace, and the garden. The whole place was totally deserted. Even from the highest vantage point in the garden, he could see no one. And no horses. Whatever Alex had done—and he was in no doubt that this was her doing—she had done it brilliantly. Like the seasoned campaigner she was, she had decided on her objective and then found exactly the right means of achieving it. He wanted to wring her beautiful neck. And yet he had to admire her presence of mind. She was beyond price.

Until the servants returned to the house, he was marooned. Alex had disappeared. She had won.

'The servants have this moment returned, your Grace.' Cooper quietly removed the untouched plate of food from the little table.

Dominic paused in his pacing. 'Have a horse saddled immediately. I am going back to St Petersburg.'

'I am afraid that is not possible, your Grace. There are no riding horses. Only the old farm horse that pulls the cart. The other servants used it to go to town and back.'

'Well, then—' Dominic stopped himself in mid-sentence. He was so desperate that he had been about to order a cart horse to be harnessed to a carriage. A useless notion, especially as the horse had already done two long journeys in the course of the day. It would not be fit for another. And it would soon be dark. What the hell had that confounded groom done with the riding horses? Dominic continued to pace the floor.

'Will there be anything else, your Grace?'

'Not until that blasted groom returns with the horses. Is there any sign of him?'

'No, your Grace.'

'I'll flay him alive,' Dominic muttered through clenched teeth.

'You will perhaps allow me to say, your Grace, that that might be unwise? Seeing as we are in a foreign country, you understand. The Russkis might not take kindly to such a thing. With one of their own.' He spoke with such an expression of concern on his face that Dominic was forced to laugh.

'Thank you, Cooper.' He shook his head. 'I can assure you that I am not totally insane. Yet. Though, if I am forced to pace this floor for much longer, you may have need of the strait-jacket before the night is out.'

Cooper allowed himself a wry smile. He had served Dominic for many years. They understood each other. 'I believe it is at the bottom of one of the trunks, your Grace. I'll break it out, and press it, shall I? Just in case?'

Dominic knew he could not win this exchange. 'Oh, very well. Put that plate down again. If it will stop your damned impertinence, I'll even eat something.'

'And that is the truth, Meg. All of it.'

Alex's old nurse shook her head sorrowfully. Then she came to sit beside Alex on the window seat and patted her hand. 'Look on the bright side, dearie. At least you now know you are not carrying his child.'

Alex swallowed a sob. She knew it was better this way. Once Dominic had left Russia, she could rejoin her regiment and resume her career as if nothing had changed. No one but Meg knew what had happened. No one else need ever know.

But everything had changed. Alex was a different person. Her longing for the army life had lessened now. And the war was over. Her remaining career in the cavalry, such as it was, would consist of guard duty, and drills and exercises. And interminable jests from her fellow officers about her lack of beard. If there had been a babe, it would all have been different.

If there had been a babe, she would not have been sorry.

'There, there, dearie. Chin up. Your papa will be waiting for you downstairs. He wanted to ride out with you, remember? He wants the whole district to see you in your fine uniform, and your decorations. I'd never have imagined he would be so proud of you, not after you ran away, without a word.'

Alex sniffed and scrabbled around for her handkerchief. 'You're right, Meg.' She blew her nose. 'It's just— Well, it's over now, and I must put it all behind me. I am back in the bosom of my family and more than happy to be so. Papa has been so kind and forbearing since I returned. He has never once mentioned the broken betrothal. Nor has my stepmother. I must admit, I thought they would at least insist on my wearing women's dress.'

'No, no, dearie. You're a Hussar. And your father is delighted to have you back home. He accepts you as you are.'

Meg was right. Alex rose and went to stand in front of the glass. She was wearing her second-best uniform, just as she had done when she arrived. Her father had welcomed her with open arms, tears pouring down his old, lined cheeks. Ever since, he had treated her like an honoured guest and had never once upbraided her for her disobedience or her years of silence. It was much, much more than she deserved, but she had accepted it all, her heart warmed by his love.

'Today, since he wills it, I shall ride in my uniform. But tomorrow, Meg, I want to wear the Cossack tunic that Papa had made for me years ago. I know it would fit. Do you have it still?'

Meg went to the clothes chest and dug out the Cossack *chekmen* that Alex had worn more than five years before. It looked almost as good as new when she held it up.

Alex smiled. It brought back so many memories. 'When I wear it, Papa will remember how we rode together and how he filled my head full of stories about his life in the Hussars. It will be as if the years of my absence had never been.'

Meg shook her head. 'If you say so, Miss Alex. I'm sure your papa will smile on you, whatever you wear. Now, off you go. Don't keep him waiting.'

Alex looked at her old nurse and saw sorrow in her eyes. Meg knew, as Alex knew, that it was not possible to turn back time. Alex was a woman now, a woman with a sore heart. No matter how she tried to right it, nothing would ever be the same again.

Alex. Dominic wanted her—he needed her—but she was lost to him. As if she had never been. At first, he had been near despair, but then he had recovered just enough self-control to try to pursue her. He knew he had become as surly as a bear, but it had been nearly three weeks now, and still he had no news of her. The officers of her regiment had stubbornly refused to provide any information about Captain Alexandrov. Major Zass had been equally unforthcoming. Everyone said that Alexandrov was on leave, and would return in a month or two, in the normal way.

After a while, Dominic had had to stop making enquiries. It had begun to look so peculiar, that a visiting English Duke should concern himself with a mere captain of Hussars. Dominic was desperate to find her, but not at the cost of ruining her reputation. He owed her that.

Her reputation might already be beyond repair, if she was carrying his child. That idea was haunting him. He had made love to her without thought for the consequences, but only for his own pleasure, his own need. It had never occurred to him that she might be a virgin. Dear God, he had behaved worse than the worst rakehell in Europe. If he had lost her, it was no more than he deserved. But it was not right to punish Alex, for she was not at fault. He had to find her, and make amends for what he had done. If she was carrying his child, he would marry her. And if she was not, he would still offer for her, though the choice would be hers. After the cavalier way he had treated her, he would not be surprised if she preferred to return to her life as a soldier. If she insisted on that, he would have to let her go.

But first, he must find her. It now seemed that his only hope was the Emperor himself. Dominic had presented himself to Prince Volkonsky every day for more than a week. On each occasion, Volkonsky had noted Dominic's request for an audience. On each occasion, the audience had been denied. And in two days' time, the Emperor was leaving for Vienna.

Dominic adjusted his cravat, tucked his hat under his arm and climbed into his carriage for one more journey to St Petersburg.

'Good morning, Duke.' Prince Volkonsky bowed, exactly as he always did.

Dominic returned the bow. 'Good morning, your Excellency. May I hope that today his Imperial Majesty might have time to receive me?'

'It is difficult, I fear. His Majesty has many matters on his mind just at present. If you would confide your business to me, Duke, I might be able to help you, or to persuade his Majesty to give you a few moments. Without knowing the nature of the matter…' He raised an eyebrow.

Dominic was shaking his head. 'I am afraid that my

business is of a very private nature. I can confide it only to his Majesty.'

Volkonsky pursed his lips. 'Pray take a seat in the anteroom, Duke. I shall call you, if your presence is required.'

Dominic nodded and complied. He had no choice. He sat, he paced, he gazed out of the window, and then he sat again. It was the routine he had adopted on each occasion to pass the hours until Volkonsky came to tell him that the Emperor would receive no more visitors that day.

As he paced, he remembered. He remembered her bravery and her wit, her intelligence and her passion. He remembered how it had felt to be holding her glorious body, pliant in his arms. He remembered that his joining with Alex had taken him to a level of ecstasy he had never before experienced. And he remembered that he had lost her.

'The Emperor will receive you now, Duke.'

'What?' Dominic spun round from the window. Volkonsky was standing in the open doorway with a rather wry smile on his face. 'I beg your pardon, your Excellency. You startled me. Did you say that the Emperor would receive me?'

'Yes, Duke. Pray follow me.' He led Dominic through into his own office and then to the door in the far wall, where he knocked. He opened the door, bowed, and said quietly, 'His Grace the Duke of Calder, your Majesty.' Then he stood back to allow Dominic to pass through into the Emperor's room.

It was a huge room, hung with paintings and mirrors. To Dominic's surprise, it contained almost no furniture. It was dominated by an enormous gilded desk, and by the man who sat behind it. The Emperor waved Dominic forward. Obediently, Dominic walked to within two paces of the desk and bowed low.

'You have been asking to see me for many days, Duke. I take it that it is business of some import?'

'I believe so, your Majesty.'

'On behalf of your Government?'

'No, your Majesty.' Dominic knew better than to lie about that. 'It is a…a family matter. It is imperative that I talk to Captain Alexandrov of the Mariupol Hussars. I have enquired at his regiment, but it appears that the Captain is on leave. No one can tell me where I may find him.'

'You wish to write to him?'

'No, your Majesty. In this particular matter, I need to speak to him, face to face. If I had his direction, I would travel to meet him, but no one seems to have it.'

'Hmm.' The Emperor tapped a fingernail thoughtfully on his desk. Then he looked up, straight into Dominic's face, and said, 'Why is it, Duke, that you come to me with this request? It is not normal for an Emperor to act as a enquiry point for junior cavalry officers.'

Dominic tried to think quickly, though it was difficult when fixed by that steely gaze. This was not the same affable man who had been a guest at the Pulteney Hotel. In his own realm, he was formidable. 'Alexandrov mentioned to me that he had been commissioned at your Majesty's own hands. I therefore thought—forgive me if this is an impertinence, sir—that you might know his likely whereabouts.' That was a pretty lame explanation, and Dominic knew it.

The Emperor knew it, too. It was obvious from the incredulous expression on his face. 'I do not accuse you of lying, Duke. I know you for a man of honour. But I am of the opinion that you have not told me the whole. I may be in a position to assist you, but without the full facts, I am afraid I could not do so.' He clasped his hands together on the desk and waited.

In the silence, Dominic saw that he had two stark choices. He could betray Alex's secret to the Emperor, explaining that he wished to find her in order to marry her; or he could say nothing, and lose her.

The Emperor's gaze was very stern. Did he know that Captain Alexandrov was a woman? Almost certainly not. It was unthinkable that he would have allowed a woman to serve as a cavalry officer. If Dominic betrayed Alex's secret, he would ruin her. She could certainly never return to the Hussars. He had thought he could offer her a choice about marriage to him. In truth, the moment he said a word to the Emperor, her choice would be gone. She would have to marry Dominic or become a social outcast. In order to save her—and perhaps also the babe she carried—he had to betray her. The alternative was to lose her for good. He felt a terrible weight descend on his shoulders. It grew heavier by the second.

He had no choice. He took a deep breath. 'Sir—'

The words died on his lips. It was not for him to decide the future of the woman he loved. It would be for his own selfish reasons, because he wanted her for himself. In that moment of bleak self-knowledge, Dominic understood much. He had followed her to Russia because he loved her. She meant more to him than any woman ever could, past, present or future. If he truly loved her, he would prove it by keeping her secret and allowing her to decide her own future. Even if it meant that Dominic would never set eyes on her again.

'Are you unwell, Duke?'

Damnation! He must have turned pale. It was no wonder. His gut was churning and he felt quite light-headed. How was it that he had been so blind? He had been haunted by Alex for weeks and yet he had never realised that he was in love with her. 'No, your Majesty,' he said, a little hoarsely. 'Thank you, I am perfectly well. It is that…I find I am in something of a dilemma. It is a matter of honour. The reason I need to see Captain Alexandrov relates to a confidence. I fear it is not mine to share, even with your Majesty. I ask your pardon for having troubled you.'

The Emperor raised a hand to his chin and stared at Dominic for what seemed a very long time. Then he nodded. 'Very well, Duke. That being the case, you may withdraw.

Perhaps you would ask Volkonsky to attend me for a moment, as you go out? He still has some matters to discuss with you, I imagine, but I shall not detain him for many minutes. You will be able to wait?'

'Of course, your Majesty.' Dominic bowed low, took a few steps backwards and left the room. In the antechamber, he relayed the Emperor's message.

Volkonsky made for the door. 'Will you wait, Duke?' he asked, turning for a moment. 'I do not expect to be long with his Majesty.'

Dominic bowed, and Volkonsky disappeared into the Emperor's room.

Dominic, alone but for the lackey stationed at the door, began to pace. Suddenly, he wanted to scream out his frustration. He had found the woman he loved, though it had taken him long enough to recognise it, and now he had lost her. Faced with a choice between her honour and his desire, he had had to let her go. A shaft of indescribable pain lanced through him. He stumbled and put a hand to the panelled wall for support. If only…if only he had told her while she lay in his arms. Then, at least, he would have known whether she could ever begin to return his love. As it was, he would never know. There was passion between them—of course there was—sudden, flaring, consuming passion, but that did not prove that she loved him. The fact that she had fled from him made it much more likely that she did not.

'Ah, Duke, you are still here. Good.' Volkonsky hurried back to his desk and began to write. 'I shall not keep you above a moment.'

Dominic had forced himself to straighten at the Court Minister's entrance. Now he murmured a polite response and turned to stare out of the window. He needed to be away from here, away from Russia. If he could not have her love, he needed to put at least a thousand miles between them.

Volkonsky rose, holding several papers in his hand, some of which bore wax seals. 'I think these are what you need, Duke.' He held them out.

Puzzled, Dominic took the papers and looked at them. They were in Russian and meant nothing to him. 'I am sorry, your Excellency, but I speak no Russian.'

Volkonsky smiled. 'They are travel permits, Duke, and orders to allow you to requisition the Imperial horses at the relay stations. You will find them invaluable. Since you have no Russian, his Majesty has commanded that an Imperial courier should be provided who speaks both Russian and French. He will wait on you at first light tomorrow.'

Dominic did not dare to hope. 'May I ask where his Majesty wishes me to go?'

Volkonsky chuckled and his smile broadened. 'Your destination is written on the topmost sheet, Duke. His Majesty has decided that you shall be permitted—nay, assisted—to travel to meet Alexei Ivanovich Alexandrov. He is to be found at the estate of Count Ivan Kuralkin. His father.'

Chapter Twenty

The door closed behind the servant. Dominic was alone at last, for almost the first time in several hundred miles of travelling. The Emperor's French-speaking courier had been indispensable, but the man was incapable of taking the hint that his endless flow of conversation was unwelcome.

Dominic surveyed the room impatiently in hopes that it might tell him something about Alex's family. It contained the usual stove, unlit in the fine weather, a number of slightly worn leather sofas and chairs, a splendid French clock on top of a gilded table, and a pianoforte. There were portraits on the walls and an icon opposite the door. There were also three statues dotted around and some rather splendid vases, in wildly different styles. It struck Dominic that they might all have been collected by Alex's father, during his travels with the army. And Alex had been at his side. No wonder she loved the nomadic military life.

The door opened at his back. She was here! He spun round, the words of greeting rising to his lips.

The woman in the doorway was old, and wearing the apron and cap of a servant. Dominic frowned down at her. She ignored it. Closing the door behind her, she advanced into the room and dropped a tiny, impudent curtsy. 'Good afternoon, your Grace,' she said, in English. 'My name is Meg Fraser. I was personal maid to Captain Alexandrov's mother, and nurse to the Captain.'

Dominic waited. If Alex had not come herself, it boded ill.

'Captain Alexandrov presents his compliments, but regrets that he is indisposed and will be unable to see you. He is extremely sorry that you have had a wasted journey.' She turned to leave.

'Alex is ill?' Damn! He had not meant to say her name. Was it the babe?

'Captain Alexandrov is indisposed,' the woman repeated flatly.

'Is there any indication of when he will be well enough to receive visitors?'

She shook her head. 'I am afraid not.'

'I... Forgive me, but are you in the Captain's confidence, Mrs Fraser?'

She stared at him with narrowed eyes. 'Why do you ask that, your Grace?'

'Because I have come a great way to see him. And, after this, I must leave Russia. There are...things that must be said between us, before I go. Could you...would you convey that message to Captain Alexandrov?' He felt in his pocket for some coins and held them out to her.

She sniffed loudly and put her hands behind her back. 'I will convey your message, your Grace, but I will not take your silver.'

Alex had decided she would not see him. Perhaps she hated him now. He had to know the truth of it, but this old woman stood between them. And he was making a very poor fist of turning her into an ally. 'I beg your pardon, Mrs Fraser. It was certainly not my intention to insult you. I have come a long way to plead my case with Alex...Alexei Ivanovich. I would esteem it a favour if you would convey my very strong desire to see him. Please.'

She looked him up and down assessingly. 'I will tell Captain Alexandrov,' she said with a tiny nod, and whisked herself out of the door.

Dominic was alone again, to wait, and wonder, and worry. Would she really deny him? If she was ill, in the early stages of pregnancy, she needed a husband who would take care of her. She needed Dominic. She must—

The door opened. It was barely two minutes since the servant had left, but Alex herself was standing in the threshold. She was no longer in uniform, but she was not in female garb either. She was wearing some sort of long tunic, in the Cossack style, over loose trousers and boots. Her head was bare. The flowing tunic, so unlike her gold-trimmed Hussar uniform, reminded him of the soft, feminine gowns he longed to provide for her. He caught his breath at the thought of her in silk and satin.

She was gazing levelly at him. She looked perfectly calm, apart from the slight hint of a blush on her cheekbones. She closed the door quietly at her back and faced him. 'You have travelled a very long way on the chance that I might be here, Duke,' she said calmly, in French. 'Was that altogether wise?'

Her glorious voice rippled through him like the sudden melting of winter snow into a rushing stream. 'I would have travelled across half the world, on the chance of seeing you, of hearing your voice,' he replied softly. Nothing but the truth would do now.

'Indeed?' She sounded cold and distant. She was going to turn him away.

His words flooded out. 'Alex. Listen to me, Alex, I beg you. I have come to ask you to be my wife. After what passed between us, I know that you may be carrying my child. If that is so, you stand in need of a husband. And I…I should be the man to support you. I would never desert you. Will you not accept my offer?'

She walked slowly into the room but, instead of stopping beside him, she continued to the window. She stood there, with her back to him, looking out. 'I am very sensible of the honour you do me, Duke,' she said tightly, 'but you must know that I could not accept.'

Dominic clenched his fists and bit his tongue. He must hear her out.

'His Grace the Duke of Calder, to marry a foreign woman, of little pedigree, and one who has disgraced herself by serving in the army, for years, as a man? I think not, Duke. You would not wish to have it said that your wife had warmed the beds of half the Russian army before she warmed yours.'

That was too much. 'You did not,' he growled. 'You were an innocent when I took you to my bed. We both know that. You may be carrying my child, Alex, and yet you refuse me? You are a stubborn, mutton-headed woman. Why do you insist on taking such a risk?'

She whirled on him. 'How dare you insult me so?' she said, suddenly reverting to English. 'The mutton-headed member of this company is you! As it happens, I am *not* carrying your child. And I would not marry you even if I were! Of all the arrogant, overbearing, cork-brained—'

With a gasp of relief, Dominic seized her in a ruthless grip. The moment she had begun to speak English again, he had understood what she felt, and what he should do. He began to kiss her with the fervour of desperation. For several seconds, she resisted, trying to push herself out of his embrace, but then he gentled the kiss and she responded to him. Her balled fists unclenched against his chest and one arm stole around his neck. Their kiss deepened even more, driven by their gnawing hunger for each other.

After a long time, Dominic put her from him. He was

laughing. Half-relief, half-joy. 'I have you now, Alex, my love. The moment you began to berate me, you betrayed what you felt.' He lifted her hand to his lips. The hand that had haunted him for so long. Strong, lean, beautiful. Then, kissing one brown knuckle after every word, he said softly, 'I—love—you—Alex.' His final kiss brought an answering sigh from her. He raised his head. And waited. He did not let go of her hand.

'I will not try to deceive you. I know I could not succeed. I do love you, Dominic, but I am not carrying your child. And I will not marry you. I am not fit.'

He ignored that. She loved him. Nothing else mattered. He lifted her off her feet and whirled her round and round. As he set her down again, she staggered a little. He put a steadying arm around her and drew her down to sit beside him on one of the leather sofas. 'We love each other, Alex. Is that not enough? I could never love another woman as I love you. If you reject me, you will not spare me from the dishonour you fear. You will consign me to despair. I cannot live without you, Alex. I need you to be my wife.'

She gave a little mew of pain.

'But if you are determined to refuse me, if you wish to return to your army life, I will not continue to press you. I have too much respect for everything you are, and everything you have achieved, to plague you any more. I will leave and return to England. Alone. But I promise you, there is no reason on earth why you cannot be my wife, in all honour. If you love me enough. If you wish it. It is my dearest wish in all the world that you will accept me. In all honour. But the choice is yours.' He removed his arm from her shoulders. He must not touch her any more. He clasped both hands in his lap and stared down at them, waiting. Her next words would seal his future—happiness or despair—but the decision was hers alone. He owed her that much. There was nothing more he could do.

The silence stretched between them.

Alex gazed at his bent head, the tension in his fingers and the muscles of his neck. He was not fully in control any more. Even though he was a powerful man, a Duke, he could not force Alex to agree to marry him. He could only ask. And wait.

He had said he loved her! He had kissed her as though she were all the world to him. And he had spoken of marriage, in honour. Could it be honourable to accept him? Would she not bring disgrace on his ancient name? It seemed that *he* did not think so.

She knew—for she knew him—that his love was real, that he did want her as his wife. She had a sudden vision of how it could be. A life together, a loving union, children at their feet. Oh, it was so very difficult to refuse him, to send him away. To consign him to despair.

He had not moved, not even a fraction. He was not looking at her. Perhaps he did not dare?

Oh, Dominic, my love, I want to believe. I do.

His words echoed calmly through her confusion. Strong, certain. If he was so sure, could she not trust his judgement? He loved her, after all, with his whole being, as she did him.

She took a deep breath and broke the silence at last. 'In all honour?'

He looked up. His eyes were shining with hope. She gazed at him, bereft of words now, trying to convey the depth of emotion she felt. It seemed she succeeded. He offered his hand. 'In all honour, my love,' he repeated softly. It was a vow.

She smiled and laid her hand in his.

'And now, my lady wife, it is time for an English custom.'

Alex blinked up at him.

'We have had a Russian day, full of jewels and pomp and incense. We have exchanged the rings, and sipped the wine, and worn the crowns. Now that we are alone at last, I have a great longing for something simple. And intimate.'

She gasped and blushed again. She seemed to have been doing so all day long. This time, she could not mistake his meaning. They were standing at the entrance of his St Petersburg house, the place where they had first made love. And it was their wedding night.

'I love your blushes, my sweet. Come—' he swung her into his arms, strode into the hallway and started up the stairs '—let me show you to our bedchamber.'

'Dominic! You cannot carry me! What of the servants?'

'If they know what's good for them, they will keep well out of the way,' he growled. 'Besides, it is the custom. The blushing bride must be carried over the threshold.'

She nestled her cheek against his shoulder and smiled into his coat. This was how it should be between a man and a woman who loved each other. She was a woman now, with a woman's needs.

He shouldered the door open and carried her to the enormous bed, laying her down on it with infinite care. Then he sat on the edge and smiled down at her. Lovingly. 'May I suggest, my sweet, that I remove all the jewels your family have hung about you? I should not wish them to…er…intrude on our embraces.' With gentle fingers, he removed the bracelets from her arms and the brooches from her breast. Then the diamond bandeau that had secured the veil concealing her cropped hair. He smiled as it was revealed once more. 'I shall be sorry when your hair has grown. I fancy I shall miss your boyish charms.'

'Oh! You wretch!' She sat up and lunged at him, but he caught her hands in his and placed them round his neck. That brought their lips very close. Temptingly, irresistibly close. 'My boyish charms,' she breathed, running her fingers into his hair, 'may diminish one day, husband mine, but my love is for always.' She offered her mouth for his kiss, but it was not enough, not for either of them. She needed to touch him everywhere, to possess him, to be one with him. And she sensed the same urgency in him.

His put his hand to her ankle and slid it slowly up the length of her leg until the silk and lace of her wedding gown bunched into a foaming waterfall about her thighs.

'Dominic, I need you. I need you now, my love.'

His groan was all the response she needed. She pulled him down on to the bed, revelling in the feel of his weight as he settled into the cradle of her hips. It felt so familiar, somehow, as if—

'Now, love?'

She put her hands to his buttocks and drove her fingers hard into his flesh, though the layers of clothing. 'Now!'

'Satisfied?'

'Mmm. For the present.' She smiled lazily up at him, trying to fix every detail of his face. She wanted to remember this moment, to be able to picture it when she was an old, old woman.

Smiling self-indulgently, Dominic began to stroke the froth of silk and lace down her thighs. 'What on earth…?' With a frown, he separated the layers of fine petticoats and extracted the contents of her secret pocket.

Alex lay very still.

'Well, well.' His frown had cleared in an instant. 'Green kid gloves.' He latched a finger over the top of one cuff and lazily pushed the leather down towards the wrist. It still folded obediently. His eyes softened as he gazed first at the gloves and then at Alex's blushing face. 'In your wedding gown, love?' he murmured, his voice very deep.

Alex could not tear her eyes from his. 'A…a talisman, Dominic. They were all I could keep of our…our first time together. I was so sure it would be our last.' She reached up for one of the gloves and held it to her lips, inhaling its scent. 'I was going to put them under our pillow tonight. It seemed fitting.'

He kissed the remaining glove. 'Mmm. Yes. I can smell

your scent on them still. And I can never forget how much those gloves frustrated me that night,' he added with a sly grin, offering her the second glove.

She took it reverently, folded the pair together and tucked them under the pillow of their marriage bed. Then she lay back once more, smiling up at him. Her husband. The gloves had indeed been a talisman. Their love had come full circle. They were together now for always.

He dropped a gentle kiss on her mouth and lay down beside her. For a long moment, neither moved. It was enough that they were together, touching, loving. The fires of their passion were banked now, for a while, though they would be reignited soon.

Dominic broke the soft silence at last. 'I have something to confess to you, too, Alex. I forgot to congratulate you.'

Her languid mood evaporated instantly. 'For what?'

'For that trick with the horses. It took me days to discover that you had ordered the groom to take them all to the village to be shod.'

Alex laughed, deep in her throat.

'And the groom is now convinced the English are all stark mad.'

'Quite right. Just look at you! And the French probably think the same, too.'

'The French?'

'It was you who saved all the horses at the Lion d'Or, was it not?' The look on his face confirmed her suspicion. She had known, as soon as she felt the weight of his body on hers.

'The little *bourgeoise*…' he breathed. 'That was you?'

She nodded. The wonder in his face was balm to her soul. So she had haunted him, as he had haunted her.

He frowned, shaking his head. 'I could not get her—you—out of my mind. I dreamed about you, your hand with that knife… Oh, you wretch, Alex. You were my obsession.'

He paused. 'Until you were replaced by someone even more seductive.'

'Oh? Who?' She was trying to hide her smile.

'By a little Scottish lady in a very inconveniently laced dress,' he grinned.

She smiled then. It was most satisfactory.

'What a very ill-assorted pair we are,' he said, on the thread of a laugh. He rolled on to his back, staring up at the bed canopy. 'And yet we are married. Dominic Aikenhead, the English Duke, and his wife, the captain of Hussars.' He shook his head against the pillow. It seemed he still could not believe it.

Alex kissed his cheek softly. 'Major Zass suspected you might be a spy.'

He was suddenly motionless. 'I am a spy,' he said quietly.

Alex froze. The taste of him in her mouth had turned bitter as gall. She could neither move nor speak.

'And you are a spy, too, Alexei Ivanovich Alexandrov.'

She stiffened even more.

'Else why did you lie to me about your ability to speak English?'

'I...I did not lie to you, Dominic. Not exactly,' she managed at last, rather lamely. A moment ago, she had been full of righteous anger. Now she was unsure. She was in his power now. What was he going to do?

'I had wondered why you were attached to the Emperor's suite at the last moment. The reason was obvious once I learned of your knowledge of English. Your task was to spy on us, as mine was to spy on you. We are even, I think.'

He pulled her into the crook of his body and held her close, his arm across her breasts. She could feel his steady heartbeat against her back, contrasting starkly with her own racing pulse.

'There is nothing to fear, Alex. You are mine, now—'

She tensed. She was not to be possessed like a chattel!

'—and I am yours,' he continued, almost without a pause.

'We are like two sides of the same coin. Take one, and you must take the other, too. Different, but equal.' He dropped a kiss on the top of her head. 'Trust me, Alex.'

She could not speak. She had no words. Instead, she raised his hand to her lips and nuzzled his palm. Then she returned it to her breast. Where it belonged. 'You have never asked me why, Dominic,' she whispered at last.

'No. One day, when you are ready, you will tell me. I am content to wait.'

'Oh.' She could not have asked for a clearer declaration of how their union would be. He loved her, he had married her, and yet he would wait to learn her secrets. Until she was ready to share them. 'I think you have been patient enough, my love,' she said softly, turning in his arms so that she could see his face.

And then she told him all of it, from her blissful army childhood to the arranged marriage she had fled, and the happiness she had found in the ranks of the Hussars. 'I could imagine nothing better than living, laughing and fighting alongside my comrades,' she finished. 'Until I met you. Then all the certainties of my life went spinning out of control. If you had not followed me here...'

He put a hand to her cheek. 'I could not do otherwise, my love. I think even Castlereagh suspected my motives.'

'Castlereagh sent you? You are here to spy against Russia?' Unlike Dominic, she could not wait to know the truth. She had to be able to trust him.

There was a long silence. 'I was. I am. But I have not done so. As it happens, I was otherwise engaged, in pursuing a remarkable young man who turned out to be...er...something other than he seemed.' He bent his head to nibble the lobe of her ear. 'I know you love your country, my darling wife, as I do mine. I offer you a pact. I will not spy *against* Russia if you, my sweetest of spies, will promise not to spy *for* Russia.'

'That is not an equal bargain, Dominic. I am not so easily gulled. If I am not to spy for Russia, then you should not spy for England.'

'I have a logic-chopping wife!' He chuckled. 'We shall have an amusing time of it, but you have forgot one factor, my love. You were only half-Russian to begin with, and now you are married to an Englishman. If there is any spying to be done, I fancy you should be doing it for England.'

She was silent, thinking. What he said was logical enough, though it turned her world upside down. She was no longer a Russian. She was English, the wife of an English duke. She could remain Russian only in a remote corner of her heart. She had accepted that when she allowed him to put his ring on her finger. Her loyalty lay with him. 'I think you are making a may-game of me, Dominic Aikenhead. An English duke would never have his wife play the spy.'

'I may tell you, madam Duchess, that the Aikenhead Honours—my brothers and I—have been very successful in our spying enterprises, these few years past. We have a tidy little band: Ace, King, Knave, Ten. We have lacked only a Queen.'

Her sharply indrawn breath betrayed her shock.

'Poor Ten. That's brother Jack's friend, Ben, you know. When we have had need of a woman in our little band, he has been forced to don his petticoats. He did it well enough, though his ability to play the woman was nothing to your ability to play the man. Your performance was matchless.'

She allowed herself a tiny smile.

'With a real female in our little group, how much easier, and safer, it would be for all of us. Just think of that.'

'You require me to help you?'

He laid his cheek against her hair. 'I do not require. You are my wife, the woman I love. I ask it of you. You have every right to refuse. If you do, I will never mention it again.'

He waited, but she said only, 'We would not spy against Russia.' It was a statement, not a question. And it was vital.

'No. We would not. You have my word on that.'

She really smiled then. 'I should warn you, husband mine, that I do have some considerable experience of spying against the French. That was the reason for the wager over the masquerade. My comrades knew I had managed to disguise myself as a peasant woman, but they did not believe I could carry it off as a lady.'

'Mmm. And the wager was the only reason you did it?' There was a definite hint of incredulity in his voice.

'I…no. I was supposed to act the spy also.'

'Mmm?'

'I…I did not. I found that there were more…um…entertaining things to do.' She put a finger across his lips to stop his question. His eyes widened and she smiled into them. 'With the man I had gone to the ball to find.'

'Ah.'

She slid her arms around his neck and brought her lips to within an inch of his. Then she sighed out his name.

He groaned in response and made to pull her closer, but she pushed him on to his back. There was something more she had to ask.

'Dominic, what will you tell the Duchess?'

'What would you have me tell you, my sweet?'

'Oh!' She pulled herself out of his arms, sat up and frowned down at him. He remained lying on his back, totally relaxed, grinning up at her. 'I meant your mother, you sapskull, as you knew very well.'

He raised his eyebrows. 'Did I?' Then he held out his arms.

Alex slid back into his embrace and allowed him to settle the bedcovers around her once more.

'I shall write to my mother, of course,' he said, with his lips against her hair. 'I shall tell her that I have discovered my

Scottish Alexandra, in Russia, just as I expected. And that I have married her.'

Alex waited for the rest of it, but he said nothing more. 'And you will tell her of my…my history?'

He laid the flat of his palm in the middle of her back and slowly, gently, let it drift down until it cupped her bare buttocks. Then he dropped a kiss on her hair. 'I shall say nothing of that,' he said quietly. 'Letters from Russia have a habit of…um…going astray, or even, on occasion, being read and resealed.'

Alex let out the breath she had been holding and allowed her body to relax into his.

'Besides,' he added, 'it is not my secret to share. It is for you to decide when, and if, my mother should be told.'

'And your brothers?'

'That is for you, also. I must warn you that I think Leo suspects. The same is true of Cousin Harriet.'

'But how could she?'

He patted her bottom. 'You betrayed yourself, my love. When you dined with me in London, you allowed her to gull you into thinking she was an old lady who was losing her wits. I did warn you that she is not. In fact, she is much like you in many ways: intelligent, and strong-minded, and as brave as a lion.'

She could not speak. Did her husband really think that of her?

'From something you did, Harriet guessed that you understood English. And she fancied there was something smoky about you in any case. I had to tell her the truth of what I suspected. But there is no need to be anxious. She can be quite as close-mouthed as Leo. When we go back to London, you may tell her yourself.'

'Hmm.' That raised another concern. Alex hoped it would be the last. 'When are we to return to London?' she asked in a small voice.

'I had thought—if you agree, my love—that we might go

travelling for a while. That would give your hair time to grow. And other things to change, too. Meg tells me she has some excellent cream for your hands, and lotion for your complexion. I should be happy to apply them for you.' He stroked a finger idly down her weather-beaten cheek.

'You have been conspiring with Meg? Good grief, I am beset by traitors! I shall have to sleep with my sabre by my side.'

'You may do so if you wish, of course. You will not, I hope, use it on your husband. I believe that is a capital crime.'

'Truly? Well, in that case, I shall have to find other means of subduing the Duke of Calder.' She rolled on top of him and pinned his shoulders to the pillow with her hands.

He did not move. He simply gazed up at her. 'I yield. What else can I do, a poor weak civilian against a seasoned cavalryman?'

She ran her tongue over lips that were suddenly parched. 'Let that be a lesson to you, Duke,' she said hoarsely, and lowered her mouth to his.

* * * * *

Author's Note

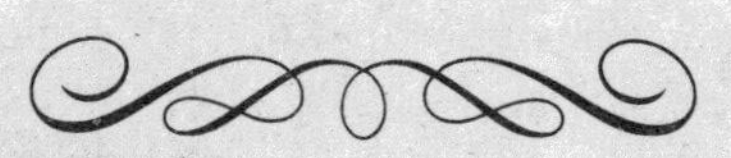

This story was inspired by the real-life Cavalry Maiden, Nadezhda Durova, who served in the Russian cavalry for about ten years, from 1806 until 1816, first as a common trooper and later as a commissioned officer. During all that time, she successfully concealed her gender from her comrades and superiors, even when she served as orderly to Kutuzov. It did not become public until she published her own story in 1836. I am indebted to Mary Fleming Zirin for the English translation of those memoirs and for her immensely helpful editorial introduction and notes, published as *The Cavalry Maiden: Journals of a Female Russian Officer in the Napoleonic Wars* (Paladin, 1990). The book is a fascinating read, as much for Durova's unembroidered view of cavalry life as for her cool descriptions of the bloody battles in which she fought.

Though inspired by Durova's story, my heroine is unlike her in many ways: Alex serves for only five years, she has a Scottish mother and speaks English, and she visits England as an aide-de-camp to Tsar Alexander. Durova did none of these. One major incident is common to both, however. The real Cavalry Maiden was summoned to meet the Tsar, to be confronted by his knowledge of who she really was; she did plead to be allowed to continue to serve in the army and she did receive her officer's commission, and the Cross of St George, at his hands. That was such a powerful scene in her memoirs that I could not resist basing the opening of my story on it. But the rest of my heroine's story is her own.

The visit of the Russian Tsar and the Prussian King in 1814 produced feverish excitement in London. For three weeks, the monarchs, particularly the Tsar, were surrounded by immense cheering crowds from which they got no peace. It was not unlike the present-day cult of celebrities. Trophy-hunters would go to incredible lengths to be able to claim that they had seen all the various royal personages. Titled ladies were known to have secreted themselves in basement kitchens in order to catch a glimpse of the passing royals through the area grating. And poor old Marshal Blücher, who was by far the crowd's favourite, got no sleep for days on end because of the noisy adulation wherever he went.

During the visit, the Prince Regent came a very poor second to the visitors, and also to his wife. It was reported that, after his encounter with her at the opera, he was hissed by the crowd on his way home. That incident actually took place at the end of the first week of the visit. In my story, I have placed it considerably later. I have also conflated two balls into one, in an attempt to distil the essence of the crowded and tumultuous programme of events that took place in the summer of 1814.

* * * * *

Celebrate 60 years
of pure reading pleasure with Harlequin®!
Silhouette® Romantic Suspense is celebrating with the
glamour-filled, adrenaline-charged series
LOVE IN 60 SECONDS *starting in April 2009.*
Six stories that promise to bring the glitz of Las Vegas, the
danger of revenge, the mystery of a missing diamond,
family scandals and ripped-from-the-headlines intrigue.
Get your heart racing as love happens in sixty seconds!

Enjoy a sneak peek of
USA TODAY *bestselling author Marie Ferrarella's*
THE HEIRESS'S 2-WEEK AFFAIR
Available April 2009 from Silhouette® Romantic Suspense.

Eight years ago Matt Shaffer had vanished out of Natalie Rothchild's life, leaving behind a one-line note tucked under a pillow that had grown cold: *I'm sorry, but this just isn't going to work.*

That was it. No explanation, no real indication of remorse. The note had been as clinical and compassionless as an eviction notice, which, in effect, it had been, Natalie thought as she navigated through the morning traffic. Matt had written the note to evict her from his life.

She'd spent the next two weeks crying, breaking down without warning as she walked down the street, or as she sat staring at a meal she couldn't bring herself to eat.

Candace, she remembered with a bittersweet pang, had tried to get her to go clubbing in order to get her to forget about Matt.

She'd turned her twin down, but she did get her act together. If Matt didn't think enough of their relationship to try to contact her, to try to make her understand why he'd changed so radically from lover to stranger, then to hell with him. He was dead to her, she resolved. And he'd remained that way.

Until twenty minutes ago.

The adrenaline in her veins kept mounting.

Natalie focused on her driving. Vegas in the daylight wasn't nearly as alluring, as magical and glitzy as it was after dark. Like an aging woman best seen in soft lighting, Vegas's imperfections were all visible in the daylight. Natalie supposed that was why people like her sister didn't like to get up until noon. They lived for the night.

Except that Candace could no longer do that.

The thought brought a fresh, sharp ache with it.

"Damn it, Candy, what a waste," Natalie murmured under her breath.

She pulled up before the Janus casino. One of the three valets currently on duty came to life and made a beeline for her vehicle.

"Welcome to the Janus," the young attendant said cheerfully as he opened her door with a flourish.

"We'll see," she replied solemnly.

As he pulled away with her car, Natalie looked up at the casino's logo. Janus was the Roman god with two faces, one pointed toward the past, the other facing the future. It struck her as rather ironic, given what she was doing here, seeking out someone from her past in order to get answers so that the future could be settled.

The moment she entered the casino, the Vegas phenomena took hold. It was like stepping into a world where time did not matter or even make an appearance. There was only a sense of "now."

Because in Natalie's experience she'd discovered that bartenders knew the inner workings of any establishment they worked for better than anyone else, she made her way to the first bar she saw within the casino.

The bartender in attendance was a gregarious man in his

early forties. He had a quick, sexy smile, which was probably one of the main reasons he'd been hired. His name tag identified him as Kevin.

Moving to her end of the bar, Kevin asked, "What'll it be, pretty lady?"

"Information." She saw a dubious look cross his brow. To counter that, she took out her badge. Granted she wasn't here in an official capacity, but Kevin didn't need to know that. "Were you on duty last night?"

Kevin began to wipe the gleaming black surface of the bar. "You mean during the gala?"

"Yes."

The smile gracing his lips was a satisfied one. Last night had obviously been profitable for him, she judged. "I caught an extra shift."

She took out Candace's photograph and carefully placed it on the bar. "Did you happen to see this woman there?"

The bartender glanced at the picture. Mild interest turned to recognition. "You mean Candace Rothchild? Yeah, she was here, loud and brassy as always. But not for long," he added, looking rather disappointed. There was always a circus when Candace was around, Natalie thought. "She and the boss had at it and then he had our head of security escort her out."

She latched onto the first part of his statement. "They argued? About what?"

He shook his head. "Couldn't tell you. Too far away for anything but body language," he confessed.

"And the head of security?" she asked.

"He got her to leave."

She leaned in over the bar. "Tell me about him."

"Don't know much," the bartender admitted. "Just that his

name's Matt Shaffer. Boss flew him in from L.A., where he was head of security for Montgomery Enterprises."

There was no avoiding it, she thought darkly. She was going to have to talk to Matt. The thought left her cold. "Do you know where I can find him right now?"

Kevin glanced at his watch. "He should be in his office. On the second floor, toward the rear." He gave her the numbers of the rooms where the monitors that kept watch over the casino guests as they tried their luck against the house were located.

Taking out a twenty, she placed it on the bar. "Thanks for your help."

Kevin slipped the bill into his vest pocket. "Any time, lovely lady," he called after her. "Any time."

She debated going up the stairs, then decided on the elevator. The car that took her up to the second floor was empty. Natalie stepped out of the elevator, looked around to get her bearings and then walked toward the rear of the floor.

"Into the Valley of Death rode the six hundred," she silently recited, digging deep for a line from a poem by Tennyson. Wrapping her hand around a brass handle, she opened one of the glass doors and walked in.

The woman whose desk was closest to the door looked up. "You can't come in here. This is a restricted area."

Natalie already had her ID in her hand and held it up. "I'm looking for Matt Shaffer," she told the woman.

God, even saying his name made her mouth go dry. She was supposed to be over him, to have moved on with her life. What happened?

The woman began to answer her. "He's—"

"Right here."

The deep voice came from behind her. Natalie felt every

single nerve ending go on tactical alert at the same moment that all the hairs at the back of her neck stood up. Eight years had passed, but she would have recognized his voice anywhere.

* * * * *

COMING NEXT MONTH FROM
HARLEQUIN® HISTORICAL

Available March 31, 2009

- **THE SUBSTITUTE BRIDE**
  by **Elizabeth Lane**
  (Western)
  Dashing reporter Quint Seavers, disappointed in love before, is unaware that independent, practical Annie Gustavson holds a secret longtime love for him. Living together in close proximity, the attraction between them is undeniable, and suddenly Quint knows that Annie is exactly what's been missing in his life—till now….

- **HIS RELUCTANT MISTRESS**
  by **Joanna Maitland**
  (Regency)
  Renowned rake Leo Aikenhead rescues Sophie Pietre, the famous "Venetian Nightingale," from a bad assault. Resilient and self-reliant, Sophie has never succumbed to a man's desires before. But dangerously attractive Leo soon becomes the only man she would risk all her secrets for!
  Second in The Aikenhead Honours *trilogy. Three gentlemen spies; bound by duty, undone by women!*

- **THE RAKE'S INHERITED COURTESAN**
  by **Ann Lethbridge**
  (Regency)
  Daughter of a Parisian courtesan, Sylvia Boisette thirsts for respectability. But, charged as her guardian, wealthy, conservative Christopher Evernden finds himself on the brink of scandal as his body cannot ignore Sylvia's tempting sensuality….

Unlaced, Undressed, Undone!

- **THE KNIGHT'S RETURN**
  by **Joanne Rock**
  (Medieval)
  Needing a protector and escort, Irish princess Sorcha agrees to allow a striking mercenary to fulfill this role. But Hugh de Montagne is unsettled by his immediate attraction to the princess of the realm….

HHCNMBPA0309